MW00439715

APPARENT
HORIZON

Also from Phase Publishing

by
Dr. Robert Melillo & Domenic Melillo

Einstein's Desk

by
Christopher Bailey

Without Chance
Whisper

by
Bree Moore

Woven
Bound

by
Colleen Kelly-Eiding

Favoured by Fortune
Face of Fortune

APPARENT
HORIZON

by

PATRICK MORGAN

Phase Publishing, LLC
Seattle

If you purchased this book without a cover, you should be aware that this book is stolen property. It was reported as "unsold and destroyed" to the publisher, and neither the author nor the publisher has received any payment for this "stripped" book.

Text copyright © 2020 by Patrick Morgan
Cover art copyright © 2020 by Patrick Morgan

Cover art by Paper & Sage
http://www.paperandsage.com

All rights reserved. Published by Phase Publishing, LLC. No part of this book may be reproduced or transmitted in any form, or by any means, electronic or mechanical, including photocopying or recording or by any information storage and retrieval system, without written permission from the publisher.

This is a work of fiction. Names, places, events, and incidents are either the products of the author's imagination or are used in a fictitious manner. Any resemblance to actual persons, living or dead, or actual events is purely coincidental.

Phase Publishing, LLC first paperback edition
October 2020

ISBN 978-1-952103-15-5
Library of Congress Control Number 2020916813
Cataloging-in-Publication Data on file.

ACKNOWLEDGEMENTS

First off, I would like to thank Christopher Bailey and the entire publishing team at Phase Publishing for giving me the unique opportunity to share this story with a broader audience. You've made the process so easy, fun, and collaborative from start to finish, and I'll forever be grateful for this chance to realize a lifelong dream.

On that note, I'd also like to thank Connor Kelly-Eiding for connecting me with Christopher. If you haven't already, please be sure to check out Connor's incredible book, *Feelings for Days*, which is also available through Phase Publishing.

I'd be remiss if I didn't express my heartfelt appreciation to every school-teacher I had growing up for encouraging my creative writing, as well as every theatre teacher throughout high school and college for instructing me in the magical artform of storytelling.

Thank you to all my loving, supportive, and supremely-talented friends who did me the honor of reading and critiquing my works. There's no way I'd be in this position today without each and every one of you helping me grow as a writer and as a human being.

Finally, I would like to share my profound gratitude to my family members for their endless encouragement, guidance, and belief – particularly my parents John and Sue, my sister Megan, and my brother-in-law Paul. Everything I am is because of you guys, so this is as much your work as it is mine.

CHAPTER ONE

Michael Cavanaugh sat alone on his balcony, slowly sliding the soles of his bare feet forward and backward, forward and backward along the bumpy surface.

Was it stucco? He stared down at the strange texture, which was reminiscent of the moon. Michael had never thought to question what his balcony was made of; he had never found a need to. After the earthquake, however, he found himself subconsciously investigating the quality of his surroundings more and more frequently.

When it had happened four days ago, he had been in Las Vegas for his best friend Drew Baskin's bachelor party. Safe and sound almost three hundred miles away, he had first seen the breaking news reports from the relative sanctuary of a blackjack table at the Excalibur Hotel and Casino.

Within twenty-four hours of arriving in Sin City, Michael's gambling funds had completely dried up. He had bought two different books on blackjack and Texas hold'em, neither one of which had come to much use. The concepts were easy enough to understand for a man of Michael's intelligence, but two factors prevented him from mastery.

First, it could never be said of Michael that he was a particularly daring individual. He had skydived once as a graduation present from college, and on his only other sojourn to Vegas, he had tried cocaine only after *significant* peer pressure from his fraternity brothers.

Beyond these two isolated incidents, however, he hadn't done anything truly hazardous or courageous since he was struck by a car in childhood.

As a third grader, Michael had been dared into a game of human Frogger by his classmates. Growing up in the San Fernando Valley, he had found himself quivering on the sidewalk facing the afternoon commute along Victory Boulevard, sweat seeping into his red polo shirt beneath his underarms and along his collarbone. The sequence of events that followed had been nightmarish, and they would prove to have a permanent effect on Michael's psyche when it came to matters of bravery and risk assessment.

After all, Frogger is only a game because of the inherent obstacles. Accordingly, it wasn't enough for Michael to just make a break for the other side of the road when the traffic was still a distance away; there was no honor in that. No, the true talent came from weaving your way through oncoming traffic by knowing when to stop and when to start again on your perpendicular journey through six lanes of rush hour.

There were two boys and one girl on hand to goad Michael into this feat of valor that fateful day, and whether their intentions were malicious or benign, Michael could not quite remember. All he could remember was making it successfully three-quarters of the way across the street, through blaring horns and numerous shouts of obscenities, before finally being struck by a Volkswagen beetle.

Michael remembered turning his head at the last possible second and seeing the silver 'VW' insignia on the front of the vehicle before a jarring impact, and then darkness. He had woken up in the hospital with a broken leg, a ruptured spleen, and a concussion. Even as a nine-year-old, it was then that Michael realized his own mortality.

From that moment on, he rationalized that if something seemed dangerous, it probably was also stupid and therefore not worth doing. Especially if he wanted to have any chance of living a long and full life.

The second major factor that had prevented Michael from any kind of gambling prowess in Vegas was his poker face; or, more appropriately, his lack thereof. Michael's face was notoriously expressive, and even from an early age, it was apparent that he was never going to be any good at lying. His parents would later tell him many stories of his childhood, recounting how poorly he had concealed the truth, time and time again.

For example, when he discovered his teenage brother Everett stealing money from their mother's purse one evening, Michael had pledged his silence and dutifully buried himself in his homework. His mother discovered the missing cash less than an hour later, and after thorough searches of the purse and her pockets, as well as several minutes of retracing her steps around the house, she had finally put two and two together and suspected her eldest of the petty theft.

Noticing Michael was in the vicinity of the purse while working at the kitchen table on his arithmetic, she had questioned him for all of thirty seconds before apparently reading something telltale and obvious in his face, leading her to pick up her phone and dial Everett to confront him.

Everett obviously blamed his brother for his getting grounded, and Michael's punishment was one of the worst sibling beat-downs he could remember.

On another occasion, Michael had attempted to convince his parents that he was going to a friend's house for dinner and to play video games. Something in his delivery must have come across as suspicious though, because his father, a longtime deputy sheriff, decided to follow Michael at a distance that evening. When he discovered his son's car parked at a local liquor store, the charade was up, and Michael realized that perhaps fibbing wasn't his strong suit after all.

And so, Michael had sat, bored and utterly broke on a stiff leather stool in Vegas, watching his more talented blackjack-playing cohorts wage war against each other and the dealer, trading chips and lewd quips while sipping on watered-down screwdrivers and dollar beers. The games had been interesting enough, so Michael was a bit surprised when he found his eyes wandering around the smoky casino interior.

He had just been staring longingly at the black leotard-covered buttocks of a mildly pretty cocktail server, who was bent over asking a small old lady at a slot machine if she wanted another mojito, when a bright orange headline beneath a panorama of Los Angeles had caught his attention.

Michael had been drinking quite heavily that night (or had it been morning?), always chipping in a drink request when one of the cocktail waitresses came over to get more booze for his card-playing companions. He remembered blinking in disbelief and drunken stupor at the television screen, but still, the image had remained.

The earthquake registered a 5.9 on the Richter scale. Less than the Northridge quake, but still significant. No lives had been lost, but several people were injured, and many buildings had been damaged throughout L.A.

He remembered wondering about his own apartment complex and whether it was still standing. Hopefully, it was. No, surely it was. And then he had thought of his dog Tucker, who had been boarded for the weekend. He would be safe there, too. The place was up in the hills near Altadena, far away from significant development.

And finally, he remembered surprising himself by randomly thinking of Jeanette Dailey, his pretty coworker from the credit union where Michael was employed and spent most of his days. Once upon a time, she had told Michael she lived in a loft downtown. He wondered if she was all right, if she had been home or out and about, if she had any animals of her own, if they had felt the earthquake coming and warned her beforehand, if such things were even possible...

For numerous silent minutes, Michael had watched stoically while the sounds of laughter, bells, whistles, and other electronic machinery swirled around him. Finally, he must have gotten the attention of his three friends, and they all went into motion, walking en masse from the green felt table to a sticky mahogany bar where the volume was playing just loud enough to make out words like "casualties," "rubble," "gas," "damaged," and "harmed."

Later, calls had been made to loved ones, both within Los Angeles and elsewhere around the country. These phone calls were meant to either ensure the wellbeing of those dwelling in Southern California or to assure those living in other places of their own respective wellbeing and safety in Las Vegas.

Most of the phone calls had been brief and amusing conversations, due in no small part to the inebriation of the callers at such an early time of day, with Drew having the most difficult time of the bunch trying to convince his fiancée that they were not going to cut their time in Vegas short just because of the earthquake.

His bride-to-be, Michelle, was spending that same weekend with her girlfriends at a spa resort in Santa Barbara. Michelle had said they were not sure if they felt anything up north, but most of the women were leaning toward no. They were all, of course, safe. They were all, of course, concerned as well for friends and family in the Los Angeles area.

Drew had repeatedly dismissed the need for the ladies to cut their own time in Santa Barbara short, as there was "no chance in hell that me and my boys are coming back before Sunday, at the earliest."

After that, the rest of their time in Vegas had proceeded according to plan, with days and nights running together in a hazy watercolor wash of strippers, gambling, and alcohol.

His mind coming back to the present, Michael stopped massaging his feet against the bumpy ground and lifted his right foot up toward his waist, catching it with his left hand to inspect the sole. It was a filthy, sooty black. He wondered how this balcony could have gotten so dirty, and just how exactly he was supposed to clean it.

It was barely large enough for him to fit two patio chairs on it, let alone to allow for any kind of garden hose or power washing. He ruminated that maybe he would just have to get a bucket of soapy water and scrub it down on his hands and knees with a sponge to get all the dirt and ash out – although there was no real place for the water to drain. Perhaps it would just have to evaporate over time, especially with the recent heat wave and the ever-steadfast California sunshine beating down.

There was no denying now that Michael was back to reality and back to the daily grind. He did have Drew's wedding to look forward to on Saturday, but that was not nearly the same kind of "looking forward to" that he had felt for their bachelor party weekend in Vegas... and now that weekend was long since over and done with.

To further complicate things, he was planning to attend the wedding dateless. Michael thought he had caught one of Michelle's bridesmaids staring at him at their engagement party, but she also seemed to be a bit of a shoe-gazer, and maybe even a stoner, so he wasn't quite sure how to interpret that particular situation.

Besides, as Drew's best man, he was set to be paired throughout the wedding festivities with Michelle's maid of honor, Lillian Ross – a woman Michael had actively detested since meeting her on a catastrophic blind date two years prior. He had never forgiven Drew and Michelle for setting that disaster of a date up... and now he was going to be forced to smile and lead her down the aisle at their best friends' wedding.

Things had been icy and uncomfortable for both parties ever since, as they repeatedly found themselves thrown together within the same group of friends. It seemed there was no escaping Lillian, and the idea of her continuing on in Michael's life as an extension of Michelle, who was to become an extension of Drew, sickened him even now and made him reach for a cigarette with disgust. He slid one out and lit it with contempt, watching the sunset settle into dusk from his perch on the fourth-floor balcony.

Michael inhaled deeply through the cigarette. Planes coasted along the skyline on invisible paths, slicing like knives through fruit-jam mixtures of red and purple and orange.

His apartment had, in fact, survived the earthquake relatively unscathed. A few items in his closet had cascaded to the floor, and several books had fallen from their shelves on his entertainment center. His glassware and other kitchen items had thankfully remained unbroken and, to the best of his knowledge, undisturbed entirely. His dog Tucker had evidently slept through the quake completely in Altadena at the boarder's. As it turned out, most of the damage had happened further north on the other side of the Valley where he had grown up and spent his childhood.

Thankfully, his parents had left for Florida years ago to retire, so only the house he grew up in could have been negatively affected. His brother Everett worked on a crab fishing boat off the coast of Alaska, and Michael rarely kept in any kind of real contact with him.

He had last seen Everett at their grandmother's funeral, now almost ten years ago. His mother would occasionally relay a greeting or some other perfunctory message from his brother to Michael over the phone, but Michael secretly suspected this was just his mother's attempt at keeping up the pretense that Everett still talked to any of them.

The click of a lamp suddenly caught Michael's attention. He turned toward the sound and saw a deep amber glow emanating from his neighbor's balcony window. The sliding glass door was open, and only the screen door seemed to be shut.

His neighbor, a stocky man with oiled white hair and thin wire glasses, moved into view at the screen door. Michael had no idea what this man's name was or what he did. He knew the man lived with a small Asian lady that Michael presumed to be the man's wife, as well as a tiny terrier mix that always barked at Michael's front door whenever the Asian lady took it out for a walk. He had never seen the Asian lady's eyes; she always went everywhere in thick, dark sunglasses that obscured half her face.

Now and again, he would see her walking the dog from his car as he drove past, or even occasionally while he was out jogging. She had only spoken to him once before, to knock on his door about a week after he had first moved into his studio apartment. In broken English, she had asked rather aggressively if he was the one responsible for leaving the empty, greasy pizza boxes on her doorstep.

After some confusion, Michael had finally been able to convince her that he had no idea someone had been doing such a thing, and politely, he insisted that he would keep an eye out and notify her immediately should he catch the perpetrator in action.

His encounters with the old man had been slightly more frequent, but even more void of communication. The man worked a job that apparently required extremely early mornings, and subsequently, made him turn in very early at night – very, *very* early.

Another such encounter was occurring right now. Michael made eye contact with the man and half-attempted a smile. The man stood, stock-still, staring back at him, with his veined hands placed resolutely on his hipbones. A year ago, when Michael had first moved into the apartment, he might have been naïve enough to attempt conversation, or at the very least, a friendly wave of the hand or a cordial nod of the head.

But Michael knew better now. Holding his ground, he took another long drag of the cigarette. The old man stared back, unflinching, his only movement the occasional blink of steel eyes behind those thin silver glasses. The man stared… and stared… and stared.

They both knew what it meant; the stare, the position of the hands, the dry frown, the lamp turning on. It was a game of chicken, and both parties knew who was going to balk first… but that still didn't stop Michael from trying.

His hand started to shake, minutely at first, then growing slowly into something more noticeable. In an effort not to give himself away, he brought the cigarette again to his lips and touched the filter with the tip of his tongue. He toyed with using his free hand to scratch his head contentedly but thought better of it. His palms began to sweat, and little beads of perspiration materialized out of nowhere on his temples and hairline. A warm rush of blood and color flowed across his cheeks as he felt his heart beating like a drum way up in his throat.

Could the man see this? It was now twilight, and the last remnants of the sunset were fading fast. Michael checked his phone. 7:31 p.m. The man had no right to be doing this; not at this time. If it were midnight, eleven, ten, or maybe even nine, perhaps *then* Michael could bring himself to sympathize with, if not entirely understand, this confrontation.

It was a Wednesday night – no, a Wednesday evening. Early evening. Late, late afternoon, some might even say. People were still eating dinner, coming home from jobs. Kids were doing homework. His own bedtime growing up must have been later than this, for Christ's sake.

Yet still, the old man stared and held his ground.

With a swift movement, Michael crushed out the half-smoked cigarette and stood up abruptly, averting the man's gaze and retreating back toward his screen. With what little dignity he had left, Michael slipped through the opening and tried to slam his own sliding glass door with excessive force. The resulting thud was not nearly satisfying enough to make up for all that he had lost.

Michael ripped a sheet of paper towel from a roll in the kitchen and blotted at his forehead, now shiny with sweat. He scanned the room for his dog. Absolutely oblivious, Tucker dozed on the leather couch, one leg stretched out languidly across a throw pillow. Michael forced himself to smile and, discovering an aggressive appetite, moved back into the kitchen area to prepare a frozen linguine dinner.

After inserting the small package into his microwave and starting the cook cycle, he summoned the courage to move to his balcony window and steal a glance back across the way.

His neighbors' apartment was now dark. The lamp had been turned off, but the sliding glass door was wide open, as it always was at night, letting in the cool evening breeze along with the sounds of traffic far below. For whatever reason, the noise of cars and motorcycles on the street didn't appear to be an issue for the man's slumber cycle.

Michael wondered if it had been the smell of smoke wafting in through the screen door that had so disturbed the old man. For all he knew, it could have been the tiny orange light of his burning cigarette end.

All that really mattered though was that the old man had won. He always won… and Michael always lost.

And that was just the way of the world, as they say.

CHAPTER TWO

"So, what's the plan? Are we staying here or going out?"

"Jesus, I don't know if I can go out. At least not driving-wise."

"Are you fucked up already? It's only eleven o'clock!"

"We've been drinking since nine."

Michael smiled and grabbed another three beers from the mini-fridge, clutching the bottles by their necks with two hands and loping back into the den.

"I think the real issue here is your tolerance level, Copernicus. Mikey seems to be just fine. Right, Mike?"

Michael shrugged sheepishly as if to express, 'What can I say?', handing one of the beers to Drew in the same gesture.

"Thank you, Michael. I *will* have another."

"I don't know, man. I think I'm still feeling Vegas. It was only, what, a week ago?"

"Yeah, well, look. I don't care if we stay here or we go out... though I would really, really, *really* like to go out. But hey, I'm flexible. I know how to go with the flow. I'm a team player, and I'm not gonna pull the 'it's my last night as a free man on this Earth' card because that just seems like an asshole thing to do, but I *would* like to have some semblance of a plan for how this night is gonna go down... seeing as it is, after all, my last night as a free man on this Earth. Sooooo... what's the plan? Are we staying here and dicking around, or are we gonna go take advantage of being the three sexiest guys in Hollywood on a Friday night?"

During Drew's impassioned speech, Michael had found a place to sit that he considered fairly neutral ground. He handed off the second beer to Aaron Hillison, who looked as if he was being offered poison before at last relenting and taking hold of the beverage. Michael then strategically decided on the oversized grape-colored armchair in the corner of Drew's den, leaving his two friends on the matching grape-colored sofa.

Grinning like the Cheshire cat, he twisted off the cap of his Tecate and took a swig of the cold beer. Michael often found himself in the middle of these little debates, and he had come to relish the perks of being the wild card that he saw himself as. It was he who would usually become the deciding vote or swing state in these discussions, and it was a privilege and authority that Michael had grown to cherish.

He sat in his chair and reveled in the knowledge that the decision of whether to go out or stay in would ultimately fall to him. The fate of the evening was in his hands. His choice would affect not just his own experience, but the experience of two other people, as well.

It was responsibility. It was power. And Michael liked it.

"Michael!"

He blinked and turned to the others. "What?"

Aaron was looking at him apprehensively, but Drew's face was a politician's mask of confidence and camaraderie. It was Drew who had spoken to him.

"I said, 'What do you think, Michael?'"

Michael turned the chilled beer in his hand. "I think we should do whatever you wanna do, Drew. It's your night, after all." Aaron swallowed hard. "However, I do think we should take it fairly easy. We partied pretty hard in Vegas, and the wedding *is* tomorrow morning. You don't wanna be hungover for your own wedding, right?"

Drew's expression quickly morphed into a sneer. "I don't get 'hungover'. I didn't in Vegas, I didn't in college, and I'm definitely not gonna tonight. We were in a fucking *frat* for four years, guys. Jesus!"

He then threw his head back in exasperation, covering his eyes with his hands as if to shut out some horrid image, and rubbed at them with his fingers.

Michael was never sure if these types of outbursts were authentic or theatrical. Drew was a dramatic individual by nature, prone to grandiose gestures, expressions, and emotions. To make matters worse, he was also an actor.

Presently, the husband-to-be was easily the best-dressed of the three of them, his sharp attire a clear indication of Drew's desire to go out on the town. A tight, black button-up shirt, dark denim blue jeans, and polished leather shoes completed an ensemble you could find on just about every man out in Hollywood on a weekend night.

Still, Michael thought Drew pulled off the look well. The subdued tones complemented Drew's dark eyes and black hair, and the sleeves of his shirt – rolled up intentionally right below the elbows – gave his friend just the necessary amount of ventilation Michael knew he needed so he wouldn't be disgustingly sweaty wherever they went.

It was Aaron who finally broke the silence.

"I'm down for whatever you want to do, Drew. It is your night."

With the look of some martyr knight gallantly charging to his death, Drew took his hands away from his face, sat up with a drawn-out sigh, and reached for his beer on the coffee table. He lifted it to his thick lips and took a long, thirsty swallow, set it back down, and wiped his mouth with the back of a hairy hand.

"No, you're right. You're both right. Let's just stay here."

Michael couldn't help himself from smiling a little bit, but he was quick to disguise the expression when Drew looked in his direction. He leaned forward to peer inquisitively at his friend.

"You sure you're sure, Drew?"

"Yeah, I'm sure I'm sure. Let's change the subject before I change my mind, though." Drew paused, then stood up suddenly. "Well, *fuck*! If we're staying here tonight, then at the very least, we're gonna do it right!"

He marched over to the mini-fridge in the corner, reached in, and removed a jade-green bottle. Smiling with satisfaction and an air of mystery, Drew danced back into the den area, tilting the bottle back and forth as he walked, allowing the dark liquid inside to swoosh and swirl round and round.

When he finally arrived back at the sofa, he slammed the bottle dramatically down on the table, fell back into the cushions, and kicked off his leather shoes, apparently savoring the suspense he had created.

Both Michael and Aaron had to lean forward to read the inscriptions on the bottle's yellowed label. Michael still couldn't make out the words from his armchair, so he got up and knelt down beside the coffee table to get a better look. He realized what he was looking at wasn't English at all, but –

"French? Is this French?"

Drew couldn't have been happier with himself. *"Oui, monsieur.* This shit is old, old, old, and came from France a long time ago. You know what it is?"

Michael looked quizzically at Drew. "Absinthe?"

"Fuck yeah, it's absinthe! The real deal, too, with wormwood, or thujone, or whatever that shit is that's illegal and poisonous. But don't worry, one bottle split between the three of us isn't gonna hurt us or anything, just get us major league fucked up, that's all."

Drew gave Michael a quick look, raised his palms defensively, and manufactured a 'worried' facial expression.

"Not 'hangover fucked up', obviously," Drew added. He reached for the bottle, and with a slight tug, forced the cork stopper out with a pop. "Just the right degree of fucked up. What I need to get married in T-minus twelve hours fucked up. A little magical medical dose of ye olde green fairy."

And with that, he took the first sip, and his eyes instantly lit up with delight.

"It's even better than I imagined. Try this, Mike."

He passed the green bottle to Michael, who smelled the open neck with a little curiosity and a lot of trepidation.

Drew smirked. "It's not gonna bite. Besides, I already diluted it with water and sugar. It's traditional. You're gonna be fine, I promise."

Michael studied the French words on the bottle's label. He had taken French years ago in high school and thought he recognized two or three of the words but wasn't entirely sure. Truthfully, he was also more than a little buzzed from the three beers he had already polished off.

"Where did you get this?"

Drew brushed a lock of dark hair from his eye. "From France, man, obviously." A wolfish grin spread across his face. "No, my dad gave it to me as an early wedding gift, I guess. I don't know where or how he got his hands on it; the man has more secrets than he has back hair. But he told me it's authentic and illegal, which is all I need to know. Kinda gets the blood racing, right? I thought it might come in handy tonight, in case I got cold feet or something... give me some trippy dreams... but this seems like a better plan. Share it with my amigos as a sort of Last Supper, you know?"

After a significant period of weighing out the potential consequences, Michael surprised himself by electing to tilt the bottle to his lips and allow just a sliver of the cool liquid to run down his throat.

It was strong and indescribably potent; it also felt *old* in his mouth. He couldn't tell if he was tasting it or smelling it more, but he actually liked it; that taste, the aftertaste it left behind, the way it seemed to freeze up his blood and settle down in his lower stomach like a thick, icy pond.

"It tastes like licorice."

"Black licorice, right? Try some, Copernicus. Mr.

Strong Silent Type. This oughta straighten you out a bit; you're tense, even for you."

Aaron attempted a smile and reached for the bottle.

"I'm sorry, Drew, I'm not trying to be... you know..."

"What?" Drew looked into his friend's eyes with a piercing incision, penetrating yet not unfriendly.

Clearly uncomfortable, Aaron didn't immediately say anything, but rather looked down at his socks. Drew, however, was not one to let up when he sensed the opportunity to psychoanalyze his friends.

"Not trying to be what? A downer?" He laughed. "Look, bud, I'm the one who's getting married tomorrow, right? If anyone's gonna sit here and mope around on the verge of tears, it should be me, not you. So, what's up?" Silence. "Come on, spill... I need you to man up for me here, or I'm gonna start getting nervous, and then I'm gonna start second-guessing things, and from there on, it's absolute panic and hysteria, and I know Mikey doesn't want to have to take care of both of us in one night – *again* – so what's going on?"

Aaron kept his gaze on his toes, wriggling them beneath the white cotton, fascinated by something only he could see there. His big, brown, intelligent eyes peered out from behind his glasses. Usually handsome in a classic, all-American sort of way, Aaron somehow seemed *shrunken* to Michael right now, like a hollow, watered-down representation of what he normally was supposed to look like.

Finally, after what seemed like an eternity of vacant minutes, Aaron looked up to discover his two best friends staring at him and waiting for him to take action. It was only then that he seemed to remember what he was supposed to be doing, and quickly, he brought the bottle to his mouth and tilted his head back.

Drew kept his eyes on Aaron, ever probing. "Easy there, cowboy. We gotta make it last. There's no way I'm sleeping sober tonight." He reached over and reclaimed the absinthe.

Michael could already feel the drink tinkering with his brain. The combination of the cheap, commercial Tecates he had already consumed with this new foreign elixir was working a spell deep into the channels of his bloodstream. He swept his gaze from Aaron's pained face to the deep-drinking Drew, who again wiped his lips with the back of his hand once finished, sighed contentedly, and passed the bottle in their small rotation.

Michael reached for it, but his movements seemed slower now and dangerously haphazard. A powerful urge to retreat to the safety and shelter of his chair swept over him. Clumsily, his fingers closed around the bottle, and he brought it back with him to the cozy grape armchair, breathing heavily as he hoisted his body back into it.

Once he was snug and secure, he tilted the absinthe to his lips and took a second pull, then returned his gaze to his companions. Drew looked more than a little bit tipsy, but it was Aaron who kept hogging most of Michael's attention. He studied his friend, who was now picking nervously at a bit of skin around the cuticle of his right index finger.

Aaron had always been the smartest of their group,

excelling at all things science- or math-related in college. Even at an early age, Aaron had possessed a passion for education and a voracious appetite for knowledge. He and Michael had gone to high school together in the Valley, where they first met as lab partners in chemistry and became fast friends.

While Michael hadn't been sure what he wanted to do with his life, and still wasn't too sure to this day, Aaron had known from the very beginning that he wanted to be an astronaut. As a kid, he had been obsessed with building bottle rockets and models of space shuttles, airplanes, and fighter jets. His favorite movie was *2001: A Space Odyssey*, and he would spend long hours at night dreaming of walking on the moon, landing on Mars, or orbiting around Saturn's rings.

As he grew older, Aaron began to hone in on his dream, applying himself in every practical and strategic way he could to turn his career aspiration into a reality. He took every science class his advisers would allow him to in high school, and even volunteered as an assistant to their high school physics teacher – who really didn't need an assistant, but who was too nice to curb this young man's enthusiasm.

Michael and Aaron had coincidentally ended up getting into the same college, so they chose to be roommates freshman year. It was Michael who had convinced Aaron to rush a fraternity with him, "for the good of both our social lives."

Attractive, intelligent, and with rich parents to boot, Aaron had been snatched up by the Alpha Epsilon Pi fraternity brotherhood, the traditionally Jewish frat on campus. Michael found himself pledging to the same organization, and so their parallel journeys continued. Though neither of them were Jewish, ironically, they soon discovered that most of the frat members weren't Jewish either, and so they seemed to fit right in.

Drew Baskin, however, was Jewish, and was also the fraternity chapter president. It was through his influence that both Michael and Aaron experienced an unprecedented amount of popularity and partying that neither one of them could have ever envisioned possible. Drew was a life force, a lightning rod of energy and charisma that seemed to make those around him more magnetic and interesting themselves, and so Michael and Aaron had stayed close to this exciting figure for the bulk of their college careers.

Drew's passion was acting, and while he was brave enough to pursue this career with a theatre degree, he was also wise enough to double major in business. His parents had divorced long ago, but his father was a powerful player in Silicon Valley who often enlisted his son as a freelancer on various web projects and online collaborations. As a result, no matter what kind of state Drew's acting career was in post-graduation, he never seemed to be at a loss for money, which made him all the more desirable to women in Los Angeles.

Michael had graduated with a B.A. in Communications. Partly because as an undeclared major his sophomore year, he had found himself in the depths of a major identity crisis. On a whim, he chose Communications, thinking himself to be good with people.

Tragically, Michael had soon learned the hard way that he was not, in fact, good with people, floundering on most of his dates and struggling to make any real friends outside of his pre-ordained fraternity brothers.

It was not that Michael was shy, he just didn't seem to possess the intrinsic ability to deepen any of his social relationships. Either he found nothing in common with the people in his life, he was bored by all the small talk, or he simply just didn't care enough about most individuals to actively try and further the relationship.

Michael was not one to initiate social events, call anyone up, or want to 'just hang out'. It wasn't that he was necessarily asocial by definition; he was just more comfortable going with the flow and letting others create his experience for him.

Nevertheless, this comfort zone of human interaction soon allowed people in Michael's life to begin taking advantage of him, and it didn't take long for Michael himself to notice. Even Drew, who had quickly and somewhat surprisingly overtaken Aaron as Michael's best friend freshman year, enjoyed having Michael as a complacent sidekick and wingman, and he would never hesitate to let his buddy take the fall for his own benefit.

But Michael was not the confrontational type, so he learned over time to swallow his pride as well as his objections, and sacrifice his own needs and wants in exchange for always having people in his life who seemed to enjoy his company, despite his apparent social limitations and shortcomings.

Aaron had majored in physics and was the only one of the three of them to continue higher education after graduating in four years with their bachelor's degrees. He had gone on to Michigan to pursue a Masters in Astronomy, and after achieving that, had returned home to California to explore career opportunities.

At this point, Aaron had ruled out becoming an actual astronaut, and Michael remembered feeling distinctly disappointed when this news was revealed to him in a conversation over beers at one of their favorite L.A. watering holes. Michael had long fantasized about having an astronaut friend he could brag about to other people, and for some reason, Aaron's decision to terminate this dream seemed to be a betrayal and almost a defeat for Michael himself.

Predictably having no idea what to do with a Communications degree in the real world, Michael was also unemployed at this time. He was the one who suggested that maybe Drew could help Aaron find a job, though, and that suggestion proved to be prescient.

It turned out Drew's father had a friend who worked at Ames, a NASA research center in Silicon Valley, and after pulling some strings, that friend managed to get Aaron an interview. More than qualified, Aaron was hired as an assistant physical scientist, and at the age of twenty-five, went to work for NASA.

Drew and Michael stayed in Los Angeles, with Drew auditioning for television and commercial work while freelancing for his father to pay the bills, and Michael working as a temp at various businesses and companies before finding relative stability in a boring but steady job as a credit union teller in Glendale.

As the years passed, Michael slipped into a comfortable nine-to-five routine, Drew slept his way around Los Angeles before falling for Michelle, a costar he met in a local play, and Aaron proved himself a capable scientist, researcher, and stargazer in Northern California. Drew and Michael stayed close, and Aaron would visit when his work allowed; mainly over holidays, and less frequently on the odd vacation getaway to places like Big Bear, Palm Springs, or Joshua Tree.

And then, about a year ago, Aaron had suddenly been offered a transfer to Dryden, another NASA center, this one located on the edge of the Mojave Desert at Edwards Air Force Base. Aaron had accepted the new job, working with a team of flight research developers on new spacecraft technology that would allow scientists to better study and understand the outer edges of the Milky Way.

The project was supposedly very important, and it required Aaron to spend long hours of every day in laboratories and research facilities, lending his expertise and inquisitive mind to the forefront of NASA's more "under the radar" space exploration work.

While the job was taxing, it did allow Aaron to move back into greater Los Angeles, where he found a small apartment outside Santa Clarita that allowed him to reconnect with his friends on long weekends and holidays.

His commute to work every day was grueling, but he assured Michael and Drew that it was well worth it, because he really loved what he was doing, and he couldn't stress enough the importance of his research.

Aaron was always fond of boasting over drinks that "the things we're doing have never been done before," and that "this is something no one has ever understood, and we're finally starting to get it."

Drew would roll his eyes then and laugh, affectionately referring to Aaron as 'Copernicus'. Drew was exceptionally proud of this nickname. But Michael found he was always a bit taken aback in these moments by the earnest truth and conviction gleaming in Aaron's intelligent brown eyes. He wondered if he would ever find something in his own life he could be just as passionate about.

Now, in the present moment, the only thing that gleamed in Aaron's eyes was the threat of what looked like tears, and Michael saw nothing but stress and fear lurking behind them. His friend had always been an intellectual, prone to mental stress, headaches, and occasional anxiety. But never before had Michael seen him looking so very devastated and unsure, as if he had some massive weight pressing down upon his brain and shoulders that would not let him breathe.

Michael debated whether or not to speak, and finally decided to give it a shot. He cleared his throat, blinked a few times in an effort to steady his swaying vision, and shakily proffered the bottle of absinthe to Aaron.

"Is it about your job?"

His voice seemed unnatural to him, and Drew also looked startled by the sudden sound. Michael wasn't sure how long they had been sitting there in silence; he wasn't even sure if they had been sitting in silence. Maybe the others had been talking this whole time he was thinking. But looking at Aaron's face, it seemed as if his friend had not spoken in a very long time.

The absinthe was still in Michael's hand, outstretched across the gulf of space between his armchair and the sofa. Were they both as drunk as he was?

Aaron allowed his sightline to move from his fingernail to the bottle, and Michael couldn't help but think how old his friend suddenly looked with all those thick lines of worry etched across his forehead. Sitting perfectly still, Aaron's eyes seemed to be looking through the bottle and into some unimaginable distant specter. He worked his jaw upward, grinding his teeth together and moistening his lips, and when he finally spoke, his voice was small and frightened.

"I – I can't say…"

Drew waited expectantly, an odd, sardonic smirk playing on his features. He reached past Aaron and took the absinthe bottle from Michael.

The movement seemed to startle Aaron. His face twitched and convulsed quickly, but his body was still rigid on the couch. Drew then smacked the bottle into Aaron's stomach, leaving it resting on his lap.

"Maybe some more of this will loosen up your tongue. Seriously, man, your act's getting old."

Aaron looked down at the absinthe in his lap, and ever so slowly, began to put his hands on it. Drew watched him for a moment, and when it was clear that Aaron was making no immediate move to drink from it, he stood up abruptly.

"This is fucking ridiculous."

He walked unsteadily away from the couch and toward the large plasma TV that faced the seating area of his den. Drew reached for the remote resting on top of the screen, thought better of it, and spun back around to face his friends.

"You wanted to stay in, I stayed in. But I'm not gonna sit here and play guessing games all night. Need

I remind you guys that this is the eve of my wedding? Aaron, I'm getting *married* tomorrow. All I'm asking is for a few hours of laughs and drinks with my two best friends in the world before the biggest day of my life." He lifted his hands out to Aaron, palms up, in an exasperated pleading motion. "What do you say?"

Michael squirmed uncomfortably in his armchair, unsure of whether to look at Aaron or not. He had never seen him like this before, not in all their time together since high school. Michael stole a quick, furtive glance in his direction and saw that Aaron's eyes were closed now, as if he was trying to shut out the whole world around him.

Evidently, that was the final straw for Drew. "Okay, then." He turned to the television and reached for the remote. Michael looked down at his feet.

Quick as a flash, Drew spun and released the remote, sending it spiraling through the air like a black plastic dagger at the couch. Aaron had no time to react before the remote hit him square in the chest. The impact made his legs jerk up defensively, sending the absinthe bottle to the ground, and in a blur, Drew was at the foot of the sofa, righting the bottle before any more of its precious contents could spill out onto the floor.

Drew was on the purple couch then, one arm pinning Aaron's limbs against his sides, the other lifting the bottle to Aaron's mouth.

Michael didn't know what was going on. Everything had been so slow, so stifled, so quiet… and now things were moving way too fast. It was all he could do to stand and move to the couch, sputtering some attempt at a profanity, reaching to pull Drew off the struggling Aaron. But Drew used his left leg to shove Michael back toward the armchair, where he tripped over one of its legs and fell backward. He landed hard on his bottom, shock and pain washing over him at once.

Absinthe running down his mouth and onto his t-shirt, Aaron tried to turn his face away from the flowing liquor, but Drew kept following his mouth with the upturned bottle. A hideous choking sound finally came from Aaron's throat, and then Drew released him, backing up and away from the both of them, surveying the scene.

Aaron coughed and rubbed at his face with his wet shirt. He tried in vain to find a clean, dry part of the cloth where he could wipe the stinging alcohol from his eyes.

Michael still sat on the ground, feeling pounding pistons of pain in his lower spine and back swell up. His eyes were locked on Drew. What had happened? He felt confused and horrified at the same time.

Drew was breathing heavily, his face expressionless. After several seconds, he looked down at the now-empty green bottle in his hand and tossed it carelessly aside. The bottle landed softly on the beige carpet and rolled to a stop against a wall.

Michael eased his way up onto his legs and crossed to Aaron at the couch, who was still coughing and blotting at his eyes. He sat down heavily next to his friend and put a hand upon his shoulder.

Instantly, Aaron recoiled at the touch and opened his eyes, seeing Michael as if for the first time. His deep brown eyes were red and shining, and they appeared more sad and frightened than truly angry or confused.

Michael was certainly confused though, and plenty angry. He whirled on Drew.

"What the hell, man?! Are you crazy? Why did you do that?!"

Drew stared evenly back at him, his broad chest slowly moving up and down as he caught his breath. He didn't answer. Instead, he just wiped his wet hands on his jeans and calmly walked to the mini-fridge, opened the door, and grabbed himself another beer.

"I'm sorry."

The words came from Michael's side, not from the refrigerator. He turned and saw Aaron, hands limp in his lap, eyes boring holes into the television set. His voice was a bit clearer now, steady if not strong.

"I have to tell you. You both deserve it. You… you need to know."

CHAPTER THREE

Michael looked intently at his friend. His curiosity was beginning to slowly dwarf the shock he still felt from the incident that had just occurred.

Without warning, Aaron belched loudly and made to cover his mouth, feeling his stomach heave. He shut his eyes against the sick, swallowed, and then, out of nowhere, began to laugh. His eyes were moist, and his face was red, but he laughed to himself with a sudden wild abandon.

Michael was beginning to wonder if he was witnessing firsthand a true psychotic breakdown. Conversely, Drew looked relatively unfazed by the volatility of Aaron's emotions. He kept one hand firmly planted on his hipbone and used the other to lift his beer up to his mouth for the occasional sip, apparently content to keep waiting and watching, his face oddly expectant.

When Aaron was finally able to stymie the rollicking laughter shaking his body from head to toe, his face was flushed and wet from sweat and tears, and his eyes betrayed a hint of hysteria in the glaze.

"It's the absinthe. It finally pushed me over." Then his smile was gone, and he was sighing out, long and low. "God... where do I even begin?"

Drew now seemed a bit amused, but Michael was far too drunk to see anything funny in the situation. He knew his friends. Aaron had never acted like this before, even if he truly was severely intoxicated. It alarmed Michael and made the hairs on the back of his neck and arms stand up straight.

He kept trying to focus his vision on Aaron's face, but he was also battling a bad case of the spins himself, and the sudden change in temperature and tone of the room had done nothing to sober up his body. Only in his mind could he register a vague sense of unease, but the sensation was growing, and before long, he felt it manifesting in the pit of his stomach, too, like a lump of black dread in the basin of his belly.

Aaron brought his fingers to his temples, closed his eyes again, and opened his mouth to speak. The veins in his forehead bulged, and every time Michael was able to steady his vision, he could swear he saw rivers of blood pumping through the pipelines under Aaron's skin around his eyebrows. It was a disturbing sight, and far more detail than Michael wished to be aware of.

Aaron spoke. "You guys know a little about my work, right? What I came down here for?"

Michael turned to Drew, who made no immediate move to answer, so he responded for the two of them.

"Yeah, you're studying the galaxy, right? Working on spaceships... or probes... or something... that can explore further out in space?"

This didn't seem to be the right answer at all, as it came haltingly out of Michael's mouth, and he immediately felt guilty and foolishly unaware of what

Aaron actually did at his job.

But Aaron had always been so private, and Michael had just assumed it was his way of leaving his work at the office. Some part of Michael had always held out hope that Aaron was working with alien technology, or on some super-secret government space project that was highly classified. His imagination frequently ran wild with possibilities of what Aaron actually did for NASA.

Aaron stared down at the floor. "That's close enough." He turned to look at Drew, then back at Michael. "Do you guys know what gamma rays are?"

Michael's brows furrowed. "Yeah, I think so. Like UV rays, or microwave... waves?"

"Similar enough. They're rays of electromagnetic radiation, the strongest kind. At one end of the electromagnetic spectrum, you've got things like radio waves and microwaves. As the wavelengths get shorter, their frequencies get higher, and you start having infrared light, visible light, and then – even higher – UV waves and X-rays. Higher still are gamma rays. Most all of these rays are screened by the Earth's atmosphere, which is a good thing, since they're basically high-energy radiation. But it means that to study some of them, we have to send out spacecraft into the galaxy."

Michael was working hard to process everything Aaron was saying. This sort of 'tech talk', as he referred to it, seldom made much sense to Michael, and Drew would often get impatient and cut Aaron off mid-speech with an interjection of "to the point, Copernicus," or just flat-out change the subject.

But something in Aaron's voice brooked no

interruption this time, and so the two other men were silent for the time being, waiting to see where their friend would lead them.

"My team has been studying gamma rays in the universe for over two decades now. They brought me onto the project as a fresh perspective, and because they were interested in the work I had been doing on gamma ray bursts at Ames. These bursts are the brightest, most powerful events in the universe that we know of. They come from massive radiation released during a supernova, when giant stars collapse into black holes. But they've always been completely unpredictable and virtually unknowable. People have been studying them since they were first discovered in the late 60s, but always without coming to any real explanation."

"To the point, Copernicus." Drew broke the spell Aaron's words had created, and Michael was startled to hear his husky voice chop in.

Aaron only smiled ruefully. "I'm sorry. Of course, you're going to say that." He took a deep breath and then stared out straight in front of him.

"Well, we've found something. After all this time of not knowing, we... well, we *know* now. Through data collection and analysis, my team was able to accurately predict our first gamma ray burst five years ago. This is something that had never, ever been done before. Over the past five years, we've been trying to perfect our methods, striving for greater understanding of these things. Our goal was to find a way to forecast cosmic events like a meteorologist does the weekly weather. We got more and more accurate and precise. If we saw a star that looked like it was ready for collapse, we analyzed the factors at play, and within a short amount of days, we could tell you exactly how much radiation would be released, how big the burst would be, how long it'd last for, and most importantly, which planets or objects would be affected by it."

Aaron paused to collect his thoughts, bent forward slightly, and allowed his hands to grasp his shins.

"These gamma ray bursts have never been a danger to our planet, but it's been hypothesized that if one were to occur within our galaxy, and if the energy beam of the burst just happened to line up perfectly with us... it would be the end of the world."

Silence descended momentarily on the den.

"Well... *fuck*!"

Michael turned to face Drew, who had set his empty beer bottle down on top of the fridge and was now applauding vigorously with both hands.

"I'm scared! I mean... forget about the wedding, right? That'll have to wait. But what about building a bomb shelter? Or maybe we can go to one of those earthquake supply stores or a Home Depot and see if they have a shelter that'll protect us from gamma rays, UV rays, fucking *beta zappa theta* waves, an all-in-one deluxe package, and get it delivered and installed in my backyard before Y2K2 comes along and shit really hits the fan. Whattaya say, boys?" Neither responded, so Drew just sneered and went on. "No time but the present. New Orleans wasn't ready for Katrina and look what happened to that shithole... and that was just *water*. We're talking heavy shit up here tonight, the real deal; a hurricane from *space*. 'Radiation' and 'supernovas' and 'black holes', oh my!"

Slowly, Aaron stood up then, and Michael realized

that his friend had been sitting there in that exact same spot on the couch since they first arrived at Drew's place earlier that evening around nine. Hours had passed, and Aaron had not moved from the sofa. Not once.

He looked down at Michael gravely, then across the den to where Drew was still standing by the mini-fridge. His gaze was level and steady, but his expression was pained, almost apologetic. When he spoke, his voice sounded tired.

"What I'm trying to tell you is that this is going to happen to us. And it's going to happen tomorrow morning, at precisely 11:13 a.m. From the new data collected, we determined that the star WR 104 went supernova and emitted a massive GRB that lasted about twenty seconds in duration. That burst is set to finally reach Earth tomorrow morning after traveling over seventy-five hundred light-years to reach us.

"It will strike our planet directly in the southern hemisphere. The damage sustained will eradicate up to a full quarter of the ozone layer, which will also fatally rupture the food chain. From there on out, it's a steady spread of radiation and lethal UV rays. If the rays don't kill us, we'll all starve to death."

Michael couldn't believe what he was hearing. Surely, this was some kind of prank; a sick joke Aaron had planned for Drew on the eve of his nuptial. Aaron had always had an offbeat sense of humor, often illustrated through bizarre, nerdy fantasies and antiquated puns. It would not be a stretch for him to dream up this sci-fi doomsday scenario and think it a funny complement to Drew's last night as a single man. Michael understood the obvious parallels and decided to laugh it all off.

"Jesus, Aaron! You are one sick man." He stood up then, clapping a hand on Aaron's shoulder and crossing to where Drew stood by the fridge. "But he's not marrying Godzilla or the Antichrist. This is Michelle we're talking about! I don't think we'll be seeing any of the Four Horsemen tomorrow... unless one of them is Lillian." He laughed at his own joke and reached around Drew to open the fridge.

Aaron looked from one man to the other, his eyes deathly serious, his face strained.

"Mike, I'm not kidding. I wish I was, believe me. I wish this whole thing was a dumb joke, but it's not. You have to believe me. Everything I'm telling you guys is true, and it's all going to happen tomorrow morning. My team and I, we finalized our calculations and figured all this out just... just a day ago, and the higher-ups immediately swore us to silence. They don't want riots, panic, hysteria in the streets. But this is real, and it's going to happen... and there's nothing we can do to stop it.

"I'm sorry, I wasn't going to say anything; I'm not supposed to say anything. But how can I not? How can someone who knows something like this not tell other people? Not tell their family, their loved ones? I mean, you guys are all I have left, and... I don't know. I thought you deserved to know..."

There was silence. Michael held an unopened beer in his right hand. Drew was staring levelly at Aaron, his expression hard to read for once.

Michael looked deep into Aaron's coffee-brown eyes, questioning, desperately searching for a sign that would betray the earnestness there and reveal Aaron to be lying, to be only joking about all of this.

What was he even saying anyway? None of it made any sense anymore. He had taken things too far, and now the night had become unsteady and uncertain.

All Michael felt was cold dread and confusion... and a pressure in his head. The pain in his tailbone shot up his spine and reminded him of his hard fall, and he felt discomfort ripple through his body and down his appendages like white-hot electricity.

Quietly, Drew moved to the wooden door at the other side of the room and opened it, spilling light onto the soft carpeted steps that led up to the foyer and the rest of his luxury townhouse, then turned back to face his friends.

"Get out."

Michael looked at Drew, then back at Aaron. The Tecate in his hand was perspiring and suddenly felt precariously slippery in his hand.

"Get out. I'm not fucking around. Get out." Nobody moved. "It's not funny anymore. It really wasn't funny to begin with. I don't know what your problem is, but don't try and make it my problem. Not tonight of all nights."

Drew looked dangerously rigid standing in front of the doorway, one hand still gripping the doorknob, knuckles white and tight.

"I've had it. Go home and sleep it off, both of you. I don't care if you have to call a cab, or call two cabs, but do it. Tomorrow is the biggest day of my life, and I need you guys to be there looking fresh and dewy at nine o'clock."

Michael took a small step toward Drew. "Hey, Drew, look... this isn't a big deal, we don't have to call it a night yet. Everyone just needs to calm down a bit, have another beer—"

"You've drunk enough of my beer for one night. Why don't you stop trying to play peacemaker and start playing caretaker to your sick friend, okay?"

Michael slowly set the beer bottle back down on the fridge and then turned around. Aaron did, in fact, look sick. His eyes were glassy, and his skin was pale as cream. He looked like a cancer patient, but there was still a desperation and a fever in his frantic gaze that unnerved Michael.

Before he could move toward him, though, Aaron walked unsteadily past both of them to the stairs. He reached the foot of the steps, stopped short, and turned to face Drew, less than an arm's length away from the future groom. Aaron swallowed hard and blinked to steady his vision, and then coughed quietly to clear his throat.

"I'm sorry, Drew. I think what I've said tonight… was without tact. I'll see you tomorrow." And then he was up the stairs and out of sight. Ten seconds later, Michael heard the front door open and close.

He turned his attention back to Drew. "I don't know what that was all about, but I'm sure he was just trying to be funny in his own weird way, and it didn't come out right. He's had so much to drink… We all have, really."

"Well, then, go take care of him."

Michael wanted to say something more to displace the tension in the room. He didn't want the night to end on this bizarre low note, not just hours before Drew's wedding. What would tomorrow look like after tonight? Would things be awkward between them?

Surely, Drew would be able to laugh off the night… and Aaron, too. They'd all blame it on the absinthe; strange chemicals making people say and do strange things.

Michael thought to touch Drew's shoulder, but decided against it.

"You gonna be all right?"

"Of course, I'm going to be all right. I'm getting married tomorrow. Now, go home and get some sleep."

Drew released the knob, walked past Michael to the refrigerator, and wrapped a hand around the bottle Michael had left there. Without looking back, he twisted the cap off and plopped down in the armchair, pushing back in it to recline and kicking his legs out in front of him.

Clearly, Michael had been dismissed. He stood there for another uncomfortable moment, wondering what else he could say to salvage the night and pave the way for an easier reconciliation tomorrow.

But the vibe he got from Drew now was one of irritation and stony silence, so Michael realized that nothing he could say would likely alter the mood that had fallen on his friend and on the night itself. Defeated, he moved slowly over to the steps.

"Night, buddy. I'll see you tomorrow, front and center."

"You'll see me before that, I hope. I'm gonna need a hell of a pep talk after tonight's shitshow."

CHAPTER FOUR

Michelle was beautiful, glistening and twinkling in folds of soft white fabric, the easy California sunlight reflecting playfully off pearls and tiny diamonds woven through her perfectly constructed hair. Lillian had reportedly taken almost two hours with the bride's hairstyle and presentation, and even Michael had to admit that she had done exceptional work.

He had never seen Michelle like this, so breathtakingly stunning in a classic, ageless sort of way. And so very happy. Her smile seemed ready to burst from her face, and the whites of her teeth rivaled her dress for color and clarity.

The morning was crisp and slightly cool, but not uncomfortable. It had been unseasonably hot for October in L.A., so Michael was relieved that the sun had not yet burned off the morning's misty pleasantness.

Standing in his rented black tuxedo, he mentally thanked the universe that he would not be sweating through his expensive clothes for the entire event. At least not so long as the temperature remained mild. Michael felt stiff and uncertain in the outfit nonetheless, but he did his best to conceal this discomfort by burying his hands in his pockets and focusing on the approaching bride.

The wedding party was not enormous, but one couldn't say it was a small, private ceremony, either. Michael thought he recognized the faces of more than a couple of his old fraternity brothers, men he hadn't kept in contact with since graduation.

Surely, Drew had, though; especially as chapter president, and especially considering how popular he had always been in school. These men now were flanked by bronzed trophy wives, all sporting tasteful yet effortlessly sexy dresses or skirts. The men looked rich, too, and somehow, even more smug and self-important than they had looked in college.

Michael couldn't fight off the feelings of envy and resentment that clawed at his insides. No matter, he thought. At least *he* was Drew's best friend, and his best man, standing at the front of this wedding. That was something that not a one of them could say, and it was enough to temporarily content Michael and soothe his growing pangs of jealousy.

Past rows and rows of family and friends, Michelle had found her way down the grassy aisle. Her father kissed her on both cheeks, gave her hands one last squeeze, and then sat down beside his wife in the first row.

Across the way, Michael saw Drew's mother wipe a tear from her eye with a handkerchief. Her ex-husband, Drew's father, patted her leg good-naturedly with a furry paw, and then gave Michael the slightest of winks. Michael smiled back.

Drew had never looked better himself. If he was at all still rattled from the happenings of the previous night, he didn't show it one bit. His face was a picture of calm, cool confidence, his eyes locked on his bride's.

Drew's hair was slick but not oily, and he filled his tuxedo out perfectly with his broad shoulders and chest. Michael couldn't help but admire his friend's weight loss; Drew had always been muscular, but he had allowed himself a bit of a beer belly before getting engaged. He had spent the past year living at the gym though, and it showed now.

Again, Michael felt the little green monster worming its way into his head. He looked down at his long, thin arms wrapped in the baggy tuxedo sleeves and suddenly felt very fragile.

Michael tilted his head back slightly to look at Aaron. His friend was shorter than both of them but every bit as handsome as Drew in his own tuxedo.

He also looked nothing like the man from last night. That man had seemed wild, hollow, sad, and rabid all at once. Now, Aaron was stone-faced, neither grinning nor frowning. He had barely spoken since arriving at the park, but he had shown up promptly at 9 a.m., showered, dressed, and ready to go.

Mercifully, Drew had done almost all the talking, and never once did he make any mention of the previous night's debacle. He was all dumb jokes and easy laughs, going above and beyond to put anyone and everyone else at ease.

Michael, however, knew his friend well enough to recognize a defense mechanism; Drew *was* nervous, and understandably so. But perhaps not about anything they had talked about last night. This was the most important day of his life, and though he was taking the greatest of lengths to portray absolute indifference and confident joy, Michael knew better.

Drew had always been a ladies' man and a womanizer, since long before they ever knew him. As such, he must have known that his wedding day – the beginning of an important new chapter of his life – was also the death of everything he had come to enjoy in his easy, independent bachelorhood. Accordingly, Drew had done everything possible to cover up his own insecurities by projecting an over-the-top outward poise and positivism.

Because of this, Aaron's quietness went unnoticed by everyone else... save for Michael. When Michael had greeted his oldest friend that morning, he had been wary of the reaction he would receive. Aaron put his immediate concern to bed though with a smile and a congenial response, and he had seemed relatively normal enough to be around.

For his part, Michael had not slept well the previous night. After leaving Drew's townhouse, he had searched outside vainly for Aaron. The man had disappeared entirely. Michael had tried calling out his name, and then tried calling and texting him, all with no success. His worry had quickly morphed into nausea, and Michael was embarrassed to find himself retching into the street, vomiting up all his emotions, along with the absinthe, beer, and half-digested burritos from dinner.

After that, he had decided to call a cab and flee the scene quickly, ashamed of himself. He had returned to his apartment stinking of beans and alcohol, and had checked his phone repeatedly, hoping to find a message from Aaron, but there was none to be found.

Michael then had resigned himself to a cold

shower, two Advil, a large glass of water, and his bed, where his faithful companion Tucker was snoring peacefully on his pillow. He had slept fitfully, dreaming of asteroids, zombies, and giant dinosaurs. On several occasions, he remembered sitting up sharply in a cold sweat, certain he had died gruesomely. The morning light came as a welcome relief, though, and Michael had woken and gotten ready earlier than planned just to avoid any further nightmares.

Here at the wedding now, Aaron met his gaze and tilted his chin down, an almost imperceptible nod. Then Aaron's eyes were back in front of him, watching the ceremony commence. Michael nodded back, for himself more than for Aaron, and turned to face the happy couple.

For the next half-hour, Michael tried to forget all about his own thoughts and wrap himself up entirely in the wedding. Michelle had chosen a secluded part of Angeles National Forest for this occasion. She and Drew were avid hikers and nature enthusiasts, and the weather had not let them down so far. Though the sun had now risen higher in the sky and had begun to burn off most of the morning's haze, it was still nowhere near as hot as it had been in the days leading up to the wedding. The park air was fresh and ruddy, and Michael found it to have a calming effect on his mind.

Even the young priest's voice, rich and resonant, was comforting to the ear as he spoke to bride and groom, his expression paternal and kindly, his arms often gesturing out to the wedding guests to include them in this holiest of unions.

Michael wondered if Drew's parents cared that their son was being married by a priest rather than a rabbi. Michelle was Catholic, and as she was overwhelmingly more devout than her husband-to-be, they had agreed that a priest was the better choice for the ceremony. Michael himself had been raised Catholic, but long ago had given up his faith after a short-lived and ultimately fruitless period of experimentation with Buddhism and other Eastern methodologies in college.

Seemingly of its own accord, Michael's left hand twitched. His attention wandered from the ceremony, and he wasn't sure what had brought it back until he was aware of the leather band strapped around his wrist.

No, there was no reason to even think about that. Besides, even if he wanted to check it, what would everyone else think? He was standing right next to Drew, Michelle, and the priest, the focal triangle of the wedding. He could not get away with it, not even with a quick furtive glance.

All it took was one person seeing him, and he would never be able to swallow the shame and guilt. And what if Michelle saw him check behind Drew… what would she think? Or, heaven forbid, Lillian? That would be the worst-case scenario of all.

It was too dangerous. The ceremonial part of the wedding couldn't last much longer anyway, and then it would be over, he would be leading his ice-queen partner back down the aisle, and they would all be driving to the reception hall for drinking, dancing, and cake-cutting. And that was the easy part, then, the carefree part Michael had been looking forward to the most since last night. Because it meant more than just a celebration. It meant…

He allowed his right hand to grasp his left wrist. His fingers slid over the smooth crystal surface and along the brown leather band, grazing along the inside of his shirt cuff. Michael had stopped wearing a wristwatch when Jeanette, his attractive coworker at the credit union, made an innocuous comment one day before lunch that he was "always obsessing over the time." It hadn't been a reproach so much as an innocent, not entirely untrue, observation, but it had made Michael self-conscious.

The next day, he had arrived to work sans watch, and he waited all day for her to notice. She had not, and Michael had taken to glancing frequently at his cell phone clock instead.

What it was that made Michael dig the accessory out from the back of his dresser this particular morning, he was not about to acknowledge out loud, nor even in his head, if he could help it. But he had reached for it, found it, and put it on beneath his tuxedo.

At first, the leather felt unfamiliar wrapped around his delicate wrist, an old friend he had all but forgotten. Michael had quickly gotten used to it though, and by the time he arrived at the park, it was out of his mind entirely.

Now, however, it called upon his attention and wouldn't let go, despite his best efforts to refocus on the matter at hand: his best friend's wedding.

His right hand had already done half the work for him, giving him the best possible positioning. All he had to do now was lift his left cuff ever so slightly with his fingers, and maybe he could drop his eyes for a second without moving his head down. That would be enough, he hoped, to do a quick read and put the gnawing sensation at his insides to bed once and for all.

Michael made up his mind, and without any further hesitation, made the move; lightning-fast, but with all the subtlety and economy of movement he could manage.

The little hand was only a few centimeters left of the jewel at the top... but that was not what Michael was interested in. The big hand was in between the first and second dots right of the jewel, skewed slightly more to the second dot than the first.

What, then? 11:08, probably. Maybe 11:07 or 11:09, but definitely not 11:10 yet. And, more importantly, not 11:13.

Michael relaxed his hands and eyes, and then sighed, annoyed with himself. This was ridiculous. He wanted to turn and look at Aaron, or ask him if he, too, was aware of the time.

But he didn't dare. The ceremony was almost over. He could see that Michelle was getting ready to say her vows. After that would come Drew's vows, the kiss, and then the reception. They had made it this far, and nothing had happened. Aaron had even nodded to him and hadn't looked fearful or stressed or even remotely unsettled this morning.

This whole concern over the time, the whole act of wearing a watch in the first place, now seemed absurdly ridiculous to Michael. He almost smiled at his own foolishness. Nothing but a bad dream, he told himself. The crazed ramblings of a drunken conspiracy theorist who spends too much time looking at stars and watching movies like *Deep Impact* and *Armageddon*. Last night was silliness. Absolute sloppiness and stupidity.

He marveled at the idea that he had somehow allowed the night to discomfort him to such a degree.

What did he expect? They had all had so much to drink, even before that stupid absinthe. Who even knows what that did to all of them. Maybe Aaron had actually seen the green fairy, and it was she who had whispered her lunacies into his ear.

And then, the sky pulsed.

A hundred heads turned upward, as if on strings, in perfect unison. The blue was gone, the clouds were gone, the birds were gone, the sun was gone. All was white, bright, and blinding. There was no sound, not even an echo or thunder. Nothing moved, nothing shook. All was still except for the light, which seemed to move somehow, shifting and shimmering... and it was not unbeautiful.

Michael's eyes watered, and for the briefest second, he thought to check his watch. But somewhere, deep down, he knew he didn't have to. His breathing was slow and shallow, his mouth open in half a gasp, his head tilted all the way back on its axis.

The light flickered everywhere at once.

And then the blue was returning, the clouds were returning, the birds were returning, the sun was returning. It was normal once again, as if nothing had happened, and Michael felt his eyes crying. He was aware of himself again, and lowered his head, and saw Drew. And the look on Drew's face was unmistakable.

Michael was vaguely aware of a small commotion; people in the white folding chairs were murmuring to one another and remarking on what they had just seen. The priest didn't seem to know what to say or do. For a minute, Michael thought the ceremony wouldn't continue, but then the holy man held his arms aloft, smiled widely, and spoke over the muted voices.

"Folks, folks… What we have just witnessed is a blessing from God above. Now, I didn't check the news today, or the weather, so I'm not sure if that was an eclipse or a solar flare or what exactly that was, but what I do know is this: This union between Drew and Michelle is exactly according to the Lord's plan, and He has shown us His approval of their love in one of the most tangible ways possible; with a sign. What a miracle! This is, indeed, a special day, and a holy one. Thanks be to God."

There was a polite round of applause, as well as a few scattered laughs and sounds of appreciation. Several older guests bowed their heads and made the sign of the cross. Most of the faces were mollified now, enchanted with the explanation given to them by the religious authority in their midst. A few thrill-seekers were still scanning the sky and looking for more unusual events, cameras and smartphones at the ready, just in case.

Michelle couldn't help herself; she reached across the narrow space between them and gave Drew an ecstatic hug, clearly moved by the cosmic event and the priest's interpretation. When she broke apart from him, Drew was staring at her, looking spellbound and mystified. Michelle laughed, and the priest encouraged Drew to continue on with his vows "before we get any more light shows," to another soft round of laughter from the crowd.

After a moment, Drew found his tongue, and rather breathlessly recited his part in the proceedings while exchanging rings. And then they were kissing, the guests were cheering and clapping, and before Michael knew it, Lillian begrudgingly weaved her arm through his and guided him down the soft green aisle, past all the innumerable smiles and kind looks.

All too late, Michael remembered Aaron, and he turned to look at his friend behind him, who was leading Michelle's sister down the path. Inexplicably, Aaron looked relieved.

Michael turned back around as they passed by the final row of guests and the wedding photographers standing at the back of the clearing. All of them had trained their cameras on the procession except for one, an elderly man on the outer end, who still peered through his lens at the sky.

Michael wondered if he was seeing something that all the others could not, something strange or horrifying or beautiful that was invisible to the naked eye. He glanced up at where he gauged the photographer to be looking but saw only blue and the faintest wisps of white clouds, rolling lazily along, unaware and unassuming.

CHAPTER FIVE

Two days had passed, and Michael was still alive.

He had spent hours on the internet and in front of his television, ranging through every news channel his cable subscription service would allow. The phenomenon that had occurred two days previous at 11:13 a.m. had barely been discussed at all.

Michael had tried to search for information about it on his phone at the wedding reception, but his service had been spotty and slow in the mountains outside of L.A. There were no TVs in the country club building where the reception was being held, much to Michael's incredulity. The park rangers and service staff informed him that the building was designed to mimic the great outdoors in which it was located, so despite the luxuries of having running water and enough electricity to light the structure and power the guitars and amps of the wedding rock band, there were no television sets or other "city comforts."

Every guest that Michael approached was willing to talk about the spectacle they had beheld, but none seemed the slightest bit concerned by it. It had come and gone so quickly that it seemed almost not to have occurred at all. Everyone had seen stranger things in their lifetimes. Environmentalists chalked the whole thing up to global warming and pollution. Conspiracy theorists whispered of aliens and government cover-ups. Conservatives dutifully echoed the priest's explanation, touched that God had smiled down on the marriage through the clouds.

One thing every person shared in common, though, was champagne, and it wasn't long before everyone was caught up in the celebration. Soon, the light was forgotten, and everyone was dancing, chatting happily, and toasting the newlyweds.

When Michael approached Drew, the groom had guided him good-naturedly to the bar. "We're not going to talk about this; not here, not tonight," was all he had said, speaking in a low but deliberate tone, before ordering them each a double Scotch. Michael had begun to protest, but Drew clapped a hand on his shoulder, turned to the pretty young bartender, and began flirting with her as she poured their drinks. As soon as she was finished, he winked at her, passed a drink to Michael, clinked their glasses together, and then went striding back to his bride.

Michael had found Aaron sitting at a table surrounded by guests he did not recognize. He wanted to pull him away from the group, but Aaron had entrenched himself in their midst, nodding sternly at the words of his strange companions, seeming completely engaged by whatever discussions swirled around him.

Finally, Michael had sought comfort outside on the veranda, only to discover Lillian and a tall man Michael recognized as one of the married party guests talking quietly against the railing, their physical proximity to one another completely inappropriate. For half a second, Michael had thought to find the man's wife, but then he remembered he had no idea who the man or his wife were, or what she might even look like. Ridiculously, Michael had felt embarrassed for stumbling upon them, and he'd hurriedly rushed back indoors.

When Drew and Michelle finally drove off in a beautiful black car and all the guests began to disperse, Michael had looked everywhere for Aaron, but his search had been utterly futile.

Feeling completely defeated, Michael had left the reception in a hurry, with scarce a word of goodbye to anyone. He had returned home and immediately turned on the TV, but most of the news networks seemed relatively uninterested in covering the mysterious light in the sky.

Pivoting, he had raced into his bedroom and booted up his laptop, desperate to learn more about what had happened that morning and what was happening currently around the world. Were people already dead? Was the nation in a state of emergency? The world?

For two days, Michael had searched. There were various reports explaining away the cosmic phenomenon. The general consensus of the scientific community was that a solar flare had occurred; rare, but harmless. There were numerous images of the 'flare' on the internet, trending across social media platforms and photo-sharing websites.

But no matter how hard he searched, Michael found nothing regarding gamma ray bursts, radiation, or any alarming news at all regarding the southern hemisphere. He couldn't remember the name of the star that Aaron had said would explode, and his friend wasn't returning his calls or text messages. There were no answers anywhere.

Sunday's news coverage barely addressed the astronomical event at all, ostensibly because it had happened early Saturday, and thus had been covered in more detail during the Saturday evening news. By Monday morning, everything there was to be said or written about the event had apparently been said or written, and Michael went to work utterly unsatisfied and full of cold apprehension.

He wanted to text Drew, but the man was in Thailand for his honeymoon, and Drew was not the type to return messages when on vacation anyway. Michael was at an absolute loss. Never before had he felt such an overwhelming combination of panic and loneliness. He *had* to talk to someone about Saturday morning, about the gamma ray burst and what it meant for him, for everyone, for the world.

But there was no one to talk to. At least, no one that would believe him. Nobody else knew what he knew and what Aaron had disclosed, against the orders of his superiors, in a drunken, desperate confession to his two closest friends in the world... the only two people he could talk to.

A young man was removing paper checks from a white envelope, smoothing out the creases and laying them one at a time before Michael's hands. He was saying something about a sports game, and Michael was nodding along good-naturedly, feigning interest and attention. He wasn't sure how long the man had been speaking, but he waited till there was a moment's silence, offered up a single "right" accompanied by one last head nod, and then began processing the checks and adding them to the man's bank account.

When the transaction was complete, Michael thanked the man and reached into his pants pocket. He produced his cell phone and hit a button to check for new messages. Aaron still had not responded to any of his texts, calls, or emails. With a heavy sigh, Michael leaned back in his chair and massaged his forehead with his thumb.

"Must have been one heck of a weekend, huh?"

Michael sat bolt upright in his chair and nearly knocked over his water bottle.

Jeanette Dailey was sitting about five feet from him at the neighboring teller station. She had hazel-green eyes and olive skin, with rich, black hair kept tight in a professional bun behind her head. Jeanette was dressed fashionably for work in a form-fitting, pale blue blouse, and her slender legs were crossed easily in front of her, naked shins peeking out from underneath a charcoal grey pencil skirt.

She laughed girlishly. "I'm sorry, I didn't mean to scare you."

"Back from lunch already?"

"Someone's got to keep an eye on you." Her green-gold eyes glinted mischievously. "You look like you didn't get any sleep at all this weekend. Was the wedding that fun?"

Michael reached for his water bottle and unscrewed the cap with one hand.

"It was eventful, to say the least. Did you hear about that light in the sky?"

"Hear about it? I saw it firsthand. Wasn't it

gorgeous?" She paused. "Wait – did that happen during the wedding? It was an outdoor ceremony, right?" Michael nodded. "Oh my God, that must have been so spectacular! Talk about the most unforgettable day of your life…"

Michael quickly debated how he wanted this conversation to proceed. He had to be delicate, if nothing else.

"What do you think it was?"

Jeanette smiled. "The light? Didn't the news say it was a solar flare or something?"

Michael wanted to say, 'And you believe that?' But he knew that he would have believed that explanation himself, had it not been for his NASA scientist friend and all that had been disclosed in confidence three nights ago.

He took a swig from his water bottle and shrugged. "I guess so. I've never seen a solar flare before, but it didn't really look like what pictures of solar flares are supposed to look like, you know?"

Jeanette looked amused. "No, I don't know. This may come across as something of a shock to you, Michael, but I'm actually *not* the world's leading authority on solar flares, believe it or not. I hate to disappoint you and all of my family members, but it's time that I start being honest with myself."

Whatever she was doing, it was lost on Michael.

"So… you didn't think there was anything weird about it?"

"Other than being abducted by aliens that morning, probed and tested aboard their UFO mothership, and then returned home before lunchtime? No, nothing out of the ordinary."

Michael had to remember to smile. "Gotcha. I suppose it's my turn for lunch, then?"

Jeanette folded her arms across her chest and gave Michael a challenging look.

"Nothing? No response to my little alien joke? You didn't even blush when I said the word 'probed'. Tell me that's not the most inappropriate thing someone has said to you today."

Michael stood and began gathering his things.

"No, you're right. It definitely takes the cake." His mind was everywhere at once. "Want anything while I'm out?"

Jeanette studied his face from her chair, swiveling slightly from side to side with one spiked black heel on the ground, chewing on a pen. After a moment, she stopped and rotated back to face her computer.

"I already ate, remember?"

Michael hadn't remembered, but now he did, and all he wanted to do was get out of the fluorescent-lit credit union office and out into fresh air.

"That's right. Well, I'll be right back. Hold down the fort, okay?"

Jeanette was typing at her computer, but she stopped long enough to give him a thumbs-up gesture without actually turning to look at him, before continuing on with whatever she was doing.

He watched her long fingers fly across the keyboard, her soft, full lips working as they silently formed the words that she was typing, as they always did when she was concentrating. It was one of his favorite things about her.

Michael took a last sip of water and tossed the empty bottle into the garbage can beneath his desk –

except he missed, and the plastic container bounced and rolled beneath a nest of power cords. Mortified, he stole a glance in Jeanette's direction to see if she had noticed. Seemingly, she had not, so Michael quickly decided to flee the scene and stole out through a door behind the teller bank.

The mild weather had lingered after Drew and Michelle's wedding, and today was another comfortable October day. The fresh air felt good on Michael's face as he exited his workplace, and he decided to walk to a local sub sandwich shop for lunch rather than drive anywhere.

He looked up at the sky as he walked. Everything seemed normal. The blue was there, the sun was there... the clouds, the birds. People were out driving to and from their jobs, their appointments, their errands. A teenager on a bicycle rode toward Michael on the sidewalk, and he stepped aside politely to wait and let the young man pass.

"Excuse me," Michael murmured as the rider rolled up.

The boy looked at him queerly as he cycled past, and Michael wondered why. When the teen had ridden off, Michael stepped back up on the sidewalk and continued on, sparing a quick glance back at the boy.

He was surprised to feel his heart starting to race and his palms beginning to sweat. What had just happened? Why did he feel so angry all of a sudden, so victimized? He couldn't explain the sensation of cold fury that was bubbling up inside him.

Michael felt wronged, manipulated... *trodden upon.* His mind raced, feverish, and the world seemed to shut itself out and then in again, a din of noise that found a single frequency and hummed in his brain. Michael's eyes watered, and his teeth clenched and unclenched, and then clenched harder. His breathing became ragged and short, and his muscles tightened and quivered. Down below, his two feet stopped moving forward altogether, and he came to a sudden halt, turning again to look in the direction of the teenager.

Without knowing why, Michael turned completely around and began walking in the direction he had just come. The boy was riding toward the stoplight, moving faster on his bike than Michael was on foot.

In a blur, Michael found that he was jogging, and then running. Something was trying to wrench itself free from his chest and his throat; something that felt closed in and suffocated and abused. He couldn't see straight all of a sudden, and his vision was trembling. Michael grunted something, and then the word broke free in a froth.

"Hey!" At first the boy didn't hear him, so Michael spat and called again. "Hey!"

This time, the boy whipped his head back and saw Michael. He put a foot down to stop the bicycle before the intersection and turned in his seat, curious.

Michael sped up. He didn't know what else to say, but something harsh was egging him on, pushing him forward, blurring his eyes.

The teenager saw it, too, and quick as a flash, turned back around and began cycling through the crosswalk.

Michael was enraged. Was he ignoring him? Trying to get away with it?

"HEY!"

The word was all Michael could say, but this time,

it was louder, harder, stronger. He felt his heart thumping a million miles an hour against his heaving chest, and his legs felt like burning ropes of jelly, but he kept running and snarling. Over and over, his leather shoes pounded the pavement through the crosswalk, and Michael was for the first time vaguely aware of startled faces as they passed through his vision, pedestrians who were quick to step back and duck away from him.

That felt good. The world was letting him come first, and he was moving like an unstoppable arrow through its midst, for the first time in a long time.

And then he was laughing, and he was aware of what he had left behind in his wake: rippling waves of concerned faces, annoyed faces, frightened faces, judgmental faces. But they had parted and were now in the past, behind him. And the biker was wheeling off down a side street, away from the danger and the scene of the crime. Most important of all, the kid was defeated.

Michael laughed and rubbed the tears from his eyes, and his legs stopped moving forward. There were side stitches in his ribs, but they were worth it, because he hadn't felt elation like this in years. Rivulets of cool, wet salt moved down the sides of his nose and to the corners of his lips. He tasted his tears, his sweat, his pain, and his pleasure... and felt like falling.

Michael thought of Jeanette then; of her smooth, copper legs beneath the skirt, and of her full, round breasts budding beneath that pale blue blouse. He wanted to march back up into the office and rip her clothes off and fuck her, right there on her desk, from behind. Michael imagined the young man with the personal checks waiting in line, and what his face would look like when he saw them. He imagined his fat Armenian boss looking on in horror, shouting for them to stop, shouting for the police.

The fantasy grew in population. Michael now imagined Drew and Aaron as they were in college, cheering him on, drinking beers out of plastic Solo cups and shouting words of encouragement. He imagined Lillian walking into the credit union and being mortified and then disgusted at the vulgarity of his hedonism, spitting out words of rage and cruelty and judgment.

And then Michael imagined walking right up to Lillian in retaliation and punching her full in the face, so hard that her teeth shattered. In his mind's eye, he then turned her around and threw her body through a plate glass window, watching her fall until her bones splintered as she hit the asphalt with a sickening crunch and an explosion of blood.

"Hey!"

The speaker was an old man waiting at a bus stop. He had taken one cautionary step toward Michael, but no more. His eyes were sharp and wary, but slightly tired.

Slowly, Michael allowed himself to revert back to reality. His bony fists relaxed into clammy open palms, and the wet sheen that covered his vision cleared and smoothed over. Gradually, his breathing slowed and his jaw loosened, until finally he was overtaken by a wave of immense release and relief.

"Are you all right?" The old man was peering suspiciously at him.

He had to answer. "Of course I am."

Michael walked back to work. There were dark pit stains beneath the arms of his dress shirt when he entered the credit union, and a faint coat of sweat still covered his forehead and upper lip. He certainly could not have smelled good. Michael had not eaten, but that was fine, because he no longer had any appetite.

Without meeting the faces of any of his coworkers or the faces of the credit union guests, he made his way silently back to his assigned station and found his seat.

Michael allowed himself a slow, exploratory look at Jeanette. She was in the middle of a transaction with a guest, leaning forward slightly while explaining a receipt. His eyes roved the exposed space between the buttons of her blouse and wondered at what was beneath the shadows of the fabric.

And then there was another woman in front of him who was clearing her throat impatiently, and Michael had to snap back and remember where he was and what he was supposed to be doing.

All at once, the momentum crumbled… and Michael felt ashamed, and nervously apologized to the guest for making her wait. He mopped his brow, smiled subserviently, though it didn't reach his eyes, and began the second half of his workday.

By 5 p.m., everything Michael had felt earlier was gone. The unnatural high he had experienced on his lunch break had long since worn off, and try as he might to rekindle the pleasure of the accompanying sensations, nothing would trigger them. He tried to conjure up the mental fantasies he'd had of Jeanette, Drew, Aaron, Lillian, his boss… but none of them elicited the same kind of visceral, excitable thrill he'd felt everywhere in his body before. Michael tried to remember what had made the visions seem so real, so forbidden and taboo, yet so mysteriously plausible and tangible at the same time.

He focused on the bike rider. What had caused the entire episode? What was it about that teenager that had started him off? What did the boy do to make him *feel* the way he had that afternoon? So powerful, so in control, while being so utterly and helplessly out of control at the same time. It was wonderful.

Unfortunately, all Michael could really think about was the light in the sky. How could anyone in his situation think about anything else?

At the end of the workday, as he packed up his things and organized his desk, Michael felt sad. He looked over at Jeanette, at all the other credit union tellers, at the remaining guests left in the lobby, and at his fat Armenian boss talking on the phone in his private office. Then, Michael looked outside at the setting sun and wondered for the first time how many more sunsets he would see... or sunrises.

He thought about his parents, and how he didn't speak to them as much as he wanted to anymore. Michael wondered if they were happy down in Florida, if their marriage was still strong, and if they were both tan. He wondered if his brother Everett was still alive and still enjoying Alaska and being a crab fisherman.

Would they have a chance to ever speak again? Would he have a chance to speak to any of them? And if so, how many more chances?

Absolutely drained emotionally, Michael truly felt like he could cry. As a matter of fact, he couldn't remember if he had ever *felt* more in a single day of his life.

In a daze of thoughts and feelings, Michael flipped the power switch on the monitor of his computer and pushed his chair back under his desk. When he turned, he was surprised to see that Jeanette was watching him.

She held a small purse over her shoulder which she gripped with both hands, and her hazel-green eyes seemed to be reading him. When she spoke, it was different; softer, gentler than it had been earlier that day.

"I didn't offend you this morning, did I?"

Michael genuinely had no idea what she meant. "What? What are you talking about?"

"With the... alien talk... and everything? I wasn't trying to make you uncomfortable. Or make fun of you, either. I know I can be a little... aggressive... sometimes. And maybe a little too playful." She pulled her hair down out of the bun and shook it free. "I just wanted to make sure you weren't upset or anything."

"Why would I be upset?"

Jeanette fidgeted with her handbag. "I'm glad you're not. You just seemed different after lunch, and I wanted to make sure it wasn't because of me."

Michael found it hard to meet her eyes. They were so intense, so unique. The thought that they might not be around forever...

"No, it wasn't because of you."

She took the slightest of steps toward him.

"Is it something else, then? I don't mean to be nosy, but... is everything all right?"

Michael finally met her gaze, and he wondered if she could read right through him. Did she know, just by looking at him, that something terrible, something final, was coming? Could he tell her? *Should* he tell her?

Aaron had struggled with that question, the uncertainty of whether it was better to share a horrible truth or adhere to the philosophy that ignorance is bliss, particularly when fate is unavoidable. Which way caused less pain? And could Michael live with the guilt of not sharing, knowing what was still coming?

That was when Michael realized he didn't really know what was still coming… and he only knew one person that truly did.

"Yeah. Yeah, everything's fine. Thanks for asking, though. See you tomorrow?"

Jeanette smiled sadly. "You know you will."

But as she was walking away and out the door, all Michael could think was 'but I don't'.

CHAPTER SIX

'The Five' was absolutely clogged with the evening commute, and Michael, like everyone else in Los Angeles, hated stop-and-go traffic. But he needed to make this drive and sit in rush hour traffic, for hours even, if need be. He needed to know exactly how much time they all had left.

When Aaron had first revealed everything he knew about the supernova, the gamma ray burst, and its dire consequences on Earth, the three of them had been beyond drunk. Michael remembered feeling dazed and uncertain of what was going on. Drew had been disbelieving, mocking, and even violent that night.

But then Saturday morning had happened. 11:13 a.m. had come and gone, and with it, all doubt as to whether or not the whole thing had just been a sick, inebriated joke of Aaron's.

And yet, neither he nor Drew had thought to ask Aaron for more details about what this event actually meant for them, about how long it would take for the radiation to spread, for the ozone layer to burn off, for the plants and the animals to start dying, for people to start dying.

For all he knew, they already were, in places

Michael could only point to on a globe. Aaron had said that the event would be covered up, and the truth would be hidden from the masses by politicians and propaganda. The people in control would seek to avoid mass hysteria, panic, riots, uprisings, and uproar.

No wonder he had seen nothing more about the light in the sky on the news or online. It was already being covered up. People were being told to go about their lives as if nothing had happened, and why should they have any reason to disagree? For all they knew, it *was* a solar flare. They were still alive and well, still waking up, going to work, coming home, eating, drinking, laughing. It was as if nothing had changed.

But something *had* changed, and Michael needed to know exactly what, and how long he had left. He wasn't foolish enough to fervently believe that this crisis could somehow be averted, but he did need to figure out as much as he could, so as to better… spend his time.

Still, the idea of apocalypse, of the world ending, of impending and certain death, was something Michael had been struggling to accept from the moment the sky lit up. It was nearly impossible for him to even think those words in his head without slipping into a crippling fear or depression.

Despite his justifiable pessimism and the logical part of his brain that told him his fate was unavoidable, there was still a tiny, hidden part of Michael's spirit that clung desperately to some faint hope that this could all in fact somehow be fixed or changed… that the world didn't *really* have to end.

Surely, there was something he could do. Or more realistically, something Aaron or NASA could do to fix it. Hell, even the United States of America. Surely, the powers-that-be were not just going to let their lives and their great fortunes go gently into that good night without some kind of resistance?

Only Aaron would know.

Michael took an exit for Santa Clarita and followed the streets until they brought him to his old friend's apartment complex. He parked against the curb and turned the ignition off. Michael didn't like the idea of surprising Aaron, and honestly, he had no way of knowing if Aaron would even be home. But his friend had given him no choice by refusing to return any form of communication.

In the quiet darkness of his car interior, Michael pulled out his phone and tried calling Aaron one last time. As expected, it rang for a few seconds before going to voicemail. Disappointed, though not surprised, Michael hung up and got out of his car.

He hadn't been to Aaron's apartment in almost a year. Now, in the dim shade of twilight, it seemed more run-down and less inviting than he remembered it. Michael walked up the steps to the second story and found the door marked '2H', then knocked his knuckles gently against the peeling, painted wood.

Either a bat or a bird flew past him and into the shadowy foliage of a tree in the apartment's courtyard. Michael was startled by the sudden beating of its wings, but he still followed its small shape with his eyes. Studying the leaves, he waited a patient moment there in the lonely space, wondering if the nocturnal creature was also staring back at him with beady black eyes.

After some time had passed, he turned back to the door and knocked again. No response. He then put his ear up to it and tried to listen for movement. Michael thought he could hear the muted sounds of a television, but upon further investigation, he decided that the noise was actually coming from next door.

Next, he tried to look through the smoky peephole in the center of Aaron's front door, but that also proved to be a fruitless enterprise. Nearby, the window that looked in on the apartment was covered by drawn, white, vertical blinds, sealing off any chance Michael had of seeing through that.

Frustrated, he pulled out his phone and redialed the same number. It rang three times and went to voicemail. This time, he decided to leave a message.

"Hey Aaron… it's Michael. Sorry to bombard you with texts and calls, but I really need to talk to you. I'm actually outside your apartment right now, so if by any chance you're screening my calls – though I'm not sure why you would be doing that anyway – but if you are, I'm here… and like I said, I really need to talk to you. So, I'd really appreciate you taking the time to just open your door and speak to me for a few minutes. I think you can spare me that, given everything that's happened the last couple days, and considering everything you said Friday night. To say that this is an emergency is an understatement, obviously." He paused. "I'm also worried about you, man. I haven't seen or heard from you since the wedding, and we didn't really get a chance to talk there, either. I need to ask you some questions. I need to know just how much time–"

He was abruptly cut off by a recorded message saying he had used up all his time.

Now even more agitated, Michael slid the phone

back into his pocket and pounded long and hard on the door. A dog started barking a few doors down, and he checked his watch to see how late it was: almost 8 p.m. Not late enough for the neighbors to be sleeping, but then again, he couldn't even be sure of that as he reflected on his own eternal struggle with the old man who lived in the apartment next to him.

Feeling self-conscious about the noise he had created, Michael wrestled with a strong desire to flee. He took a few steps toward the staircase and then paused at the top, scanning the apartments for any sign of life.

Other than the dog's barking and the occasional rustle of whatever that winged creature was in the tree, everything around him was quiet and still. He hesitated a moment longer, and then moved back to the door marked '2H'. Michael took one last look to either side of him, made up his mind, reached for the doorknob, and turned. To his immense surprise, the door swung open easily.

It was dark inside Aaron's apartment, and Michael wondered if his friend was actually sleeping. But why would he do that with the front door unlocked? Maybe he had forgotten to lock it on his way out. Aaron wasn't the absent-minded type, but then again, he undoubtedly had a lot more than usual on his mind these days. And household security becomes less of a priority when the world is ending.

"Aaron?" Michael took a step inside. "Aaron? It's Michael. Are you home?"

He ran his fingers along the inside of the wall, searching for a light switch. Finally, they found one, and he flicked it on.

The apartment was much as he remembered it, just messier. There was an old sofa-sleeper against the far wall and a small television set with several National Geographic magazines piled on top of it. A few pairs of jeans were strewn out across the beige carpet, and there was a mug of tea on the kitchen counter, with the bag still steeping.

Michael walked over to it and put a hand on the ceramic. It was cold.

"Aaron?"

He looked down the hallway that led to the only other room in the apartment: the bedroom. Michael flicked on another light switch and crept cautiously down the hallway.

The bedroom door was shut. Again, Michael put his ear to the wood and listened for any sound on the other side.

Nothing. He knocked softly.

"Aaron? Are you asleep? It's Michael."

There was no answer. He retrieved his phone and dialed the number yet again. From the other side of the door, Michael heard the electronic tune of Beethoven's *Für Elise* start to play. The digitized piano melody repeated once more and then stopped, and Aaron's voicemail greeting played in his ear. He had to be inside.

"Aaron?"

Michael knocked again, then twisted the knob and pushed the door open timidly. He couldn't immediately find a switch on the wall, but there was a floor lamp just right of the doorway. With shaking fingers, he located the cord and pressed a small button.

Soft, orange light bathed the cream walls of the

boxy room. Aaron's bed was unmade, and his cell phone rested on top of a woolen blanket. Michael crossed over to it and illuminated the screen. There were at least a dozen missed calls, several new text messages, and a handful of voicemail notifications. But the phone's owner was nowhere in sight.

Michael saw Aaron's open laptop computer on his desk in the corner of the room. He dragged a finger across the touchpad and the screen lit up. A wallpaper image of some swirling, colorful nebula stretched across the screen, but there was no evidence that Aaron had been using any applications before the computer had gone to sleep.

The door to Aaron's bathroom was shut, as well. At the base, however, white light poured out from the crack and spilled out on the carpet's edge.

For what seemed like the fiftieth time tonight, Michael knocked and called to his friend. And once again, there was no response, so Michael turned the knob and entered.

Naked and half submerged in about sixteen inches of water, Aaron had his head tilted back, resting on the white ceramic edge of the bathtub. His eyes were closed, and the water in the tub was still. He looked pale.

Michael's first instinct was to turn away in embarrassment, but it was overruled by a growing sense of unease. He approached the bathtub and touched Aaron's shoulder lightly, then shook him. The skin was cooler than he'd expected.

"Aaron."

Aaron's eyelids didn't even flicker, and his lips remained pressed together in something vaguely resembling a smile.

Like an overinflated balloon, Michael could feel panic welling up inside his torso, the swollen latex pressing all his inner organs up against each other and the bony prison of his ribcage. He shook his friend again. The only thing that moved was the water, quick ripples gliding across the glassy surface, spreading out and away from the soggy body in the tub.

"Aaron!"

He touched two fingers to the man's neck and tried unsuccessfully to find a pulse. Michael didn't know what to do; his hands were shaking violently, and his eyesight was blurring in and out. It was getting hard to breathe, and all of a sudden, he was jerking to his knees and his chest was heaving, his stomach convulsing. He needed to throw up.

Michael's head swiveled to find the toilet bowl, but it was covered by the lid, and on top of that was a piece of paper, a half-empty bottle of Coppertone sunscreen spray, and an unopened Easy Mac packet. Michael hadn't noticed any of this when he first came into the bathroom, but now that he looked closer, he saw black ink on the paper and recognized Aaron's handwriting immediately.

Mike – I hope you don't find this, but if you do, know that I'm sorry for having ever said anything that night. No one deserves that kind of information, even if it is the truth. You might find my parting gifts to you to be in bad taste, but maybe they'll inspire you to follow my lead and save yourself a lot of pain. A lot of pain, Mike. That's why I'm cashing my chips in and taking the easy way out while I still can. We might not be able to change our fate, but at the very least, we can determine how we meet it. And for me, two dozen pills and a hot bath sure beats the hell out of skin cancer and starvation. Should you be of a like mind, I left the other half of my prescription in the medicine cabinet behind the bathroom mirror. I hope to see you in the next life, buddy. If not, well… I guess we'll always have Chem Lab with Mrs. Poole. ~Aaron

Michael read the paper four times over before finally placing it back on the toilet cover. He had a bizarre notion that he ought to cry, but he found himself nowhere near tears and wondered if it was only something he had seen in a movie, the kind of response a skilled actor would have in a traumatic moment like this. Michael imagined himself breaking down in sobs and screaming hysterically, shaking his friend's lifeless corpse.

In the mental fantasy, he saw himself pulling Aaron's naked body from the tub and hugging him to his chest on the linoleum floor as water splashed out around them. All the while, an omnipresent camera ever so slowly and dramatically pulled back from the heart-wrenching scene, underscored by a wailing symphony of strings.

Yes, that was how all this was supposed to play out. And yet, all Michael could do was stare down at the note and then over at his friend in the bathtub.

He picked up the sunscreen and the macaroni packet, twisted each of them in his two hands, and found himself reading the ingredient lists. How funny would it be to discover the same ingredient on both panels? He smiled at the notion, then replaced both the canister and the plastic package on top of the toilet lid and stood up.

Michael knew he must be in shock. He kept looking at his friend, white and lifeless in the tub, waiting for him to move, to speak, to open his eyes. The whole situation was unreal. Try as he might, Michael could not quite recognize the man sitting in the tub as his old friend, the teenager he had once known in high school and then in college. This was some imposter, some mannequin that had been switched out and made to look like his friend.

The Aaron he knew would never do this, never give up like this. That Aaron was a dreamer, a scientist, and an astronaut. Memories of their time together began to slowly trickle back, like the beginnings of snow runoff in spring, and Michael found himself sitting on the cold linoleum floor, reminiscing on thoughts and images he hadn't visited in years.

Now, the tears threatened to come, and he made no attempt to resist the salty droplets as they filmed over his eyeballs. Reality was beginning to set in, and the strange figure in the tub was starting to look more and more like his friend again.

The sight of Aaron in the still water, naked, alone, and frail, made Michael's heart heave, and his breath stuttered in and out irregularly. That queer smile on Aaron's face, if you could call it that at all, only disturbed Michael further, and made it harder for him to keep his composure. He wanted to shake his friend again, to breathe life back into his lungs or to wake him up from this gruesome nightmare... But deep down, he knew that he was too late. He was just too late.

Someone needed to be called. Obviously, the police were the best choice, since it was clear an ambulance was no longer necessary. Michael had no idea how long Aaron had been dead for; he hadn't seen him since the wedding. For all he knew, he had come home that very night and drawn this bath.

Still, a call to 911 was the inevitable next step. And yet, Michael found himself thinking instead of calling Drew. His best friend was on his honeymoon, and who knew what the service was like in Thailand, but surely the death of one of his groomsmen merited an emergency call.

Michael shuffled back into Aaron's bedroom in a kind of daze and sat down at his laptop computer. As if on autopilot, he realized why he had come here and what he had been looking for. He couldn't think about the bathroom right now, or what was in it... not anymore. Michael had to do something else before dealing further with the awful truth of that situation.

With a swipe of his finger against the touchpad, he brought the device back to life, and then double-clicked the internet browser application at the bottom of the screen. Michael clicked a drop-down menu to view Aaron's browsing history.

The first result shown was his email account. Michael selected it and waited for the page to load. To his immense relief, Aaron had stored his password and username in the login screen, so all Michael had to do was hit 'Enter', and immediately he was granted access to Aaron's inbox.

There were a handful of spam messages, but the vast majority of his email was work-related. Michael opened dozens of messages, each marked 'PRIVATE,' 'CONFIDENTIAL,' or 'URGENT,' reading through them as quickly as he could. Unfortunately, much of it seemed to go over his head, as various scientific terms and 'tech talk' kept reappearing throughout the emails.

What was plain and simple to comprehend, though, was the gravity of the dilemma at hand. None of the letter-writers minced words, and all seemed to be in either a state of shock, depression, or extreme panic and exigency. Another commonality between the messages was that not a one of them seemed to offer any practical solution whatsoever.

There were a handful dated from the previous Saturday, all right before, during, or after the time of 11:13 a.m. The emails confirmed what their authors had already foreseen, and what Aaron had explained the night before: a gamma ray burst of terrific magnitude caused by the supernova of what was WR 104 had indeed finally made its way to Earth. The blast struck the southern hemisphere of the planet, and the damage had reportedly been catastrophic. Countless lives had been lost, widespread hysteria had ensued, and the governments of the as-yet-unaffected world had united as one to conceal the nature of their planet's impending doom from its oblivious citizens.

It was all true, then. There hadn't been any real doubt left in Michael's mind, but if by chance some residual hope had been clinging by a thread, that thread was cut now.

Michael forwarded any emails he found to be pertinent or more intellectually accessible to his own account, and then debated whether or not he should delete the original messages. Surely, the police would go through this inbox. But then again, Aaron had obviously not been concerned enough with the possibility of these confidential documents being found by Michael or anyone else after his death, so perhaps it was best just to leave them. Any rational detective would likely shrug them off as conspiratorial; the crazed theories of hyper-imaginative nerds who spent way too much time staring into telescopes and watching sci-fi flicks.

One particular email gave Michael pause. His eyes found the words 'estimated timetable', and he read on like a desperate man, convinced he could find what he was looking for in the following sentences.

In the end, the key word had been 'estimated'. The letter-writer had offered her own subjective theory as to how long it would take for the UV rays to begin permeating the northern hemisphere and, by inclusion, America. Even still, there was no telling when – or if, even – the governments of the other countries would inform their citizens that it was indeed time to panic. Would the radiation grow so severe that skin cancer levels became a global epidemic? And if so, would it happen overnight? Over a few days? A few weeks? How long would it take for the food chain, and for all of Earth's natural biological processes, to begin showing signs that something was severely wrong? A few months? Or a few years? When would life become impossible and the planet become inhospitable?

Everything was conjecture... but no one gave humanity much time. The bottom line was that the doom of mankind was approaching, and it was coming much, much faster than anyone wanted to accept.

In the midst of the work emails were a few messages containing odd parting thoughts, final commendations, and other honest expressions of grief or affection. A few coworkers had listed Bible passages, most of them from Revelations, at the end of their messages. There were plenty of goodbyes, but no one said 'good luck'.

Michael began shutting the computer down. He closed Aaron's email and hit the power button, then gently lowered the screen and extracted his phone from his pocket. Calmly, he dialed 911, waited, and then relayed the situation to the responding voice on the other end of the line. The woman told him to remain where he was and informed him that both an ambulance and police were on their way.

Michael decided to wait in Aaron's living room; he couldn't bear to be close to the bathroom anymore. He did, however, take the note from the toilet lid and folded it away into his pocket. Technically, he was probably breaking some law by tampering with evidence in a crime scene, and he was sure that there would be questions of whether he found a suicide note when he discovered his friend's body. But Michael made up his mind that the answer to that question would be 'no'. The note was addressed to him anyway, it was his property now.

He did decide to leave the sunscreen and the macaroni packet on the toilet lid. What a bizarre mystery that would be to the investigators…

The police were there within ten minutes. The paramedics followed not long after and confirmed that Aaron was indeed dead. Michael went over the entire sequence of events that had led him to this apartment tonight, detailing how Aaron had not been returning any of his calls and messages for days. He told the police officers that he had gotten worried, as he had, and decided to pay his friend a visit after work. He also explained to the officers how Aaron had been acting odd the last few times he had seen him, briefly commenting that his friend had seemed more subdued than usual at the wedding and the night before the wedding.

Of course, Michael said nothing of WR 104, 11:13 a.m., or any of what Aaron had shared with him and Drew the past Friday night. He painstakingly recounted how the front door had been unlocked, and how he had entered only after knocking for several minutes and becoming increasingly worried.

The questions were tedious, and the night grew later and later, before finally, the police decided they had learned enough. They took down all of Michael's contact information, gave him their own, and asked that if there was anything else he remembered, anything at all, that he immediately give their station a call. The officers offered their condolences, promised that they would be in touch, and then offered to walk Michael out to his car. Michael politely declined.

As he stepped under the yellow police line tape that had already been applied to the front doorway of the apartment, Michael had the thought to take one last look at his friend. But by then, it was likely too late. Maybe Aaron was already zipped up in a black body bag.

There were all kinds of people swarming around apartment 2H, and it was almost midnight now. Michael still needed to drive home and attempt to process everything that had happened. Besides, he thought, he would probably get to see him at least once more, if whoever ended up being responsible for Aaron's funeral decided to do a wake or an open casket.

Both of Aaron's parents were dead. He wondered who that responsibility would fall to. Some distant uncle? Or could it fall to him, or even Drew? Michael wasn't sure how these things worked. The last funeral he remembered attending was his grandmother's, when he had been in college.

Slowly, Michael walked down the steps of the apartment complex, seeing for the first time the flashing blue, red, and white lights of the emergency vehicles parked on the street. Several of Aaron's neighbors had put on bathrobes or sweatshirts and were wandering around conversing with each other or with the officer standing at the yellow line, curious about what had happened in their quiet building.

Michael met eyes with a woman staring out from a window across the courtyard. She seemed to be scowling suspiciously at him. The effect was unnerving, and he quickly lowered his gaze.

As he reached the foot of the staircase, he heard a sharp screech and his heart stopped. Michael turned just in time to see the winged mammal flutter out from the leaves of the courtyard tree and swoop off into the night, a black silhouette against a midnight-blue sky.

He sat in his car for at least five minutes before starting the ignition. After he did, he reached his fingers into his pants pocket, just to make sure he still had Aaron's note there. Michael then took one last look in the rearview mirror back at the apartment complex before turning off of Aaron's street and finding his way back to the freeway.

Halfway home, Michael brought the note out and reread it on top of the steering wheel by the dim illumination of his car's cabin light. When he got to the part about the other half of Aaron's prescription in the medicine cabinet, he wondered if he had made a mistake by not taking the pills with him. Then again, it would have been suspicious for an autopsy to declare Aaron's death a drug overdose with investigators finding none of the drug in question at his apartment. Stranger things had happened in the history of crime, of course, but the last thing Michael wanted was to become a police suspect.

The authorities had no knowledge of Aaron's suicide note, but they did have half a bottle of prescription medication in Aaron's bathroom and the other half in Aaron's stomach. That, combined with his email inbox and Michael's account of his abnormal behavior, would probably constitute enough evidence to rule out foul play. Michael certainly didn't want to spend his remaining days in a police interrogation room, though.

He thought about calling Drew. It was 12:30 in the morning California time, but who knew what time that meant for Thailand. Michael tried to calculate time zones and figured roughly that it was probably mid-afternoon where his friend was.

He dialed the number and waited. There was a good chance that Drew wouldn't pick up, even if it was mid-day in Thailand. Long-distance communication had never been Drew's strong suit, and he was on his honeymoon, after all. The phone rang twice before being picked up.

"Yes?"

Michael was less surprised than he thought he would be to hear the husky voice on the other end. He cleared his own throat to speak.

"Hey Drew, it's me."

"I figured as much."

"Sorry to bother you on your honeymoon."

"Don't be sorry. What is it?"

Michael wasn't sure where or how to begin.

"Aaron killed himself."

It sounded like a joke saying it out loud like that, but Drew didn't laugh. He just waited for Michael to continue.

"I found him in his apartment, in the bathtub. He took a bunch of pills and overdosed."

The line was silent for a while, save for Drew's heavy breathing. He suffered from asthma and was notorious for his snoring and frequent sinus infections. Drew had once told Michael that a condition of Michelle agreeing to marry him involved the purchase of a CPAP mask and machine. Michael wondered if he had bought the device already and if he was wearing it every night to bed.

"Did you call the police?"

"I did. They're still there. The whole apartment's been taped off."

More silence on the other end. This time, Michael broke it.

"Do you think there's someone else I need to call? Like, his next of kin or something?"

"His parents are dead."

"I know, but maybe some other family member?"

"I don't know who that would be. I'm sure that's what the police are for, anyway." Drew sighed, low and long. "*Fuuuuuck.*"

Michael swallowed his saliva. "I'm sorry to have to be the one to tell you."

"Are you all right?"

The question caught Michael off-guard. "Yeah, I'm fine, I guess. Just shocked, you know? I don't think it's really sunk in yet."

"What *has*?"

It was a rhetorical question, obviously. Michael couldn't believe how much his life had changed in the past three days. He was still struggling to accept the idea that the world was ending, let alone having to deal with the sudden death of one of his oldest and closest friends.

It was far too much to handle; his head was spinning, and his eyes began to water. Michael had to blink in order to maintain his vision. He was still about five minutes away from home.

"Do you know when you're planning on coming back?"

"I'm sure that's gonna change now; it all depends on the funeral. Jesus Christ… a wedding and a funeral, back-to-back. Not to mention the fucking apocalypse."

Michael thought of Aaron's email inbox, and the messages he had forwarded to his own account.

"There are some emails I found on Aaron's computer that I want to show you when you get back. Or, I guess I could send them to you when I get home, too, if that's easier. I know you're on your honeymoon, but it's–"

"Urgent?"

Michael paused. "Nothing conclusive as far as how much time we have, but none of it looks promising."

"Of course it doesn't."

Michael couldn't help feeling incredibly awkward having this conversation. It felt bizarre and surreal.

"Have you said anything yet to Michelle?"

"Of course not." Drew sounded almost annoyed by the question.

"Well, are you going to tell her?"

"That the fucking world is ending? On our honeymoon? You're kidding, right?"

"You have to tell her at some point. Who knows how much time–"

"I don't have to do anything."

Michael grimaced. He saw the sign for his exit coming up.

"Drew–"

"No, listen to me. I don't have to do anything. And neither do you. No one *has* to do anything anymore. Ever again." The tone of his voice was commanding. "You understand that, don't you?"

Michael wasn't sure that he did. "Yeah."

"I'm gonna talk to Michelle about Aaron. Send me those emails when you get home, and keep me up to speed with what's happening as far as the funeral goes. If we need to change our flight, we'll change our flight. Otherwise, don't call me again. I'm trying to enjoy my romantic getaway."

Michael switched lanes to his right to let a tailgating pick-up truck barrel past him.

"I understand." He paused. "Are you all right?"

"In regards to what?"

"You know, in regards to Aaron... and... and everything else too, I guess?"

Drew surprised him by laughing. "No, Michael, of course I'm not all right. But I'm dealing, man. That's all I can do. That's all anybody can do." The tone of his voice was much lighter now, almost conversational.

"Keep it together, okay? Don't pull an Aaron on me. I'll be back before you know it, and when I am, we'll talk. I love you, kid." And then there was a click and the line went dead.

Michael turned onto his street, feeling upset by Drew's last warning not to 'pull an Aaron'. The comment was unbelievably offensive and insensitive. He wanted to call Drew back and make him apologize. The implication had clearly been made that Aaron had not 'kept it together', and even the phrase 'to pull an Aaron' in regards to suicide made Michael fume. It was beyond tasteless, it was inhumane.

This was their best friend, a groomsman at Drew's own wedding, and he had horrifically decided to take his own life. The reaction from Drew should have been one of shock and disbelief. Either that, or sadness and hysteria. But he certainly should not have made light of the situation. Using Aaron's death as a joke, as the punchline of some finger-wagging warning, was just heartless.

Michael parked his car in the garage beneath the apartment complex, put Aaron's letter back in his pocket, and walked to the elevator. He stepped inside and rode it up to the fourth floor. When he made it inside his home, he found his dog Tucker where he usually was this time of night, sleeping on the pillows at the top of his bed.

"You don't seem too concerned by any of this, do you?"

Tucker's only answer was a soft, wheezy snoring sound. Michael gently eased the animal off one of the pillows and onto the other before sliding under the sheets himself and turning the lights off.

After a while, he reached a hand out from beneath the covers and stroked the dog's fur softly, careful not to wake him. Michael realized he had forgotten to brush his teeth, but then he remembered it didn't matter anymore. He thought back to something Drew had said on the phone earlier and kept repeating it over and over again in his head: "No one *has* to do anything anymore. Ever again."

Michael fell asleep thinking about those words.

CHAPTER SEVEN

Drew was shaking an inordinate amount of salt onto his steak and eggs. Michael hadn't been counting, but he was sure at least ten to fifteen seconds had elapsed since Drew first started salting his breakfast, and still, his big, furry fist rained sodium on his plate.

When a small, white dune began to take shape on the bloody meat, Drew took his fork with his free hand and smoothed the mound out across the chop. He finally put the shaker down and replaced it with a knife caked in butter, which he then proceeded to grease across the contents of his platter. After the slab had melted away into his meat and eggs, he opened another butter packet and slid his knife under that one as well and repeated the whole ordeal.

Michael watched him, half fascinated and half repulsed. When the second slab of butter had melted to Drew's satisfaction, he picked up his fork and began to cut the steak into long, large strips. Once he was finished with that, he speared two of the strips on the end of his fork, used the bare fingers of his left hand to scoop some scrambled eggs onto the fork prongs, and shoved the whole greasy mixture between his thick lips.

Drew then chewed luxuriously for at least another

twenty seconds or so before swallowing the hefty mouthful, rinsing it down with the last of his second Bloody Mary, and flagging their server down with the empty glass.

"I'll have another."

The waitress, a pretty young blonde with skinny legs and rich almond eyes, smiled, nodded, and scampered away.

Drew was still holding the dirty glass away from his body in her direction. He scowled.

"She forgot to take the glass."

"I'm sure she'll take it when she brings you back the new one." Michael reached for the straw of his own Bloody Mary with his mouth, found it, and sipped.

From the look on Drew's face, he wasn't satisfied with his friend's explanation. But instead of saying anything, he just stabbed two more strips of steak with his fork and shoveled them into his mouth, chewing in contemplation.

Michael picked up his own utensils and began dissecting his breakfast omelet. For as long as he could remember, this was just the way he chose to consume certain foods. He'd been doing it since he was a boy.

Drew watched him with undisguised disgust. "You're ripping that thing apart."

Michael kept working at it, pulling bits of spinach, tomatoes, peppers, ham, and onions from the cheesy egg, and separating them out into separate portions arranged evenly around his ceramic plate.

"Seriously, Mike. Don't mutilate the flavors."

Michael looked up from his project and raised his eyebrows incredulously.

"Don't mutilate the flavors?" He used his fork to

gesture over at Drew's plate. "You drowned your breakfast in butter and salt, and you're worried that *I'm* mutilating the flavors?"

The waitress returned with a fresh Bloody Mary. Drew saw her coming, picked up the dirty glass, and exchanged it mid-air without looking at the girl.

"Thanks, doll."

She smiled shyly and skipped off. Drew turned and watched her leave, then abruptly brought his gaze back to Michael.

"She's shit as a waitress, but I bet she knows a few ways to make up for it, huh?"

Michael smiled and nodded his head in agreement. Truthfully, he thought she looked way too young; she was probably still in high school, or just barely starting college.

Drew looked in the direction she had disappeared and whistled to himself.

"Fuck, do I miss that. I really do." He leaned forward over the table, dropping his voice to a conspiratorial whisper. "You should go for it, Mikey."

Michael laughed. "Go for it?"

"Yeah, man! Why not?" Drew's eyes glinted lasciviously. "I bet she's tighter than a fucking Chinese finger trap. And she's got legs for days, too. Great legs." He leaned back in the wicker chair and ran his hands through his black hair. "Imagine those strong, slender thighs wrapped around your neck, man. *Mmmm.* Tell me you don't like that image."

Michael tried to imagine it in his mind. The girl was definitely attractive, but when he started picturing her naked, it just felt creepy and wrong.

"She's too young."

Drew was aghast. "Too young? She's fucking *nineteen*! She's perfect!"

"You talk to her, then." Michael lowered his eyes to his plate and began working on his omelet again.

Drew continued to watch Michael tear the omelet to shreds, his facial expression revealing unmitigated contempt.

"This is a perfect segue." He took one last bite of eggs and put his fork down, clasped his hands together, and rested them in a giant hairy fist on the table.

"A perfect segue for what?"

"To talk." Drew never seemed to mind talking with his mouth full, another habit Michael found particularly annoying.

"Isn't that what we've been doing?"

"No, I mean to *talk* talk."

Michael knew exactly what Drew was alluding to. At Aaron's funeral, they had planned this brunch with the sole intention of being able to have a conversation somewhere relatively private that was also far away from Michelle. Michael had suggested Drew come over to his apartment one night in order to keep the nature of what they intended to talk about as secret as possible.

Drew had quickly shot that suggestion down though, saying it was a "needless precaution," and claiming that they could just as easily have this conversation outside at his favorite café… which ended up being exactly where they decided to meet, per his recommendation, of course.

Michael was uneasy at first about the idea of this meeting taking place so publicly, surrounded by so many people who were still innocently unaware of what was happening in the world. But Drew had beaten him into submission by guaranteeing that none of them would have any idea what they were talking about anyway, so it really didn't matter.

"The way I see it, we have three choices." Drew spoke slowly and deliberately, but his eyes betrayed a hint of amusement, as if he wasn't really taking himself entirely seriously.

"Option A: We do nothing. We continue on as if nothing's happened. This is probably the choice you'd default to normally, but of course, it's not the right choice, and I won't let it happen, for your own sake. After everything we've been told, everything we've read in those emails, everything we've seen happen with our own eyes, it would be beyond senseless to go on with our heads up our own asses, pretending like we're not all already dead."

Drew paused to bring the Bloody Mary to his lips, take a long gulp, and set it back down again. He wiped red tomato juice residue from his upper lip with the back of his hand.

"Option B: We pull an Aaron."

Michael fidgeted in his chair. "You know I don't like it when you say that—"

Drew immediately put his hands up defensively and warped his face into a contortion of affronted hurt.

"Relax! I'm not trying to offend you or spit on Aaron's grave or anything. I love and miss him as much as you do. All I'm saying is that he took the easy way out, all right?" Michael opened his mouth to protest. "He did, Michael. You don't have to defend the guy; he's dead, okay? Don't make me feel like an insensitive prick just because I'm the only one who's got the balls to call it like it is. Offing yourself in the face of global armageddon is taking the easy way out."

"Maybe it's the best way out. You read his letter."

"Yeah, I read his letter. And forgive me for not running out to the nearest Walgreens to pilfer half a hundred Xanax. I've still got things in this life that I enjoy, that I care about, that I'm not ready to leave behind yet. I've still got things I want to do – a whole lot of things I want to do – things I can do, should do, and am going to do."

He smiled majestically. "Which brings me to Option C; the option I've already chosen for myself, and the option you're going to choose before I have my fourth Bloody Mary. Option C is we embrace the very real truth that our time is limited and the end is nigh... but we do the opposite of Aaron. We choose life, in spite of death. And we *live*, Mikey. We live like we've never lived before. Like kings. Like there is no God."

He raised his drink on the word "kings" in a grinning salute, tossed back the last of his cocktail, and lazily stretched his arm out off the table where it was sure to be in someone's path, but also where the waitress would have no choice but to notice it.

Michael was staring at the glass when he realized Drew had stopped talking and was waiting for a reaction. He met his waiting eyes and tried to formulate his thoughts.

"What exactly do you have in mind?"

Drew laughed and forked more steak and eggs into his mouth with his right hand, his left still clutching the empty outstretched glass.

"What exactly do I have in mind?" He chewed and

spoke at the same time. "What exactly do *you* have in mind, Mikey? Because whatever you have locked away up there, it's time to open it up. And no time but the present. Literally." He stopped chewing and swallowed, and suddenly looked pensive. "This just might be the best thing that's ever happened to you. And me, too, I guess…"

Michael couldn't believe what he was hearing. "What are you talking about?"

"You don't get it, do you?"

Drew groaned with impatience and made a big show of collapsing his face into his arms on the table, slamming the empty cocktail glass on its side. It rolled over to Michael's side of the table, where Michael had to put a hand out to stop it from going off the end.

After a moment, Drew slowly brought himself back up and grabbed a bottle of hot sauce that was resting near the condiments in the center of their table, and began dribbling it all over what remained of his breakfast.

"This is a once-in-a-lifetime opportunity— *Jeeeeesuuus*! I am killing it with these puns today!"

He burst into rollicking, drunken laughter and was soon wiping tears out of the corners of his eyes with his free hand. Michael placed the fallen glassware upright. When Drew finally regained control of his mirth, he pressed on, pausing intermittently only to admit more sauce-drenched food into his mouth.

"But it is though. Once in a lifetime. We don't know how much time we have, but we do know it's not a lot. So, what do we do? We do whatever we want, and we do *everything* we want. Never been bungee jumping? Let's go. Wanna rob a bank? Why not.

Always wanted to see Paris… or Hawaii… or *Omaha, Nebraska?* Now's your chance. There's nothing holding you back. No rules, no limitations, nothing."

"Except time."

"Except time. But again, we don't know when this whole thing is going to happen. We could be dead tomorrow. And I, for one, don't want to spend my last night alive eating Easy Mac out of the microwave and applying sunscreen to your white ass."

"I understand what you're saying, but I also don't want to spend my last night in jail, and that's exactly where I'd be if I robbed a bank."

Drew looked exasperated. "It was a fucking example, Mike, *Jesus.* If you don't wanna rob a bank, then don't rob a bank. If your idea of really living is stepping outside your front door with your shoes untied, then be my guest, but don't come crying to me when you fall flat on your face. I'm going to be too busy doing lines off of hookers in Vegas and having an orgy." Drew noticed the glass by Michael's hand. "Where the fuck is our waitress?" He looked around wildly. "This girl is killing me today…"

The girl was taking an order two tables away. Drew reached across the table and retrieved the empty glass, turned around, and tried to assess how much longer she was going to take with her other guests. He turned back to make a face at Michael.

"This is ridiculous."

Michael was still finishing his first Bloody Mary. "It looks like she's got a lot of tables."

"That's not my fault, nor should it be any of my concern as a paying customer."

He turned back to face her and waved an arm to

get her attention. She was speaking with an elderly lady, but still managed to make brief eye contact with Drew, nod her head, and raise an index finger before looking down to write an order on her notepad.

"I don't believe it. She wants me to wait a minute? Did she just give me the finger?"

"She gave you *a* finger, not *the* finger."

"I almost would have preferred the other one. This is absurd. Michelle and I have been coming here at least once a week now for months." Drew turned once again to face Michael, and gingerly placed the glass on top of his head.

Michael's eyes widened in horror. "What are you doing?"

Drew's hands moved away from the sides of the glass, and his eyes screwed upward in concentration.

"I'm entertaining myself while I wait." He balanced the glass on his skull for maybe five full seconds before it slipped to one side. Drew craned his neck quickly to compensate, but it was too late. The cocktail glass crashed to the ground and shattered noisily.

Immediately, the young waitress started moving in their direction. Drew noticed and smirked to Michael, proud of this accomplishment. She came over to survey the glass wreckage at their feet, her brow furrowed.

"Oh no! Are you all right?" The waitress seemed genuinely concerned.

"I'm actually not all right. Now, I'm not only without a Bloody Mary, but I'm without a glass, as well."

"I'm so sorry about that. Can I bring you another one?"

"I don't know. *Can* you? I'm wondering the same thing, as a matter of fact."

The waitress didn't seem to get it. "Oh, absolutely. People spill things here all the time. We just can't help it; we're only human, I suppose." She smiled good-naturedly.

"I didn't spill it; there was nothing to spill. It was empty, so I dropped it. Or rather, I *allowed it to fall*, would be the more accurate phrasing."

That finally struck something. The pretty blonde's smile fell from her face faster than the glass had hit the ground.

"Oh."

Drew leaned in to her. "Yes… 'oh'. My wife and I have been coming here for months, and I've never had to wait this long for a refill. Are you new or something?"

The waitress blushed. Michael felt terribly uncomfortable, and his heart reached out to her, yet he didn't know what to say. And it was not in his nature to curtail Drew, especially not when he was in a mood like this.

She looked down at her feet. "I'm sorry, sir. I'll get a busser over here right away to clean this up, and I'll bring you a fresh one, on the house."

But Drew would not be mollified. "Why send a busser over? It's not his fault the glass is broken."

The young woman didn't know what else to say. She attempted one last feeble, miserably apologetic little smile, and then turned to escape. Drew reached for her though and caught her wrist.

"I asked you a question."

Now the server was definitely at a loss for words.

She looked genuinely shocked that he was touching her, her eyes quickly taking in the strong fingers wrapped around her flesh, squeezing tightly.

"You're hurting me." Her voice was meek, but there was a clear sense of alarm to it. She tried to tug free of him, but Drew pulled her in roughly, forcing her to take a halting step toward him.

"Is this the only way to get your attention?"

Even from the other side of the table, Michael could smell the tomato juice and the vodka on Drew's breath. He opened his mouth to intercede, but found he had no tongue. Drew had pulled the girl within a foot of him, and she was beginning to tear up, panic written in the lines on her forehead.

"Please let go of me." She looked desperately around for help. Drew's fingers were leaving bright white splotches on the pink skin of her wrist.

"We'll take the check." His voice was low, firm, and dripping with acid.

And with that, he let go of her, simultaneously spinning her around. She took a frightened step away from him, but not fast enough. Drew slapped her buttocks with the palm of his hand... *hard*. She squealed in pain and horror, then shuffled quickly away, already choking back sobs. Several guests who had become vaguely aware of the incident heard or saw the slap and were now rising to protect her. A couple individuals threw accusatory looks at Drew, but no one said anything.

Drew just pushed his chair back loudly from the table and stood slowly. He picked up the last strip of steak from his plate with his hand, tilted his head back, and dropped it in his open mouth. Chewing, he started moving toward the exit.

"Come on, Mikey."

Michael didn't move a muscle. Most of the café had gone silent. The waitress had disappeared inside the kitchen.

"What about the bill?"

Drew snorted. "You think she wants us to pay or you think she wants us to leave?"

Mechanically, Michael reached for his wallet. "Probably both."

"Whatever, Mike. The steak was overcooked, the drinks were watered down, and the service was…" He guffawed, shaking his head as he stepped from the patio onto the sidewalk outside the café. "I have no words for it. Whatever. If you wanna pay for your experience, go ahead." And without another word, he stepped out of sight.

Michael stood shakily, opened his wallet, and realized he had no cash, only a credit card. He could feel the eyes of the whole restaurant on him. It made him nauseous, and his palms started sweating. Michael looked at where the girl had disappeared, then to where Drew had disappeared, and then quickly at some of the faces staring back at him. He swallowed hard, made a decision, put his wallet back in his pocket, and hastily made his way to the exit.

When he was out on the sidewalk, Michael saw Drew waiting for him across the street at their cars. He had half a mind to walk the other direction; the last thing he wanted right now was to be seen with Drew and to be guilty by association. But walking away would only create more drama, and where was he supposed to go? His car was parked right behind Drew's, and he was on the other side of town from his apartment.

Michael hid his hands in his pockets, checked the traffic in the street, waited for it to ebb, and then scampered across. Drew watched him with interest, stretched casually out against the hard metal body of his Land Rover.

"Did I embarrass you in there?"

Without answering or acknowledging the question, Michael beelined for his own vehicle, an older black Toyota Corolla that was parked too close for comfort to the shining silver bumper of Drew's SUV. He drew his keys from his pocket and started for the driver's side door.

"You embarrassed yourself in there, Drew. That was completely unnecessary."

Languidly, Drew straightened his spine, looked up at the sun, and then walked over to Michael. He rested a hand on the driver's window of the Corolla, propping himself up. The gesture in itself was not innately threatening, but Michael knew better. He finally turned from the car to face his friend.

Drew was waiting for him with a look that seemed gentle, almost paternal.

"It felt kinda good though, didn't it?"

Michael didn't have to lie. "No, Drew, it did not. She's probably calling the cops right now. We could get arrested for sexual harassment, or assault, or something."

"She's probably complaining to Larry, the big, fat, boring manager, who is always flirting with Michelle, and who honestly considers himself to be a friend of mine. The worst that could possibly happen is maybe I'm not welcome there anymore, but I doubt it.

Regardless, I'm sure I don't wanna eat there again anyway. Not after today. So, it seems like a win-win to me, huh?"

Michael was not following Drew's logic. "Is this what you're suggesting we do with ourselves? Spend our last days on Earth tormenting some poor waitress just because we *can*? That sounds an awful lot like bullying to me."

Drew's expression hardened. He had always hated being called a bully, and Michael knew it.

"Mike, I'm not saying we should be intentionally cruel just for the sake of it. I'm not advocating that. All I'm saying is that life is very literally too short to sit for an hour in a café, waiting for some little shit waitress to walk by so I can get another Bloody Mary. If I overreacted, it's because I'm acutely aware of my own mortality these days. Can you empathize with that for a second?"

Michael fidgeted with his keys. "Of course, I can. But why the ass slap, then?"

Drew stared at him blankly as if he was speaking another language.

"Why the ass slap? Because she had a nice ass. And because I'd been wanting to slap it from the moment she walked up and I noticed she had a nice ass. And because, *most importantly*, I knew I wouldn't get another chance." His dark eyes bored holes into Michael's. "You don't have to like it. I just need to know if you understand *why* I did it. Do you?" Michael was silent. "Do you, Mikey?"

"Yes, yeah…"

"Good. What are you doing right now?"

"Going home, if you'll let me."

Drew's face was pained. "Don't hold this against me, Mikey, I'm trying to teach you something here—"

"STOP! Just stop, okay?!"

Michael accidentally dropped his keys in the heat of the outburst, but he didn't care. All of the pent-up wrath and frustration he had felt during the course of their brunch was suddenly bursting out of his pores like a volcanic eruption, and he was aware of his muscles quaking violently beneath his skin.

"I don't need you to teach me anything! I'm perfectly capable of making my own decisions and coming to my own conclusions. You always act like I'm some little pledge brother you're trying to take under your wing and show me the ropes. I'm twenty-nine years old! Okay?!"

Michael was breathing heavily now and was furious to discover that his eyes were watering. To conceal this embarrassing fact, he reached down and scooped up his keys from the pavement, stabbed the key into the door hole, and turned it, keeping his face toward the car the whole time while he tried to calm himself. He opened the car door with a heavy sigh. Michael closed his eyes and took a deep breath, and wondered what Drew was thinking, and what his facial expression looked like right now.

He probably thinks I'm losing it, Michael thought to himself remorsefully. His muscles were finally beginning to relax a bit. After what felt like a very long time, Michael cleared his throat and turned to face Drew.

His friend was smiling appreciatively. "There it is."

And that was all he said, nodding his head with satisfaction as he moved off to his own car. Michael stood still, watching him open the door to his expensive luxury SUV. Before Drew disappeared inside the cabin, he took one last look back at Michael.

"*Carpe diem*, Mikey. We'll be in touch." And then he started the engine and began to drive off.

Michael watched the Land Rover turn a corner and vanish out of sight before turning his gaze back toward the restaurant. It seemed, at least from the other side of the street, that business was back to normal. No one seemed to be paying him any mind, and the young waitress was nowhere to be seen. She probably had gone back to work though, or, at worst, was still taking a short break to compose herself.

At the end of the day, Michael seriously doubted the young woman would suffer any lasting psychological damage from the morning's episode. She would chalk it up as a terrible day at work, and probably complain to her parents or to her boyfriend, and then leave it at that. It was not the type of thing to put a person in the psychiatric ward, after all.

Every server must experience terrible customers from time to time. She had probably never been spanked at work before, but even that, he could not be entirely sure of. Michael had no idea what the risks and occupational hazards of being a beautiful young woman in the service industry entailed. He stepped inside his car and began the long drive home.

CHAPTER EIGHT

When Michael was back in his apartment, he fed Tucker and decided to have a smoke out on the balcony. As he shut the sliding glass door, he looked out of habit over to his neighbor's apartment to check and see if the old man was there. He was not. It was barely 1:00 p.m. on a Sunday afternoon, and he knew the man did not work weekends. He thought he could hear the sounds of a muffled conversation coming from inside the neighboring space.

Losing interest, Michael sat down in a black patio chair and reached for his lighter on the end table next to him. He produced a cigarette and lit it deftly, bringing the stick to his mouth and relaxing back into the chair.

The sun was beating down on his balcony directly, and the warmth felt good on Michael's skin. This was the perfect time of day to be out on the balcony, and he so seldom was because of work. In an hour or so, he knew the sun's position would change, and long shadows would begin to creep across the stucco floor. Soon, it would grow too chilly again to be outside.

Michael longed for the spring and summer months when Los Angeles would be warm, even in the shade.

He had always enjoyed basking in the sun, and sometimes even imagined himself to be a cold-blooded reptile, a scaly creature that needed the sunlight to warm its body and store up energy for the long night. Michael closed his eyes and took another drag, stretching his legs out in front of him.

Eight days. It had been eight days now since the wedding… since the sky had lit up and changed his life forever.

The responsibility of planning Aaron's funeral had fallen to a distant aunt. She had originally wanted the service to take place on Thursday, but Drew had intervened from his phone in Thailand, convincing her to push it back to Saturday so that he and his new bride could attend. They had flown into LAX late Friday night, cutting their honeymoon short by a day.

The funeral had been a quiet, sparsely attended affair that Saturday morning. Most of the guests were estranged relatives of Aaron's, and none of them seemed to have kept in much contact with him over the last ten years.

The aunt responsible for planning the whole event made it seem otherwise, however, often referring to Aaron on a very tender, personal basis, and crying frequently and without reservation. Michael had never heard Aaron speak of the woman. Not once.

He was not surprised that not a single one of Aaron's coworkers showed up. Drew had even made the same observation aloud to Michael at one point, just before they made plans to do brunch the next day and discuss all that had transpired over the past week.

Michael stared up above him now, scanning the air for weaknesses. Maybe if he looked hard and long enough, he would be able to detect warning signs of the coming apocalypse. The color of the sky was an unreal platinum blue, but that was nothing out of the ordinary for the City of Angels. He couldn't find anything noticeably different about his surroundings, so he looked over at the sun again. It was still just as bright and blinding as it had ever been. Seemingly, nothing had changed.

Michael allowed his mind to wander. Soon, he was reflecting back on his conversation with Drew over brunch, and then on Aaron's note to him. Michael had shared the note with Drew and then stored it safely away in the drawer of his nightstand. Unintentionally, he found himself opening the drawer and re-reading the letter at least once a day, nearly every day since he had discovered it. Michael had also laboriously studied the contents of all the email correspondence he had forwarded from Aaron's laptop to his own, and it was not uncommon for him to wake up in the middle of the night and open the messages once again, searching for any clues he might have somehow missed.

What did he want to do with his time? He had already gone skydiving. He had no interest in "doing lines off of hookers in Vegas," nor in "having an orgy." Michael set his cigarette down on the edge of the end table and went inside to find a yellow notepad of paper and a ballpoint pen, before returning back to his balcony roost and the burning cigarette.

This was how his brain worked, and how he had always made important life decisions. Michael was a 'pros and cons' type of guy, all too familiar with the practice of drawing a line down the center of a page and making two opposing columns to help him solve the greatest conundrums of existence. This time, though, he didn't need the line or the columns... he just needed a list.

Michael sat and stared at the faded yellow paper, letting time tick by and his cigarette burn down to the filter before stubbing it out and rubbing his forehead with his other hand. So far, he hadn't thought of anything.

What did that say about him as a human being? There had to be plenty of things in his life that he valued. He loved his dog. Most of the time, he liked Drew... when he wasn't drunk, bullying, or overdramatic. He did not like his job, but he tolerated it.

Michael tried to remember old dreams he had once had but couldn't think of anything meaningful enough to merit being written down now. He remembered always wanting to go to Disneyworld as a kid, but nowadays, the idea didn't excite him. In fact, no tourist destination, no matter how trip-worthy, felt like a must-see to him.

He had never really cared about visiting Europe. Michael had no burning desire to see other parts of the world, and he knew relaxing alone on a tropical beach somewhere would probably just make him anxious and stir-crazy. Besides, he would never be able to afford a vacation... unless he actually did decide to rob a bank.

No, he needed to be more realistic. What did he want to do with his time that he *could* do? Michael began subconsciously doodling on the pad while he racked his brain for inspiration.

A couple birds flew past his balcony, and he looked up to watch them circle round one another and then dart out of view above him. Michael scratched his head with the tip of the pen and tried to focus in on his wants and on his innermost desires.

And then, out of nowhere, he saw her face materialize in his mind's eye… and he knew he wanted Jeanette. He had always wanted her, for as long as he had been employed at the credit union, from the moment he first saw her. And if there was ever a time to make a move, it was certainly now.

Michael pulled out his cell phone. He had stored her number in his contacts list long, long ago, when he had first begun work at the business and been given an employee contact sheet. Looking back, he was ashamed to say he had never called her. Nor had he ever asked her out in person. Not on a date, not for coffee, not even to grab lunch together during a work break. And she had given him signs for years, he was sure of it. He had just always been too clueless or too afraid to reciprocate.

Now, Michael stared down at the name and number glowing on the screen, his insides churning. He wasn't sure what to say, or how to begin. Michael tried to reflect back on memories he shared with Drew inside bars or at college parties, and on the pick-up lines his friend had used so successfully on so many women.

This was a different situation, though. Jeanette wasn't a complete stranger, she was a woman Michael had known for quite some time now, and she was someone he would have to continue to see almost every day at work for the foreseeable future.

Granted, the foreseeable future wasn't as scary or as endless as it once seemed.

Michael dialed the number and waited, holding his breath and silently hoping Jeanette wouldn't be able to hear the thumping of his heart over the receiver. *If* she even picked up... and Michael half-hoped she wouldn't.

Just as he was about to hang up, he heard a voice come from the other end.

"Hello?"

"Jeanette?"

"Yes. Who's this?"

Michael swallowed. "It's Michael."

"Michael who?"

His heart sank, and he realized immediately this was a major mistake. Again, he battled the impulse to hang up, but he knew that even if he did, there was a strong chance she would eventually put it together and realize who had called her and then hung up mid-conversation. She couldn't know *that* many Michaels, after all.

"Michael Cavanaugh. You know, from work?"

There was a moment of silence on the other end as Jeanette took in the information.

"Michael! How are you?"

She at least sounded somewhat excited that it was him. Michael exhaled a little bit.

"I'm fine, thanks. How are you?"

Jeanette laughed. "Great, great. Just enjoying my weekend. I love this sunshine, don't you?"

Michael smiled and nodded. "I'm outside on my balcony right now. It feels so good. Great weather for October."

"Definitely."

Several seconds passed by as Michael struggled to

find the right words he was looking for.

Finally, Jeanette spoke. "So... what's up? I didn't know you had my number."

"Oh, I found it on the employee contact sheet."

"You still have that thing? I have no idea where mine is." She laughed again. He liked her laugh. "Well, aren't you just the model employee!"

Michael laughed with her. His anxiety was starting to recede, and he was remembering to breathe again. She had a calming effect on him, even now, over the phone.

"I try to be." His mouth was dry as he prepared to ask the question. "The reason I'm calling is because I was wondering if you wanted to do something sometime."

The words came out in a breathless rush. Michael was finished speaking before he thought he wanted to be, but it was too late now. He was utterly lost for words, and all he could do was wait in agony for a response.

"Okay. What did you have in mind, Michael?"

He liked the way she said his name. It was a struggle to formulate and order his thoughts before answering her question.

"Well, I was wondering if you wanted to grab dinner sometime. Or lunch, if that's easier. Or drinks. Or coffee. Or whatever works for you, actually."

"Lunch might be a little difficult to take together right now, since we're so short-staffed."

He hadn't thought of that. "True. I hadn't thought of that."

"Maybe we should start with dinner, and then depending on how that goes, decide if we still want to do drinks later. Are you a good cook?"

Michael wasn't certain if he qualified as a 'good' cook. He had always assumed that he was a better-than-average cook, and he had enjoyed learning different recipes and honing his skills in the kitchen after spending most of his adult life as a bachelor living alone in a single apartment.

That said, he also knew plenty of people with more sophisticated palates than himself, so he couldn't be too sure of his own culinary prowess. His meals had always impressed himself, and Drew and Michelle were always complimentary on the rare occasion he had them over for dinner in the past. Tucker always ate whatever morsels were left over, and the dog never seemed to complain.

Cautiously, Michael made up his mind. "I know my way around the kitchen, yes. And I've been told I make a mean lemon pepper chicken dish."

The lie came out easier than expected. No one had ever told him any such thing, but Michael had always enjoyed that recipe above all others.

"Well, I'm sold. Does tomorrow at your place work for you? I'm not trying to invite myself over, but I'm having my floors redone and my place is a mess. Through no fault of my own, obviously."

"Yeah, my place sounds good. What time works for you?"

"You're the gourmet chef. What time works for you?"

Michael blushed and even laughed a little. "Nine?"

"*Ooooh*, the late dinner. How European of you! I'll have to dig my finest evening gown out of my closet." Jeanette laughed flirtatiously. "Nine o'clock it is, then. I look forward to it." She paused. "I'm glad you called, Michael. This was a very nice surprise. Completely unexpected, I have to say, but definitely a nice surprise."

Michael felt his heart flying up and out of his chest. He was lightheaded and giddy with emotion.

"Well, I'm just glad you picked up the phone. Do you need my address for tomorrow?"

"No… *I know where you live.*" Jeanette said it in the deepest, gruffest voice she could manage. She gave it a moment or two to register, and when he didn't laugh, she finally did.

"I'm kidding, Michael. It's a joke! I'll just get your address from you tomorrow at work." She paused. "Unless, of course, I stumble across my copy of the employee contact list while I'm looking for my evening gown." This time, he did laugh. "Have a good night, Michael! See you tomorrow."

"See you tomorrow, Jeanette." And he hung up the phone.

CHAPTER NINE

"So, this is the famous Tucker. He's shorter in person than I expected, I won't lie to you."

The famous Tucker was in absolute paradise. He rolled over onto his back and allowed her fingers to rub his soft belly up and down as his pink tongue lolled out the side of his mouth with pleasure.

Michael took in the scene from the stove in his small kitchen. He was carefully monitoring the progress of a pot of rice and trying desperately to conceal his nervousness and excitement. Watching Jeanette pet and play with his dog gave him all sorts of crazy ideas, including a vision of the future where the two of them were walking Tucker in a park somewhere, hand-in-hand, a happy couple. He wondered if there was still enough time left for that.

"Is he a collie? Like Lassie?"

"No, he's a Sheltie. Shetland Sheepdog. They're basically smaller versions of collies. But he does look a lot like Lassie. Whenever I take him to the dog park, if there are ever little kids around, they always like to call him that."

Jeanette lifted her green-gold eyes from the happy animal and met Michael's gaze.

"I'm surprised little kids today even know who Lassie is. I feel like she's a product of a different generation."

Michael turned back to the stove and resumed stirring the rice with a long wooden ladle. "I guess she's not entirely forgotten. Maybe their parents were big fans of the TV show as kids."

"Or their grandparents."

Jeanette had stopped scratching Tucker's stomach during the conversation, and he licked her hand to remind her he was still there and available for more attention. She laughed and began rubbing him behind his ears.

Michael stopped stirring and opened the oven door slightly to check on his lemon pepper chicken. It looked like it was just about ready.

"You can stop petting him whenever you decide enough is enough. If you don't, he never will. He'll lay there all night."

Jeanette didn't seem to mind. She sat down on the carpet next to Tucker, keeping one hand working on him while the other unclasped her shoes. Deftly, she removed both of her heels and placed them under the coffee table in Michael's living room. He caught himself looking at her bare feet and went to the cupboards to begin setting the kitchen table.

"Do you have any animals?"

Jeanette shook her head. "My lease doesn't allow them. Normally, I wouldn't give a fuck, but one of my best friends just got evicted from her place because her neighbors reported her and her cocker spaniel to the landlord."

Michael meticulously arranged the silverware on

either side of the two plates he had set out.

"I can sympathize. My neighbors here are an absolute nightmare. Thankfully, they have a dog too, so I'm not really worried about having Tucker. Although, we're not supposed to have animals here, either."

Jeanette gave Tucker one last scratch and then rose to her feet.

"*Ooooh*, so you're a bit of a rebel then, huh?"

She crossed into the kitchen and turned the faucet on to wash her hands in the sink. Tucker stared longingly up and over at her, clearly not finished being pampered. Jeanette noticed and smiled down at him.

"Nothing personal, Tucker, I just don't want your hair in my chicken." She tore off a paper towel to dry her hands. "Can I help you with anything?"

Michael shook his head. "Nope, not a thing. Just have a seat and relax."

He still could hardly believe she was actually in his apartment right now.

Work had been mercifully busy for a Monday, so they had hardly shared anything more than a smile all day at the credit union. Michael was thankful for that. After their phone conversation, he had suddenly realized in a cold panic that they had a whole day of work together to get through before 'the date'.

Michael wasn't even sure whether it was a date, but he hadn't counted on having to make conversation with Jeanette before she came over. He had been looking forward to the hours between his job and dinner as a time to prepare and calm his nerves, but instead, he found himself burying his face in his computer screen when he arrived at his workstation the next morning, pretending to be thoroughly engrossed with his email inbox.

Jeanette had walked past his chair, lightly touched him on the back, politely mentioned that she was happy he had called, asked if she could bring anything over and offering to bring wine, and finally ended the conversation by saying she was looking forward to their dinner. Michael curtly nodded and agreed the whole time, then busied himself once more with his inbox.

And that had been it. Eight hours later, he had collected his things, powered down his computer, and as casually as he could, strolled over to her station and slipped her a torn piece of scrap paper with his address scribbled down on it. He had strategically waited till she was on the phone; she smiled, waved goodbye, and mouthed "see you tonight." Then, Michael was off and running, eager to prepare himself for what was already feeling like the biggest night of his life.

Jeanette pulled out a chair and sat down at the kitchen table. Tucker immediately roused himself and trotted over to sit beneath her. She rubbed her foot through his fur and watched Michael mix the chicken in with the pot of rice.

"I know you've got your hands full, but don't forget to open that Cab and let it breathe a little. I'd do it myself, but I've been ordered to sit and relax, and I don't want to disturb my new best friend down here."

"He sure does have a thing for you."

Michael laughed as he emptied the chicken and rice into a large, ceramic serving bowl, rested the ladle inside, and carried it over to the table.

"You're positive he's not bothering you?"

"Not at all! He's an absolute sweetheart."

Michael retrieved a wine key from one of the drawers in the kitchen and proceeded to open the bottle she had brought over. When he finally got the cork out, he poured two small glasses and brought them to the table, along with the bottle itself.

Jeanette smiled slyly up at him. "Not gonna let it breathe, huh? Eager beaver."

Turning as red as his Cabernet, Michael sat down sheepishly.

"I am *so* sorry! I completely forgot. Just not used to having wine, I guess."

She reached across the table and patted his hand sympathetically.

"I suppose I'll let it slide this one time." Jeanette sighed wistfully. "It was a three-hundred-dollar bottle of wine, but no worries. Let's enjoy ourselves, right?" She raised her glass and smirked at him playfully.

Her unique sense of humor, a clever mix of flirty sarcasm, was sometimes lost on Michael, but when it struck home, he found himself incredibly turned on. He clinked his wine glass with hers and took a drink, maintaining eye contact with Jeanette the whole way through.

As he brought the glass back to the table, he was surprised to see her tip her own glass back and finish it off with a last swallow. She returned the glass to the table and pretended to notice he was watching her.

"Oh, relax. I got it from Ralph's for ten dollars. Is it tacky that I just told you that?" She reached for the ladle and began to fill her plate with the chicken dish. "I'm not trying to be cheap, and don't worry, I'm not a lush. It was just a longer, busier Monday than I was prepared for at work, and I just found out today that my mom's in the hospital."

Michael was completely taken off-guard. Before he could blurt something out, Jeanette saw his expression and put up a hand.

"Don't worry, they don't think it's anything serious. She's had some heart problems over the past couple years, and this looks like a minor flare-up. She'll probably be out in a couple days. She's old and she smokes like a four-alarm fire, so it's not too surprising."

Michael didn't know what to say or do. "Well, I hope she's ok." He was still frozen in his seat.

Jeanette's brows furrowed as she nodded and replaced the ladle.

"She will be. It's just frustrating to hear, that's all. She needs to be taking better care of herself. I've told her that, God knows how many times, and yet, she's so stubborn. She lives like she's still a teenager. I guess that's where I get it from."

Jeanette poured herself another glass of wine. Michael quickly drained his own to keep pace and nodded when she offered to refill it for him.

"I'm sorry. I don't want to kill the mood, and I promise I'll change the subject. I just hate feeling powerless, you know? She's on the other side of the country, and there's nothing I can do to really help her. That's the worst part, I think."

Michael began filling his own plate with the chicken dish, keeping his eyes on Jeanette. "Well, maybe you could take some time off? Go out and see her, make sure she's okay?"

Jeanette shook her head and took another drink of wine, this time a sip.

"I don't have the vacation days left, unfortunately. I just *had* to go to Mexico this summer with my old college roommates, and now I'm out of luck. It's all right. Like I said, I'm sure she's fine. She's probably just being overdramatic."

Michael's face was a picture of sympathy. "If I could give you some of my days, I would. I'm not using them for anything anytime soon."

Jeanette laughed. "Don't you want to take a vacation? Isn't there someplace you'd like to see, or family you'd like to visit?" She forked a piece of chicken with some rice, blew softly to cool it, and took a bite.

Michael watched her closely. "How is it?"

Her face lit up. "Amazing!" She continued to chew it down and then went for another bite. "You undersold yourself, Mr. Lagasse."

Michael beamed with pride. "I'm glad you like it. This is about all I know how to do. It's an old recipe of my grandmother's, actually, which I somehow have memorized; don't ask me how. I'm no chef. Anyway, I'm not a big traveler, and my family's kind of spread out. My parents are in Florida, and my brother's a reclusive crab fisher off the coast of Alaska. I haven't seen him in ten years, and I only talk to my mom over the phone on rare occasions, like anniversaries and birthdays and things. My dad's kind of... aloof, I guess? That's pretty much it in terms of family." He took a bite from his own plate. "This is pretty good, if I do say so myself."

Jeanette had been listening intently. "Please say so yourself; it's delicious. Thank you for having me over tonight, by the way. This is so much better than watching reruns of *Grey's Anatomy* and eating a Lean Cuisine meal. I told you I'm getting my floors redone right now, too, right?"

Michael nodded. "Do you know when it's supposed to be finished?"

Jeanette groaned into her wine glass and set it down. "Well, 'supposed to' and 'going to be' are two completely different timeframes. It was *supposed* to be finished last month, but here we are in October, and my apartment still looks like Dresden. I think it's *going to be* finished, hopefully, by the first of November. We'll see. If Thanksgiving rolls around and it's still not done, you might be hosting me again sooner than you thought."

Michael laughed and took a sip of wine. "I wouldn't mind. I like having you here."

It was not the right thing to say. Michael realized it almost as soon as it came out and immediately regretted it.

Jeanette just smiled and tried her best to not seem surprised by the remark, but he could tell it had landed on her, and he quickly racked his brain for a way to recover. Words weren't coming, though, and Michael felt a hot flush creep up his neck and burn into his cheeks. His mouth was dry as he took another swallow of wine. Things had been going so nicely, and all of a sudden, he had embarrassed himself.

To make matters worse, Jeanette had locked her eyes right on him now. He squirmed uncomfortably in his wooden chair and looked anywhere but at her. Even Tucker seemed to be watching him now... waiting for him to say something – say anything – to fix the situation and make everything right.

Jeanette found her tongue first. "So, why did you call me, Michael? Why now, after all this time? If you don't mind my asking…"

She wasn't making things any easier on him. What was he supposed to say to that? Even if the world was ending, something told him *this* was not the right moment in time to confess his feelings of love for his coworker, not on a Monday night over lemon pepper chicken and rice. Michael worked his mouth into a thin smile and shrugged.

"I don't know. I guess I just figured that it might be nice… you know, to do something outside of work. I mean, we talk at the credit union, and we've known each other for a while now. You know I'm not some psycho killer—"

"I don't know that yet, actually. I brought my pepper spray and my rape whistle, just in case." She nodded in the direction of the purse she had left on the kitchen counter. "Don't think that just because you have a cute dog, I'll let my guard down. I *know* men like you, Michael Cavanaugh." Her face was deadly serious.

Michael raised an eyebrow and began to feel his unease recede, ever so slowly, away from him.

"And what kind of a man am I, Jeanette Dailey?"

She took her time before responding, chewing and swallowing a mouthful of rice, then washing it down with the rest of her wine. Finally, she inhaled a deep breath before suddenly bursting into a fit of girlish laughter.

"I don't know! I was trying to think of something clever to say back, and nothing came out. That's so embarrassing! I'm usually so witty."

Michael joined in the laughter. "I still think you're

witty."

"You're just saying that because you want to sleep with me."

Michael almost choked. He turned bright red as his laughter caught in his throat.

Jeanette picked up the bottle and refilled their glasses, keeping her eyes on her work. "Breathe, Michael. I'm just joking with you." She finished pouring and replaced the bottle at the table's edge. It was almost gone. "I feel like I have a habit of shocking you. Is that true?"

Michael reached automatically for his wine glass. He was beginning to realize just how much more liquid courage he was going to need to make it through this dinner alive. Jeanette took another drink herself, and then scooped more chicken and rice onto her plate.

"Did I offend you? I know I can come across a little... sensational sometimes, but really, I'm just trying to have a good time. We work in a bank, for fuck's sake. We have to spice up what we can." Her expression softened, and she reached out to grasp Michael's wrist, lightly but firmly, across the table. "I know you're not just trying to get into my pants. This is a lovely dinner, and I'm so happy you called me. Really. I think this was a great idea."

Her tenderness was meant to be a reassurance and a comfort, but the sudden physical contact had only disrupted Michael even further. The wine was beginning to soak into his senses, and he suddenly felt the need to excuse himself to the bathroom.

"I'm sorry, I have to pee real quick."

He stood up abruptly, breaking the contact, and without another word, scrambled down the hallway and into the sanctuary of his bathroom.

When the door was shut, Michael finally allowed himself to breathe again. He reached for a cotton hand towel by the sink and mopped away the light sheen of sweat that had formed on his forehead. There was no question that he was definitively drunk already. He could feel his eyes moving faster than his brain, and his vision seemed to lag. He closed his eyes and reopened them several times, splashed some water on his face, and moved to the toilet to unzip his fly and relieve his bladder.

Michael slowly began to process the awkwardness of his exit line and overall departure from the kitchen table, and when he was done urinating, he flushed and rested his palms against the wall in front of him, sinking his forehead like a wilting flower against the bumpy white surface. Again, he closed his eyes and attempted to pull himself together.

He was embarrassing himself, and they had only just made it through dinner... and not even completely yet. How could he possibly be feeling so disjointed after less than half a bottle of wine? He was a grown man, and though Michael was not a heavy drinker, he had certainly never been considered a lightweight.

It was more than just the alcohol, though. Jeanette was being uncharacteristically forward, even for her... he was sure of it. She had pried into the reason for him asking her to this dinner, she had removed her heels in his living room, she had made that comment about him wanting to sleep with her and get in her pants... and she had touched him, grabbed and held onto his wrist across the table, and looked into his eyes in a way she had never looked before. There was no misinterpreting the signs.

Jeanette had come on much stronger than he had expected, but then again, she had always been flirtatious at work. She *did* have a habit of shocking him by saying the most sensational and often the most inappropriate things. And now she was here, in his apartment, on a Monday night, at who knows what time anymore, polishing off a bottle of wine between the two of them.

Drew's face appeared in Michael's mind, complete with a knowing smile and a lascivious wink. *You won't get another chance.* The words came from out of his memory somewhere and reverberated through his head in Drew's deep voice. He had said something yesterday at brunch, something to try and justify why he had abused their poor waitress. Drew had wanted to do it, to slap her ass. And so, he had done it. Without a second thought and with no regard for the consequences. Drew had done it simply because he knew he wouldn't get another chance.

Michael moved to the mirror to wash his hands and examined the reflection staring back at him. Why was he being so mousey, so shocked, so *meek* all the time? Nothing Jeanette had done warranted this kind of response: a cowardly retreat to the bathroom, right when things had been getting really interesting between them.

What was he so afraid of? He should have stayed, he should have fought through the uneasiness in his stomach and his shortness of breath, and he should have told her how he felt about her, right there and then.

No time but the present. Literally. Drew was right.

Michael stared hard into the eyes looking back at him, hating the weakness that he saw there, the insecurity, the doubt. This was what Drew had been trying to tell him all along; that there was simply no time for this kind of indecision and uncertainty.

What did he want to do with the time he had left, however long that might be?

Did he want to end it prematurely, like Aaron had? It was already ending prematurely enough.

Did he want to do nothing, and just wait for the end to come, whenever that might be?

Or did he want to follow Drew's example and grab the bull by the horns, asserting his will and his way and finally beginning to live life to the fullest, on his own terms and conditions, for as long as he had air left to breathe?

This could be his last night on Earth... and he had called Jeanette for a reason.

The bathroom door opened swiftly, and Jeanette looked up from the kitchen table to see Michael moving back into the room. She smiled playfully.

"Well, I guess when you gotta go, you gotta—"

Her words were cut short by Michael's mouth. He grabbed the back of her head with both of his hands and pressed her lips against his own. Standing over her, Michael had to bend forward at the waist to bring his face level with hers. Her head tilted on her neck and over the back of the wooden chair uncomfortably, and her arms rose awkwardly for balance.

Michael didn't see the motion, though, because his eyes were closed tightly, all his energy concentrated in this one effort, and he pushed his tongue through her lips and into her mouth. One of his hands moved down her neck and he felt himself reaching for her breast, but then she was pushing him off and sliding her chair back with a jolt.

There was a terrible yelp and Tucker ran from beneath the chair, tail between his legs, and disappeared into Michael's bedroom. Jeanette rose to her feet, turned her head in the direction of the dog, and uttered a quick sound of alarm. Then, just as quickly, she turned back toward Michael and was backing away from him and from the table, her face a perfect combination of shock, disappointment, and anger.

"What are you doing, Michael?!"

He stood there, rigid, quivering slightly... and was mortified to find that he had an erection and no answers for her. Michael took a step toward her, and a swift drop of her eyes told him that she was as aware of the protrusion in his pants as he was.

Jeanette was moving then, first to the coffee table to retrieve her shoes, and then to her purse on the kitchen counter.

"I think I should go."

Some primal instinct flared at the idea of her leaving, and Michael took another step, meeting her at the counter. He touched her shoulder lightly.

"Wait."

She recoiled from his hand as if it was on fire, and her eyes flashed dangerously.

"Don't touch me!"

Jeanette slung the purse over her shoulder and made to move around him. His mind worked quickly, and he finally was able to form speech, the words tumbling out fast and furiously slurred, but still comprehensible.

"Are you kidding me? After all the signs you've given me, the way you act at work, and now tonight... *now* that's too much? What the fuck?"

She maneuvered around him and made her way to his front door, talking as she walked, careful to avoid eye contact.

"I'm going home, Michael. You're drunk, and we can talk about this in the morning or something. Goodnight."

He grabbed her roughly by the shoulder then and spun her around to face him.

"There might not be a morning!"

She slapped him hard across the face – a purely physical reaction to being grabbed and turned against her will. Equally reactive but without any real thought, Michael slapped her back. The *crack* of his palm against her soft cheek bounced off the walls of his apartment.

Jeanette's eyes watered from the stinging pain, but her jaw set hard as stone, and she shoved him roughly in the chest away from her, survival mode kicking in over the absolute stunned disbelief of what had happened. In desperation, she wrenched the door open and slammed it shut behind her, and Michael could hear her footsteps flying down the hallway as she retreated from him.

He stood there for at least five minutes; his head spinning, his cheek throbbing, his heart racing. All too late, he went to open the door and call after her, but she had long since vanished into the night. He felt a mixture of so many things all at once: astonished, ashamed, enraged, excited, and even horny.

Despite everything that had happened, Michael

was smiling… an absurd, big, bright, white smile that refused to acknowledge anything had gone amiss. Before he knew it, his smile had morphed into a slight giggle, and then he was releasing tension and frustration by laughing wholeheartedly and manically from his diaphragm, and tears were running down his reddened cheeks.

He moved unsteadily into his living room and collapsed in a heap upon his sofa. Michael tried to call for Tucker, but the dog would not come, perhaps still licking his wounds from the kitchen chair accident.

In a moment of stunning clarity, then, Michael knew exactly what he wanted to do. He pried his cell phone from his pants pocket and dialed a number. On the third ring, Drew picked up.

"You really can't live without me, can you?"

"What are you doing right now?"

"Whatever it was, I have a feeling I won't be doing it much longer."

Michael was already grabbing a jacket from his closet. "Do you want to go out?"

"Where?"

Michael slipped the jacket on over his phone hand, and then brought it back to his ear as he wrestled into the other sleeve.

"I don't fucking care. Anywhere."

"Are you drunk?"

"Yes. So what? Not enough, though. Where are you?"

Drew laughed. "I'm at home. Where should I be on a Monday night?"

"Not at fucking home. *Carpe diem*, right?"

There was the briefest pause from the other end.

"More like *carpe noctem*. You gonna pick me up? Michelle's asleep, but she'll wake up if she hears the garage door open."

"Yeah. I'll be there in ten."

"Just don't do anything stupid like ring the doorbell or honk the horn once you're here. Text me, and I'll come out." And then Drew hung up.

The next five minutes were a runny mess of blurred vision and action. Michael brushed his teeth furiously in the bathroom, hard enough to make his gums bleed. He vaguely made a mental note to see his dentist soon, remembering he was long overdue for a checkup and cleaning. And then he remembered what was happening to the world, and he quickly dismissed concerns of dental hygiene with a frenzied bark of a laugh.

Michael tried not to dwell on what had just transpired with Jeanette, but when the memories did manage to infiltrate his sodden brain, he found his knuckles getting whiter and his eyes watering. As quick as the reactions occurred, he would allow his merry-go-round mind to light upon a new thought or image, and then he was moving again, mentally and physically, misting his neck with more aftershave and grabbing his keys from the kitchen counter.

The last thing he did was call for Tucker again, but the dog was still nowhere to be found, and Michael didn't feel like searching all over for him just to apologize and say goodnight. So, he flipped the light switch, locked the door, and headed down to his car.

Michael couldn't remember the last time he drove drunk; it must have been college. He wasn't the kind of guy who went out that often, and when he drank, it was usually with Drew and sometimes with Aaron, and they almost always did it in someone's house or apartment. If they did go out, they walked to a local bar, or split the cab fare between them. It felt like a new adventure with an old friend; sliding into the driver's seat, turning the ignition on, and finding the right radio station before backing out of the garage and wheeling off into the night.

He pulled up in front of Drew's house smoking a cigarette and blasting an 80s rock ballad. Before Michael could write a text message, Drew slipped out his front door and jogged up to the car. He wore black slacks and an olive-green dress shirt, untucked, with the sleeves rolled up and the neck left open, displaying a tuft of coarse, curly black hair.

Michael smiled expectantly as Drew reached the car, opened the door, and stepped inside, speaking as he lowered his body down into the car seat.

"Turn the fucking radio down! I could hear you from inside."

Michael cranked the volume down a few notches and stepped on the gas, lurching the car forward and down the street.

Drew scrutinized his face. "How many have you had?"

"Not enough. Like I said."

"I'll bet. You look wasted."

"I am wasted."

Drew sighed and turned the radio back up. "Just don't kill me. I don't want to go out riding shotgun in a Toyota Corolla and listening to *The Scorpions*."

Michael grinned and turned the music louder. The alcohol had warped his sense of hearing.

"There are worse ways to go."

"Yeah, and there are definitely better. Where are we going, by the way?"

Michael hadn't really thought of that yet. All he had known was that he needed to get out; out of his apartment, out of the situation with Jeanette, out of his whole great big boring life. The alcohol he had consumed at dinner made him want to drink more, and so he racked his brain for local hotspots.

"I don't know. Where do you wanna go?"

Drew rolled his window down and spat. "This is your party, Mikey. You're calling the shots tonight, not me."

Michael liked the idea of that. Whenever they had gone out in the past, it was almost always at Drew's insistence and the place was always of his choosing. Not that Michael minded most of the time. He was always impressed with the locations Drew had discovered, and enjoyed not having to make any major decisions regarding their nightly activities; it was easier to follow than to lead.

But now Michael found himself in the driver's seat, quite literally, and he was exhilarated by the idea of controlling the fate of their nights. He thought again for a moment as he piloted the car out of Drew's subdivision.

"Hollywood?"

Drew turned his head and raised an eyebrow in surprise. "Hollywood? *You* want to go party in Hollywood, on a Monday night?"

Michael was already on the way. "*Carpe noctem.*"

Drew snorted, looked back out his window, and spat again. He moved his right arm out into the wind, drummed the side of the car door, and then rested his hand on the metal frame above his open window.

Michael couldn't contain the smile spreading across his face, and he, too, stuck an arm out the window and felt the wind ripping past his limb as the car sped down the road. His stomach was full of butterflies, and for the first time in a very, very long time, he felt happy. Really, truly happy... and free.

CHAPTER TEN

Hollywood Boulevard was deserted for the most part. Michael found parking easily enough, remembering that few people went out at midnight on a Monday, even in a city as big as Los Angeles. He and Drew walked unmolested along the dirty, star-tiled sidewalk, passing only the occasional sleeping homeless person nestled beneath ripped pieces of cardboard or filthy blankets.

Hollywood was neither glamorous nor beautiful, as Michael imagined the rest of the country must think. It was grimy and far too bright for that time of night, littered with souvenir shops, fast food restaurants, strip clubs, and newspaper stands. Most of the street performers and celebrity impersonators had gone home, the tourists had retreated to their hotels, the streets were empty, and the shops were closed... but still, the neon lights glowed, and giant video screens lit up the night air with an obnoxious white-purple haze.

After walking aimlessly for a few blocks, Drew pointed out a small little building crammed between a decrepit Chinese restaurant and a run-down condominium. A radiant yellow sign identified the place as Power Surge, underlined with a lightning bolt and a green martini glass that flashed on and off every two seconds. Michael thought it looked perfect.

A large Black man in an oversized pea coat was perched on an iron stool outside the entrance. He nodded lazily at the two of them, apparently seeing no need to check their IDs. Drew looked at least a dozen years older than he actually was anyway, so that probably helped. Michael led the way past the bouncer and into the bar.

Calling the place a 'dive' would have been an understatement. Michael knew Hollywood was seedy at night, but Power Surge was almost frighteningly so. Half of the walls were covered in cheap photo reproductions of classic Hollywood movie stars and starlets, the edges of the headshots yellowed and cracked. The other half of the bar had no decorations whatsoever, and Michael wondered whether the establishment's owner had simply run out of funds or if he/she was just too lazy to finish with the décor.

It wasn't as if there was a lot of square footage. The bar was even smaller on the inside than it had looked from the street. The place smelled strongly of tobacco, even though no one could legally smoke inside. Along the wall lined with photographs were half a dozen small booths, all of which were surprisingly occupied.

Across from the booths was the bar, complete with about fifteen stools, many of which had torn, padded seats. Michael noticed the stuffing coming out from beneath the imitation leather on more than a few of them, but again, he was surprised by just how many seats were taken for a Monday night.

Above all else, the place was dark... very dark. A

busty L.A. native worked by herself behind the bar, deftly filling milky glasses from the small beer rail or mixing cheap but strong cocktails in stained rocks glasses. Drew ambled over to an empty pair of bar stools after quickly surveying the scene and proceeded to order three shots of decent tequila from the bartender. Michael looked at him curiously, but Drew only winked.

"One for you, two for me. You've got a helluva head start."

Michael nodded sluggishly. He realized he had to pee again and slipped off the barstool with a couple mumbled words of explanation to his friend. Drew either didn't notice or didn't care.

After a quick glance around, Michael located the single bathroom at the end of a small, bleak corridor and stumbled his way toward it. The door was locked when he reached it, so he took a step back to wait. He leaned heavily against the wall, looked at it, swayed away and looked at the spot where his arm had made contact with the textured surface.

Sure enough, his skin was darker there, and he rubbed the dirt and dust off his flesh. He wondered if Power Surge had ever been cleaned. How old was this place, anyway?

After what felt like way too long a time, the lock finally clicked and the door swung inward. A man swathed in black leather and a mask stepped out from the smoky gloom, scaring Michael and making his heart skip half a beat before he realized it was just a cheap Batman costume. The man stared at Michael as he exited the bathroom and then walked back to his place at the bar, brushing his thin black cape out behind him as he sat back down.

Michael laughed at the absurdity of the sight, but his humor died as soon as he caught whiff of the rank odor emanating from the tiny bathroom. With great trepidation, he flipped the light switch on and entered, shutting and locking the door behind him. Knowing now why the room had been occupied for so long, Michael made up his mind to hold his breath while he relieved himself in the discolored toilet. It was not an easy task, as he found himself urinating far longer than he normally would.

Finally, he was forced to take a quick breath as he flushed the toilet with his foot, halfheartedly rinsed his palms in the small sink, and hit the lights on his hurried escape out. He wiped his still-dripping hands on his jeans as he moved back beside Drew.

"What took you so long? I took my shots already."

Michael reached for the one shot glass still filled with liquid, tossed it back, made a gagging face, and then placed it next to the two empty shot glasses in front of Drew. He tilted his head as subtly as he could toward the other end of the bar.

"The Caped Crusader over there took forever to take a shit."

Drew turned on his stool and noticed the man for the first time since arriving. He sputtered out a low laugh.

"Holy smokes, Batman!" He leaned forward in his seat to better attract the bartender's attention and spoke under his breath. "This place is a fucking freak show. I love it."

Drew was not wrong. Everyone in the bar looked like some kind of cartoon caricature or social misfit.

Batman was not the only patron in costume, either. He was flanked by a young woman trying desperately to conjure up a resemblance to Marilyn Monroe in her iconic white dress and blonde wig. She wore the dress well enough, but the wig was very obviously a wig, and the woman herself had much darker features than the famous Tinseltown bombshell.

The two characters must have arrived moments before Michael and Drew had, perhaps at the end of a long day spent taking pictures and collecting small bills, as they were just now settling in at the bar. "Marilyn" took off the wig, for a split second revealing a flesh-toned skullcap beneath. The sight disarmed Michael, and he suddenly felt like he was dreaming. Quickly though, she peeled off that head covering and shook out her natural black locks, which were sweaty and stiff from their long hours of imprisonment.

Batman, in turn, removed his rubbery cowl… revealing a face that more closely resembled Alfred's than it did Bruce Wayne's. Michael wondered at their relationship to one another, and then let his gaze roll over to some of the other guests.

Out of the six booths along the wall, half were occupied by couples. One pair of young twentysomethings had abandoned their beers to make out and were slowly feeling each other up below the table. Another couple sat in the next booth over, looming over a cell phone on the table in front of them, looking at photos and giggling together. Two tattooed women in tank tops sat huddled against one another in the far booth along the wall, whispering in each other's ears as they took in the world around them.

Were they lesbians? Michael assumed as much, but there was no telling for sure these days. He thought he made eye contact with one of them and smiled warmly.

When she didn't return the smile, he began to second-guess whether or not she had actually seen him at all, and so he adjusted his position slightly to what he considered to be a more conspicuous arrangement.

Michael's attention then wandered back to the bar, where an old man in a full suit looked as if he had fallen asleep on his folded arms along the bar's edge. The other patrons seated around him paid him no mind, laughing and talking unnecessarily loudly. Even the bartender didn't seem to care; she took a drink order from the man on his right, nodded acknowledgment, and then walked over to Drew, who by now had lifted his entire rear section off the stool in his effort to lean over the bar and gain the woman's attention.

"Three more shots and a beer. Whatever's darkest. Mikey, what do you want?"

Michael looked at Drew uncertainly. Drew looked impatient.

"Tell the nice lady what you want."

Michael turned to the bartender. "I don't want any more tequila." He was surprised by his own voice, and embarrassed to hear himself slurring his speech once again. Michael looked down at his feet sheepishly.

Drew placed a strong hand on his shoulder to steady him and refocus his attention. When Michael looked up, Drew's face was sharp and pointed, and his nostrils flared.

"I didn't ask what you *don't* want, I asked what you *do* want. You want a beer or a drink?"

It took him a moment to decide. "Drink."

Drew removed his hand from Michael's shoulder and turned back to the bartender smoothly.

"He'll have a vodka tonic."

She looked at Michael for a moment, then proceeded to make all of the drinks. Michael watched her work for a while, but he had a hard time keeping up with what she was doing. He tried to follow the steps and the ingredients, making mental notes of what tools she was using and what brands of liquor and mixers, but the effort soon proved too overwhelming, and she worked too fast for him to follow.

He shook his head and turned to look at the photographs along the wall, making a game out of naming the celebrities pictured within them. Michael thought he actually did fairly well for the first couple of minutes, but then it became harder and harder to process the images in the darkened bar, at least from a distance.

One image along the top, near where the wall met the ceiling, was particularly difficult to make out. He stretched out his legs cautiously and allowed his body to slide from the barstool until he was on his feet and shambling over to the wall. Michael rested his hands along a cushioned divider between the booths and leaned forward, peering up at the picture from below.

Now, at least, he could make out that it was indeed a man, dressed in a trench coat with a grey fedora and holding a gun. The photo had a white border around it with no caption or label, but someone had used a permanent marker to scribble a signature over the image itself.

The handwriting was terribly sloppy, though, and

in the dim light, it was nearly impossible to decipher any of the letters at all. They just looked like black squiggles, lines, and curves, and it frustrated Michael that he still could not recognize the man in the picture, either.

"What are you looking at?"

Michael was startled by the voice and surprised to learn that it came from the booth he was leaning against with his right hand. Three young women sat there, and from the look of it, they had been watching him with curiosity. Michael was also taken aback by how close they were in proximity to him… but then he had a thought, turned to his left, and realized his other arm was mere inches from the couple making out in the other booth, somehow still oblivious to his presence.

He pulled his arms back hastily and straightened up, turning again to the booth to his right and the three girls. Michael wasn't sure who had spoken to him, so he turned to look back up at the photo when he gave his answer.

"I was just… I was… I was trying to see who that was."

He looked back down at the girls. They looked to be about college-age; maybe a little older, but not by much.

Two of them could have passed for sisters, brunettes with dark brown eyes and thick eyebrows, although one had thicker, poutier lips than the other. The girl with the lips had a bright blue dress on that accentuated her cleavage, while her friend wore a lacy black nylon shirt over a black tube top.

The third girl was white-blonde and pale, with

heavy eyeliner and silver glitter on her neck and collarbone. Her eyes were violet and positioned above prominent cheekbones. She was the only one who did not look up at the photograph when he described it, but instead kept her eyes on him. Her mouth was set in a thin, hard frown, and she seemed to be judging him from her seat.

The other two girls didn't take very long to analyze the picture before returning their faces to him as well. The one with the tube top shrugged.

"I don't know who that is."

She must have been the one who had spoken before. Her voice was high, and she sounded like a stereotypical Southern California sorority girl, through and through.

Now all three of them were looking at him, waiting for whatever he had to say next. Michael noticed the drinks in front of their bodies and had a thought to ask if they wanted new ones. Instead, he smiled congenially, looked back up at the picture, and scoffed out loud, throwing his palms up on either side of his head before looking back down at the girls.

"Who knows?" He turned and casually walked back to his seat at the bar.

Drew was waiting expectantly, again with two empty shot glasses in front of him. His expression was equal parts pride and interest. When he spoke, his voice was low and measured so only his friend could hear him, and he slid Michael's untouched shot and cocktail over to him.

"*What was that?*" Drew couldn't help but smile conspiratorially.

Michael stole a furtive glance back toward the girls.

Their conversation had resumed, and Michael wondered if they were talking about him. He hoped they were.

"Nothing. I was just checking out that photo on the wall."

Drew smirked and looked back in the direction of the girls.

"Looks like you were checking out more than that. What did you say to them?"

Michael heard the question without really hearing it, focusing his attention instead on draining the vodka tonic in front of him. He took it in steady swallows from the thin black reed of a cocktail straw, his eyes glazed and glassy, leaning forward to connect his mouth with the straw and leaving his hands limp at his sides. His head was swimming.

Suddenly, he remembered that Drew had said something to him, so he turned in his stool to face his friend.

"I said–" He stopped short, because Drew wasn't there.

Michael turned to look on his other side, but all he saw were the faces of strangers staring at one another, or at him, or at nothing. He looked down at the bar surface in front of him. His glass was gone. He couldn't remember if he had finished it or not, but it had certainly been taken away from him one way or another.

A hot flash of anger rose up in his chest, tightening his heart muscles… and he wondered if the sun-ripened bar bitch had cut him off while he wasn't looking. He almost rose to his feet, but then he noticed his shot glass in front of him, still filled to the brim.

She had taken the liberty of putting a browning lime wedge atop it this time.

The sight of it made Michael's stomach lurch, so he extracted it with his thumb and forefinger and then tossed it dismissively onto the black rubber floor mat behind the bar. Without a moment's hesitation, he picked up the little glass cylinder and threw back its contents, gulping down whatever was inside.

Tequila. Michael hated tequila. He had told Drew that.

"I told you I hated tequila." He said the words to no one in particular, even though they were clearly meant for Drew.

Little beads of sweat formed at his temple, and he massaged them away. The tequila went down much smoother than he had anticipated, though. Still, he wanted to rinse the taste from his mouth, so he went to grab his cocktail glass.

It wasn't there… and Michael slowly remembered once again that it had been taken from him.

He realized with disgust that he had to pee *yet again*. Michael was deeply disappointed with his bladder and tried to ignore the mounting pressure, but soon gave in with a grunt. He took great pains to ease himself as gracefully and fluidly from the barstool as was possible in his condition.

Michael took half a step toward the bathroom, then stopped when he suddenly had the thought of saving their seats at the bar. Though he hadn't noticed anyone else enter the place since he and Drew had arrived, it was still a surprisingly occupied little joint, and he liked the spots they had found. He grabbed a black cocktail napkin from a small stack on the corner of the bar, found an empty drink that the bartender had not yet cleared, and moved it over to rest beside his empty shot glass. Michael delicately placed the napkin atop the stranger's glass and admired his handiwork before turning to shamble off toward the bathroom.

As he did so, he caught sight of Drew... and had to do a double take.

It was definitely Drew, lounging against the booth, one arm supporting himself while the other was outstretched and clutching a rocks glass. He shouted something to an enthusiastic echo of high-pitched cheers and clanked his glass against two similar-looking drinks, both belonging to the girls Michael had encountered earlier beneath the photo of that movie star he couldn't place. They tossed back the mint green contents of whatever shot he had ordered, slammed the empty glasses back on the table, and laughed.

Michael's eyes concentrated for a moment on the dark pit stain beneath Drew's supporting arm. He was already beginning to sweat through his olive-green dress shirt, and Michael was sure he had unbuttoned a couple more of the buttons near the collar by now. He always did that at a certain point of the night.

The young women were devouring him with their eyes, which Michael was surprised to find made him jealous. Drew was not unattractive, but he certainly wasn't gorgeous, either. He had confidence, miles of it, but was that really all it took to make their eyes light up like that? The one with the cleavage and the bright blue dress kept playing with the tips of her hair as she listened to him talk. Michael stood there watching as Drew turned to order another round of shots for the table, yelling across the short expanse between the booths and the bar. The bartender raised her eyebrows and frowned but nodded all the same.

Michael couldn't believe it. Drew didn't even seem to notice him, and just as quickly, he had resumed his conversation with the women. They drank it all up… the booze, the charisma, the confidence. Michael's jaw quivered with rage.

Someone brushed past him clumsily and muttered half an apology. He thought to hit the offender, but realized it was Marilyn Monroe, giddily dragging Batman with one hand while clutching the iconic blonde wig haphazardly with the other. She pulled him to the front door and out into the night, for a moment casting a blinding neon light into the dark cavern of the bar, and then the heavy oak door swung shut behind them and it was black again inside, and mustier still. Michael shrugged to himself and moved off toward the back corridor, beelining for the bathroom.

Halfway down the dark hallway, he was grabbed from behind. He whipped around to confront this new attacker, but the eyes that met his own were deep purple in the gloom of the dimly lit little passageway.

"Hi."

That was all she said before placing her hands on either side of his face and backing him up against the wall. He didn't try to resist, or maybe he couldn't even if he had wanted to. She stared deep into his eyes, holding his head there against the wall between her cool white hands, assessing him, all the time keeping about a foot of air between their faces.

Michael tried to meet her intense gaze for about five seconds before he began to take in the rest of her.

The blonde hair, abnormally bright even in this place; the silver glitter rubbed onto her collarbone; the sweet smell of her perfume; her thin, pale, pink lips; the angular shape of her sharp features; the dark black pupils, wide as saucers. Somehow, the pits of her eyes seemed unnaturally large, like they were trying to conquer the fine violet rims holding them in place. Her face was so unique, so striking, that it was almost intimidating. He wasn't sure if she was truly angry, or if she just naturally looked that way. Perhaps she had been sent there to kill him; to crush his fleshy skull like a melon between thin iron arms of ivory.

He stood there, powerless as putty between her long fingers, his vision zooming in and out, in and out, and then he was in a different room altogether. Michael was seeing a figure in the dark, moving in blurs in front of him. Somewhere, there was a faint knocking sound. There was also heavy breathing, and the feel of sweat sticking to different parts of his body than before.

Something cold and hard touched his hand. He looked down at the sensation and saw the bones of his knuckles clutching what looked like a dirty ceramic sink. The room was brighter than the hallway had been, but still, his eyes struggled to adjust to these surroundings. Like a piston, his heart pounded in his chest without mercy. He discovered pleasure and became aware of the skin in front of him, light and opalescent, moist and somehow still cool to the touch... but everything else was hot and sticky. How was he feeling this? Michael saw his other hand, clutching her back, and he could make out several vertebrae at the base of her spine, showing just beneath the fabric of her sweater. That was where his hand was;

that was where the feeling was coming from. His hand tightened, and he heard a soft moan in his ear.

That was when he saw the face staring back at him from behind her left shoulder. It startled him when he recognized his own reflection. The face seemed unfamiliar in the darkness, but it was undeniably him. He stopped for a moment to take in the phantom specter, but she ran her fingernails through the back of his hair and it felt like electricity, and moved herself around on him, and kissed his ear.

"Don't stop." The voice was a whisper, barely making its way out between the sound of breathing. He couldn't place it; perhaps he had never heard this voice in his life. Yet it spoke to him as if he was the only person it had ever known, and it settled into his mind and his thoughts and made him feel comfortable.

Michael slid his hand around the rest of her waist and pulled her into him, and she drew his face back to hers and kissed him deeply. He could feel his heart knocking against her chest, beating like a drum, and the blood was hot behind his ears. There was more knocking, from behind his sternum and then abruptly from behind his back, somewhere in the distant past. It faded once again. Muffled sounds of voices tried to reach him, but he was too far gone, his body given over to her in absolute surrender. They melted into each other with every motion, bodies slumping closer and closer as his mind drifted further and further away from him.

At one point, he didn't realize he had stopped moving or thinking until she was saying something in his ear, and then he was awake again and present, and all ablaze with energy and fear of what he had missed.

But despite this small resurgence, he still felt dizzy and lightheaded, like something out of a lucid fever dream.

There was a soft thud from behind him somewhere, and then a louder sound, indescribable. The girl shrieked and a bright white light lanced its way onto her face, illuminating it fully for the first time. She was much younger than he had originally thought. Low atmospheric lighting and caked-on makeup had until now serviceably concealed the indicative bumps and scars of acne, but under the searchlight, all was revealed for what it was. The whites of her eyes screamed panic as she tried to pry herself off of him and out of the light.

Michael felt an unsympathetic hand grab his upper right shoulder and yank him backwards. He tried to cry out, but he slipped instead and stumbled, gasping as he began to fall, but before he hit the ground another hand had steadied him, only for a second, and then he was pulled up way too fast and spun back into the hallway. Someone was shouting, but most everyone else was silent, though their mouths were open and their eyes were wide.

He didn't recognize any of the faces as he was shoved forward past the bar from before. The hands dug into his flesh, and he remembered that he was being moved without his consent. Michael attempted to break free from the grasp, wriggling and turning to throw a slow punch with his right fist. Instead, his arm was met by a hand that tightened forcibly around his bicep, and then he felt a stabbing pain in his kidney, and he cried out and his knees buckled. Michael wanted to reach back to feel the pain, to see what had happened, but his arms were now pinned behind his back, and he was at a door.

It burst open and he was thrown forward, and all of a sudden, he was outside and on his hands and knees, throwing up on the concrete. His stomach convulsed as he spewed out brown-yellow liquid, coughing and tearing up. The skin on his palms had torn and was bleeding slightly, and his kidney still throbbed unbearably. A hand touched his back, and he crumpled to the ground and rolled to his side defensively, rage making his veins throb. He coiled as if ready for another strike.

But it was only Drew, taking a step backward with both palms now raised, forehead wrinkling, backing off.

"Easy, Mikey, easy. Jesus Christ."

Michael felt the spins coming again, and clumsily rolled from his side onto his back. He brought his stinging hands to his face and covered his eyes, shutting his jaw tight against the bile bubbling up inside of him.

"Why did you do that?" It was all he could manage to splutter out. His voice cracked in his throat.

"Do what?"

Drew sounded very far away. Michael took a rasping inhalation and tried to steady his vision, still swirling behind his closed eyes.

"Hit me in the back."

His friend had the audacity to laugh. "Hit you in the back? Ha!"

Drew's tone was mocking, and Michael wanted more than anything to not be sick anymore, to be solid enough to stand up and beat the shit out of his best friend.

For his part, Drew sounded righteously indignant. "I got you out of there alive! That crazy bitch was calling the cops, but I talked her out of it… so, you're welcome."

Michael took a minute to process this. 'That crazy bitch' must have been the bartender. He had heard someone shouting in the bar, but it had sounded like a man's voice. Maybe it was Drew arguing with the woman. He couldn't remember.

All he could remember was getting struck in the kidney on his way out of the bar, and the way it hurt more than any pain Michael could recollect. Even now, it felt as if someone had torn a gaping hole in his organs, and there was no way to relieve the ache. His eyes glistened, so he kept them shut tightly and masked behind his shaking hands.

"Who was that, then?"

"Who was it that threw you out of there? That would be the big Black linebacker they call a doorman. You're lucky that fucker didn't kill you. I told him I was a lawyer; otherwise, you might have ended up in the ER instead. Again, you're welcome."

It took a minute for Michael to comprehend the words. A vague memory of a man in a pea coat came to mind. He removed his hands and took a tentative look back toward the bar. The iron stool was no longer there, nor was the bouncer.

Drew followed his gaze. "He's talking to the girls, man. Her friends didn't want to leave. One of them was saying something about her constitutional rights when I followed you out here. Your chick is still weeping in the bathroom." He snorted derisively, then took a few steps toward Michael and offered him a hand. "Come on, buddy. We should get out of here. You know you don't want that guy coming back out here."

Michael looked up at the proffered hand and spat before reaching up to take it as Drew pulled him onto unsteady feet.

"Maybe I do." Michael grumbled the words darkly, turning to glare at the front door of the bar.

Drew couldn't help but smile and let out a little laugh. He patted Michael on the upper back, guiding them forward as they began to move away down the street.

The streetlights marked their journey onward, and Michael was secretly thankful for Drew's occasional hand on the back or shoulder, as it steadied him and kept him moving forward. Every fiber of his body felt like collapsing to the ground, and he still felt dizzy and nauseous. He tried to replay what had happened in the bar like a film in his mind, but large chunks of time were absolutely unexplainable.

All he could recall were blurred images and the occasional sensory blip of a sound, smell, or touch. None of it fit together to form any kind of discernible narrative. Drew kept prodding at him for details of his sexual encounter with the pale young girl, but Michael could honestly tell him next to nothing of his experience. Only that it was clear, from the limited memories he did have, that she had brought him into the bathroom to have sex. And they had, for who knows how long, until the bouncer had broken in the door and wrenched Michael out into the night.

Drew filled in the blanks as much as he could, but it was soon clear that he had been oblivious throughout most of Michael's incident, too preoccupied with the girls at the table to notice his friend's absence or the absence of the third girl. He had only realized Michael was gone when someone loudly complained to the bartender about a locked door. She had sent the bouncer to investigate, but even then, Drew had not suspected that Michael was in any way involved.

It was only when he physically saw Michael being dragged out of the bathroom and down the corridor that Drew attempted to intervene, convincing the bartender not to call the cops and warning the bouncer against unnecessary violence, as he was "fully prepared to press charges" on behalf of Michael if he needed to.

This part of the story did manage to amuse Michael, and soon they were both laughing drunkenly down Hollywood Boulevard, regaling one another with old war stories from college parties that bore absolutely no resemblance to this evening's events.

And then they were gliding down the deserted streets of Los Angeles in Michael's Corolla. Only this time, he was seeing it all from a different perspective, nestled into the passenger seat as Drew sped down side streets and back roads. He didn't remember having a conversation about who would or who could drive, nor did he remember surrendering his keys to Drew… But some kind of exchange must have occurred to bring them both to this current situation.

Michael looked over at his friend. Drew had one arm on the wheel, the other bent in half against the window, elbow against the glass, hand supporting his temple. His eyes were red and tired-looking. Michael thought to turn music on, then realized the radio was already playing. Gently, he turned the volume dial up

153

just a bit, so as not to completely disturb the mood of the car cabin, and closed his eyes, nodding along to the beat of a pop song he did not recognize.

He must have fallen asleep, because when the impact came, he didn't see or hear anything. Michael felt the sudden jolt and the car come screeching to a halt, and as his eyes and ears opened, he heard Drew curse under his breath, and then he saw the empty night street in front of them.

Michael didn't immediately recognize where they were. It must have been somewhere in Drew's neighborhood. But the car had come to an abrupt stop, and Michael turned to look at Drew.

His friend's face was hard and unflinching, and his eyes were locked on the road in front of them. Both hands were now on the wheel. His back was straight against the car seat, and he sat rigidly still, devoid of any movement save for a slight trembling of his arms.

Michael wasn't sure what had happened. Obviously, they hadn't hit another car, nor could he see a tree or a lamppost or any other object in front of the vehicle. But Michael was sure he had felt a collision of sorts, so he turned back to face his friend.

"What happened?" His voice sounded groggy and timid. He tried to make it as un-accusatory as possible, but he was too drunk and too tired to completely mask his emotions in this disoriented state.

Drew kept staring straight ahead. Finally, after long seconds of silence, he spoke in a voice just above a whisper.

"*Christ.*"

His face was white, and his arms were still shaking, more noticeably now than before.

"I think I hit something."

Michael leaned forward in his car seat to look out. All was relatively dark outside the glass windshield. A lonely, white fluorescent streetlamp did its best to illuminate this particular stretch of pavement, but half of the light had burned out. As far as Michael could tell, there were no other vehicles in sight.

Somewhere up ahead on the tree-lined residential road was another street where Michael saw a car drive by and out of sight. A green reflective signpost marked the intersection, but he couldn't read the cross streets listed there. Small houses stood sentry on both sides of the road they were on – all dark, all quiet. Evidently, the crunching sound Michael had woken up to had disturbed no one else. The lights were all off in the homes and the residents had seemingly slept right through it. He looked at the clock on the dash of his car: 1:41 a.m.

"Well…" Michael didn't know what to say after that. He turned again to look at Drew, who looked as if he had seen a ghost.

Michael's vision swam in and out of focus. He wasn't sure whether his disoriented condition could be attributed to alcohol or to the sudden awakening from sleep, but he realized he had to do something. Tentatively, he reached for the handle next to him and pulled the black lever toward his body, releasing the passenger door out into the night.

A cool wind whipped into his face, with just a lick of humidity to it. He hadn't remembered it being gusty on their walk to the car, but the Santa Ana winds were certainly present now, and he shivered once as the change in temperature registered under his light jacket and shirt. Drew said nothing as Michael pulled himself out from the cozy car interior and into the brisk evening air. Michael crossed his arms in front of his chest for warmth and strode around the front end of the car to inspect for damage.

A warped tangle of cracked and bleeding limbs were massed together in a pile of beige, black, red, and volt yellow. Two Nike sneakers glowed in the reflection of the headlights, but each was in a different place than it should have been. The ground beneath the form was already stained dark and black. Michael could make out coarse, individual hairs on what looked like legs, leading into soggy brown-crimson socks and the glowing tennis shoes. And the yellow... Michael had never even seen highlighters that bright before. Everywhere not black or beige or increasingly deep red was the bright yellow of the jacket.

The sound of a door opening and shutting brought Michael's head whipping around. Drew stepped out from the car with his hands already over his nose and mouth, slowly moving forward to the front of the vehicle, eyes locked on the heap in front of it.

Michael turned back to look where Drew was looking. He couldn't believe that it was what he thought it was. It couldn't possibly be that.

The wind blew again, and Michael felt the hairs on the back of his neck go on end. Drew cautiously stepped to within a yard of the mass, and then squatted down, tucking his chin to his chest and covering the back of his head with his hands. Michael took one step, then another, and another, until he had finally moved around to the other side of the pile.

It was a man, no doubt about it. A middle-aged

man, perhaps in his late fifties or early sixties. Michael had the strangest sensation that he was looking at his own father, and he had to blink the thought away.

The man's head was bent back unnaturally on his neck so that it rested on the darkened asphalt at an impossible angle. His eyes were wet and open, and both stared straight ahead as if in shock. Michael could see gold and grey fillings in the back of the man's mouth; his lower jaw drooped open, and some of his teeth were gone altogether now. His nose dripped dark blood from crooked cartilage.

One arm was broken and in front of him, and the other was lost somewhere under the yellow nylon and polyester of his windbreaker. The man's chest had been caved in, but other parts of his body looked swollen and enlarged beneath the zippered jacket, track shorts, and mess of stained and ruptured flesh.

Michael gazed into the soft blue eyes staring out from the broken face, and his breath went out of him immediately. He sank to the ground before the body, but he could not avert his face from the man's eyes… they seemed so genuinely surprised. Was there fear there? Pain or suffering? Had his life flashed before them only moments ago?

"*Mike.*"

He heard the feeble voice croak out his name, and he scrambled forward toward the body in disbelief. Somewhere, a survival instinct kicked in, and he was aware then that this man was still alive, and perhaps he could still be saved, if they moved fast enough. Michael had heard the man speak. He had said his name… he had called to him.

But Michael paused. The man could not have

known his name. That was impossible. He looked up and across the body.

Drew was standing now, his arms at his sides, and he was looking levelly at his friend, not at the inert person between them. Michael comprehended then who had spoken his name.

"Mike, we have to go."

Although the tone was stronger now, it seemed all the more surreal. Drew didn't move a muscle. His face was still paler than Michael had ever seen it before, but his eyes were dark and hard as coal.

"We have to go right now." It was definitely not a statement, an observation, or an opinion. It was a command.

Michael stared quizzically up at him. He didn't understand what Drew was saying. He couldn't possibly mean–

"Get back in the car." This time, Drew took a step toward him.

Though Michael was meant to feel threatened, he discovered instead a grunt of a laugh that escaped out of him without warning.

"*What?*" A tear fell from his cheek, and he suddenly realized he was crying.

Drew swallowed hard and decided to try a new approach. His voice was gentler now, almost coaxing.

"Listen to me. Let's just get back in the car, and we'll talk about this and figure out what we're gonna do."

"Gonna do about what? W-w-we *killed him!*"

Michael stammered through what was quickly becoming a kind of sob. The world was spinning again, and he felt gravity slipping away and his body becoming lighter and lighter. He wanted to float off into space. That, or to fall face forward into the earth and just sink right into it like quicksand, turning end over end as he toppled downward into darkness.

Drew shushed him as quietly as he could. "Let's talk about this in the car."

"There's nothing to talk about! Can't you see that? Look at this, Drew. Look at this... this *man*. This is a person, this is a human being, and he's *dead*—"

"I know he is! I know what happened, I know what this is, and that's why I'm trying to do something about it!"

Drew was having real difficulty keeping his voice down, and now he started looking frantically from side to side every few seconds, checking the surrounding houses for any signs of light, sound, or movement.

"Listen to me, Michael. Listen to me! I know you're upset, I know you're in shock. I am, too, believe me. But think... just *think* for a second. Okay? And hear me out. Okay?"

Michael didn't respond, so Drew went on.

"What do you want to do, stay here? Call the police? Call an ambulance? What *good* will that do? The man is dead. There's no saving him. You just said that yourself. So what *good* will that do anyone? The police will come, the ambulance will come... They'll take him away in a body bag, and they'll take us to jail, Michael! For *manslaughter*. Vehicular manslaughter. Think about it. I can't pass a breathalyzer test right now. Can you?"

Drew let his words sink in. After a few seconds, Michael spoke up again, his eyes still red with tears.

"I can't believe what you're saying..."

Drew wouldn't let up, continuing right on with his

argument.

"Can you? Mike… can you prove *you* weren't the one behind the wheel tonight?"

At that, Michael looked up sharply. Drew shrugged and raised his eyebrows.

"It's your car, Michael. And your word against mine."

Michael stood up suddenly and balled his hands into fists. Drew took a step back and raised his hands out in front of him defensively.

"I'm just saying, this doesn't look good – for either of us." He paused and reconsidered. "Forget what I just said… that was stupid."

A moment passed between them. Each man sized the other up, and then Drew lowered his hands altogether. A strange smile played across his lips.

"It's the end of the world, Mikey. Remember?"

Truly, Michael had not. He had forgotten that entirely in the midst of the tragedy before them.

And now, the situation slowly began to feel different… and as much as Michael hated to admit it, he could feel his brain allowing the severity of the man's murder to lessen in the face of a newer, greater perspective. Michael lowered his head, closed his eyes, and gritted his teeth.

Drew, ever observant, noted the physical change as well, and drove the dagger home.

"We're all dead anyway, right? All we can do is decide how we want to spend our last days…"

Drew took one last look at the mangled, bloody waste in front of the car's bumper, swallowed hard, and then turned to walk back to the car. When he was at the driver's side, he put one hand on top of it, the other on the open door, and planted his right foot on the floorboard. Time seemed to stand still in that moment, and the air was oppressively thick.

When Michael finally looked up to meet Drew's gaze, he was still crying and still quivering with some combination of rage, horror, and despair. But below it all, there was also a deeper understanding and a silent acknowledgement that what Drew had said was true. All Michael could do now was make his own long, lonely walk back to the car.

When he shut the door behind him, the interior cabin lights faded out and the two men were swathed once more in darkness. Drew put the car in reverse and backed up about a dozen feet, then turned the wheel sharply to the left and swooped forward and around the bright yellow mound in the center of the street. Once clear of the obstacle, he proceeded to the end of the street and then turned out of sight.

With the headlights gone, the glow of the safety reflecting panels on the man's shoes and jacket dimmed in the half-dead gloom of the broken streetlight until they were dark altogether, and the night was quiet once again, save for the occasional rustle of the stained yellow fabric in the wind.

CHAPTER ELEVEN

The morning came without daylight. Somewhere, the sun struggled to break through a thick, woolen blanket of grey storm clouds, but its efforts were in vain. Michael only knew it was morning because the clock on his dashboard read 11:13, and the world around him was illuminated more than it had been when last he saw it. Wearily, he rubbed his eyes and took in his surroundings.

He was still parked on Drew's street, about two houses down from where he had dropped off his friend nine hours ago. Without a word, Drew had parked and then exited the car, leaving the keys in the ignition and the engine running. In a black, shadowy streak, he was up the sidewalk and staggering through his own front door.

Michael remembered wondering if Michelle was waiting up for him, or if she was still fast asleep. After several minutes, he finally had opened the passenger door and looped around to the driver's seat. He then had put the car in gear and drove all of two hundred feet before stopping and turning the engine off. That was when Michael broke down again and started crying... and that was the last thing he really remembered.

Now, he was bleary-eyed and nauseous, and his head pounded. He also realized that he had woken up to the sound of buzzing. His phone vibrated on the seat next to him.

Michael recognized the number of the credit union. He was over two hours late for work. Fearful and disoriented, he let the call go to voicemail. It was not the first time this morning his work had tried to contact him, either. There were two other missed calls from the same number in his phone's log when he checked.

For a moment, he wondered if Jeanette was worried about him, but then the memory of the night before came creeping back and extinguished that notion in a hurry. He had kissed her, slapped her, and sent her fleeing from his apartment. Maybe she was not at work today, either, after their debacle of a date last night.

Michael sat and stared out into the grey wilderness of the world beyond his car. Every now and then, a small drop of water would splat against his windshield, but the timing was irregular and inconsistent. Rarely did it rain in Los Angeles, and even when it did, the rain never seemed to know quite what it was doing.

Tentatively, Michael opened the car door and stuck out an outstretched palm. He waited for thirty seconds but felt nothing. The air itself did not even feel moist.

Slowly, he gathered himself up and out of the vehicle and shut the door behind him. In a kind of stupor, he circled to the front of the car to examine it. The events from the previous night had already taken on a dreamlike haze, and Michael needed to see the evidence for himself, here and now, in the harsh sobriety of daytime.

He kneeled to examine his bumper, the grill, and the headlights. Michael ran a hand along the metal and plastic contours of the car and felt only the occasional dent or ding. For all his suspicions, the Corolla appeared to be in decent shape, and there were no visible signs of a major impact or collision on the front of the car itself.

One headlight had a crust of reddish brown streaked across it, and for a moment, Michael's heart stopped in his chest. But upon closer examination, it looked more like dirt or soil than blood.

Michael only used the car on city streets, though, so why there would be dirt on his headlight, he could not say. Regardless, he did not touch the stain with his bare hand, but instead grabbed a few fast-food napkins from his glove compartment and rubbed away at it until it was gone. He even toured the sides and rear of the vehicle, just to make sure they were also spotless. They were.

When Michael was done, he didn't know what to do with the dirty napkins, so he tossed them on the floor mat of the passenger side in a little crumpled heap and got back in the driver's seat.

He had no idea what to do now. Briefly, he contemplated going to work, but the idea of facing his boss, or even worse, of facing Jeanette, was unbearable. Michael had no appetite, no sense of clarity or direction. He rubbed remnants of sleep and dried tears from his eyes and eyelashes and looked up into the rearview mirror to examine his reflection.

In the thin glass rectangle, he could see that his

eyes were bloodshot and milky, and his facial hair was beginning to grow out in patches of dark, springy whiskers. His lips were dry and chapped; his hair was messy and unkempt. He could smell the stale acidity of alcohol on his breath. The taste was there, too, rank and odious.

Michael hated himself like this. He hated what he had become. And yet, there was nothing he could do. He was stuck in this moment... until the moment would end.

For the first time, Michael found himself wishing for the end of the world to come faster. He stared up out of his windshield into the white stonewash that was the sky, and willed the sun to pierce through the thunderclaps and the atmosphere itself.

In his fantasy, Michael imagined one long, brilliant spear of sunlight stabbing into the earth beneath him and his car, roasting him beneath the glass panes and metal framework like an ant under a magnifying glass. Even now, he could almost feel the heat and the warm, welcome surrender into the afterlife as his skin melted away from his bones and his blood boiled. He imagined steam rising from his muscles and fat, and the searing pain of the steady death. It would be a relief, he thought, and retribution for what he had done.

If there was a hell, Michael knew that he might not escape it. But perhaps God, or whoever or whatever was waiting on the other side, could see past his recent crimes and sins, and remember the Michael who had lived for so long out of the spotlight, quietly and unassumingly going about his daily routines of middle-class, white, male, American tedium.

But Michael didn't believe in God. And if there

was ever a time to start believing in one, after last night, this probably wasn't the best time to begin.

Despite the uncertainty of tomorrow, or even today, Michael *was* certain that he should not have left the jogger in the street like he had. Deep down, he knew there was no good reason for driving away from the accident, just as there was no good reason they should have been driving in their inebriated state in the first place.

While evaluating his actions, Michael also acknowledged that he should never have forced himself upon Jeanette, and he should not have struck her when she shrunk away from him in fright and embarrassment, even though she struck him first. He should not have allowed Drew to molest the pretty waitress or to attack Aaron the night before his wedding. Michael should not have even chased the teenage boy on the bicycle down the street, screaming and laughing like a lunatic.

There were a great many things he should not have done, but he had done all of them and more since the light in the sky. Some of them, he had even done before the light.

Despite his moral convictions and newfound certitudes, Michael wasn't convinced he truly felt the requisite amount of regret, and that alarmed him. He had felt strangely justified in some of those situations and conflicts, and even in the ones where he did not, Drew had persuaded him to at least logically approve of the actions taken in consideration of the impending apocalypse.

Michael could not deny the rationale behind most everything Drew had told him, even if it went against all commonly accepted sense of right and wrong. They should not have been driving last night, the jogger should not have died at their hands, and most importantly, they should not have left him alone there and fled the scene like heartless criminals.

Even still, Drew was right. There was no sensible reason for them to stay, other than the fact that it would have been 'the right thing to do', as most everyone is taught from birth. People are supposed to be held responsible for their actions, and everyone knows that every action has a consequence.

But who was supposed to hold anyone responsible anymore? The government? Police? Parents, who are supposed to teach their children to do good and avoid being bad? Bosses, who are supposed to judge adults for being 'good' or 'bad' at their jobs? Future generations? God?

None of these people, these ideas, these institutions, or these forces mattered anymore. Not as far as Michael was concerned. Yet still, he could not shake the nagging feeling that somehow, he needed closure; he needed to make amends for what he had done.

But what could he do? He supposed the jogger must have had a family. Perhaps a wife who had been waiting for him to come home last night. Or if she had been sleeping, how must she have reacted upon waking and realizing he was not there beside her? Who had discovered the body? Had there been witnesses last night that Michael and Drew hadn't noticed? Were police searching for a black Toyota Corolla even now?

Michael stepped out of the car and began to do a second investigation of the vehicle, this time much more thoroughly. He still couldn't believe there was not more damage to the front end of it. Then again, he had never experienced a significant collision in the car before, so perhaps the automobile was built to withstand more force than he would have originally believed.

When he was fully satisfied, Michael decided it was time to get the car off the streets and out of Drew's neighborhood. He felt a sharp stab of panic when he realized that the location of the accident had seemed all too familiar to him, even last night in a compromised state. While the street's exact name had escaped him, the knowledge that he was near Drew's home had not. He could not recall just how long it had taken them to speed over to the townhouse, but it felt like it took no time at all, either.

Michael needed to get as far away as possible from this neighborhood as quickly as he could. So, he stepped back into the car a second time, started the ignition, and lurched the Corolla into motion.

He drove with caution but intention, frequently dropping his eyes to check his speed every so often. His phone began to vibrate when he was five minutes away from home. Michael picked it up and again recognized the number as work. He tossed the device dismissively onto the passenger seat and stared straight ahead, his jaw set and his grip on the steering wheel unflinching.

The last five minutes of the drive seemed to stretch on endlessly as Michael hit red light after red light. He actually did a double-take in the rearview mirror when he realized an LAPD cruiser was idling behind him at one intersection about six blocks from his apartment complex. Michael made sure to drive slower than he normally would, keeping his speed well below the limit. Before long, the cop car changed lanes and pulled around him, and then Michael was turning into the relative safety of his home building.

When at last he pulled into his parking spot and cut the engine, he allowed himself a deep exhalation and took a moment to compose himself before making his way to the elevator and then up to the safety of his apartment.

Tucker was waiting for him on the other side of the door. If the dog was still upset over being stepped on during date night, he sure didn't show it. He greeted Michael as warmly as he always had, bouncing up and down while barking and licking at his owner's hands exuberantly. Michael felt a sudden pang of guilt. He had all but forgotten his dog entirely, and Tucker was usually fed before he left for work in the mornings. Straight away, he headed for the kitchen pantry and scooped out twice the normal ration of dog food for his canine, who began wolfishly gobbling it down the minute the food hit his bowl.

Another thought dawned on Michael as he realized that Tucker had not been outside since the previous afternoon. Somewhere in his apartment was probably a puddle of urine... and maybe something worse.

After a quick inspection though, he found himself pleasantly surprised by the apparent absence of any excrement. As soon as the dog was finished eating, though, Michael fastened his leash and collar and led him back into the elevator and then outside, where Tucker wasted no time in emptying his bladder and bowels.

Michael thought he felt a raindrop and looked up expectantly toward the sky. The charcoal-grey thunderheads continued to swirl lazily off of and on top of one another, but still refused to open up and spill out their contents onto the earth.

Southern California needed the rain desperately, much like it usually did. Michael couldn't even remember the last time it had *really* rained. He wanted it to happen now; a true downpour. His mind conjured up images of large, fat raindrops falling heavily from the sky, stinging his face and soaking his shirt until it clung to his back and shoulders, cold and wet. Michael needed that kind of rain to thoroughly rinse the crust of sleep from the corners of his eyelids. More importantly, it was just what he needed to cleanse his pores and wash the filth of his crimes away forever.

Tucker gave a quick bark to break Michael from his daydream. A man and his dog were jogging up the sidewalk into view. Michael looked down and saw Tucker standing at attention, sizing up this new animal he had caught fresh scent of.

"Come on, bud."

Michael murmured to him, giving the Sheltie a quick tug on the leash as he began to walk back toward the front of his apartment building. Tucker followed obediently, resisting ever so slightly to allow the occasional glance back at the other dog.

They were halfway up the steps to the front door when the voice came.

"Hey!"

Michael instinctively turned toward the sound but kept walking up the steps. The man couldn't be talking to him, as he had no idea who he was.

But sure enough, the jogger seemed to be staring angrily in Michael's direction, and he and his dog had stopped their run. Michael looked behind himself at the complex door, and, seeing no one there, turned back to face the stranger, a bit curious now. The jogger's face was stern and accusatory.

"Yeah, you. You gonna pick this up?"

Michael's gaze followed the man's pointing hand to a spot in the grass beside the sidewalk.

At first, he didn't see anything, and Michael wondered for a moment what the man could possibly be referring to. But then he noticed a small pile of defecation, and he looked up to meet the jogger's eyes. Before he could say anything, the man was speaking again.

"Yeah, I saw you do this. Come pick it up. I almost stepped in it."

Michael had one hand on the front door, the other on Tucker's leash. He stood there for a moment, processing what was happening. A small smile played on his lips as he began to register that the man was serious, and perhaps attempting to be threatening as well.

"Are you serious?" He had to stifle a laugh.

The man was not amused, though his French bulldog appeared to be. The small creature seemed to smile up at Michael and Tucker as it caught its breath, apparently enjoying this little break from exercise. It panted ferociously and let its tongue spill out comically from its mouth, then began to sniff at where Tucker had relieved himself.

The sweaty jogger kept one hand planted on his hip as he squinted up at Michael.

"Yes, I'm serious. It's against the law, you know. Now, go get a bag and clean it up."

Michael found himself sizing the man up. He was shorter than Michael, but easily more in shape. Massive, white eyeballs bulged out of the man's sockets, and his cheeks and neck were dotted pink with razor burn. The jogger's thin lips were turned downward in a scowl that parted just wide enough for him to catch his breath. His chest heaved up and down beneath a robin egg blue tank top. Veins at the man's temples looked ready to explode out through his skin.

"Go fuck yourself."

Michael didn't yell it, nor did he say it with any great malice. The words came from a tired place but were not without a hint of humor. He felt beleaguered, and the interaction he now found himself in seemed absurd compared to everything else that had happened in the last twenty-four hours.

"Come on, Tucker."

A small part of him registered surprise at his own courage. He didn't wait for a reply, though, instead turning back to the front door and moving right along.

"Excuse me?" Of course, the jogger was not the type of person to just let it go.

Michael's heart pumped faster, and he recalled some of the physical sensations he had experienced that day with the teenager on the bicycle. A bit excited, he turned back around to face the man.

"*What?*" This time, Michael *did* say it with malice. The word was meant to be a challenge, threatening and dangerous.

Michael narrowed his eyes and locked them on the ugly, bright white balls in the man's head. He clenched his teeth and felt his muscles tighten and begin to quiver with a subtle anticipation. His breathing became quick and shallow.

Now, it was the jogger's turn to size Michael up. He looked just the slightest bit surprised by the response he had received, but quickly, he composed himself and took a step forward.

"What did you say to me?"

"I said, 'go fuck yourself', and you heard me the first time. Who made you God?"

The jogger raised an index finger and tilted his head. The effect was surely meant to be intimidating, but Michael found it comical. His finger looked like a knobby pink sausage.

"Watch it."

"No, you watch it. Why don't you just keep on jogging?"

Perhaps both men could feel the direction that this was heading in, and yet neither seemed ready to make the first move. The distance between them seemed to grow smaller in Michael's head, and he realized he was pleased to be on higher ground than his adversary.

Maybe the jogger had underestimated Michael's reaction, because his gaze seemed to waver ever so slightly, just for a moment, as if he was second-guessing this whole exchange. It happened just long enough for Michael to take note.

"Why don't you just pick up your dog's shit?" The jogger's voice broke at the end, betraying perhaps a hint of exasperation.

It was enough for Michael. He descended the steps quickly, pulling Tucker roughly behind him by the leash. Once his feet hit the sidewalk, he stopped, and the jogger took half a step back, alarm written clearly on his face. The sweaty man raised his free hand into a fist defensively, the other hand tightening on the leash leading to his oblivious French bulldog.

There was maybe three feet of vacant space left between them now, and the shrinking void felt charged and uncomfortable. The veins at the man's temples really seemed bigger now up close, as did the whites of his eyes.

And he stank. The smells of salt and sweat and freshly-mown grass all gnawed at Michael's senses and made his head swim. Everything about this man was repulsive to Michael; his sight, his smell, and certainly, his personality.

Michael felt his heart pounding faster and faster... and he liked it. He was in it now, and there was no going back.

"Why don't you make me?"

It wasn't his best line, and he grimaced a little to hear himself say it out loud. For a moment, Michael was taken out of the bloodlust, and an ounce of doubt and fear trickled through him. What was he doing? What was he saying?

The jogger sneered and issued a short sarcastic snort of a laugh.

"Come on, what is this? Third grade?" He was patronizing Michael now. The jogger took half a step closer and lowered his voice. "Hey buddy, why don't you just do the right thing and pick it up, huh?"

In a frenzied blur, Michael's knuckles crunched into the side of the man's face. The move seemed to take both men by surprise, and suddenly, Michael was awash in pain. He had thrown the punch, but he never would have expected it to be so painful to hit someone. In action movies, fists flew with reckless abandon, and the heroes never seemed to have any trouble beating the snot out of the bad guys.

But this was real life, and the pain was excruciating. Michael grabbed his right hand with his left, dropping the leash in one fluid motion. He had not tucked his thumb in the punch, and he wondered if it was broken or at least dislocated. The nail was shattered though and little beads of bright red blood began to escape from the ridge.

Before he could tend to his hand further, he saw a beige blur out of the corner of his left eye, and then Michael was seeing stars. He almost fainted from the impact. It felt like someone had taken a sledgehammer to his face, and he gasped with surprise, letting out an audible grunt.

Then there was a hand grabbing at his left shoulder, tearing clumsily at his shirtsleeve. He felt the fingers trying to pull him back up, and he spat and reached out for the body in front of him. All he could see was the bright blue of the man's tank top, so he used his left hand, his good hand, to pummel at the man's side.

The movements were sloppy and disjointed, nothing like the punches he had seen boxers throw, or even action stars in the cinema. He felt strong arms reach around him like a vise, and Michael struggled to free his own limbs from the grip. Wildly, he threw his skull against the jogger's torso. All he could hear were his own grunts and the sound of dogs barking.

For a second, he wondered if Tucker was fighting with him, or perhaps warring with the French bulldog.

Then the man was shoving him off and to the ground. Michael fell on his backside heavily, but quickly began to find his feet and rise again.

Before he could get back upright, however, the jogger had shoved him down again. Michael tried to resist, flailing at him with both arms and squirming like a snake, but the jogger was stronger than him.

The hulking man followed Michael to the ground this time, grabbing one of his wrists and pinning it to the ground. He reached for the other wrist, but Michael was frantically swinging his fist at the man's body, aiming for anywhere and everywhere. Every impact sent waves of pain up Michael's thumb and arm, and he was sure he had broken the digit now, but it was his only free hand and he had to use it.

Finally, the man pinned him down with both arms, digging his elbows sharply into Michael's chest and planting his left knee into Michael's groin.

That was just too much. The breath went out of Michael all at once, but his fight did not, and still he wriggled helplessly under the weight of his assailant, coughing and sputtering and moaning.

"Stop. Stop! *Stop it*!" The jogger spat the command inches from Michael's face, and spittle flecked across Michael's nose and onto his lips.

Enraged, Michael gurgled out half a scream, but the man shoved his body back into the ground with a last heave. He released Michael's left wrist and used his free hand to slap Michael hard across the face. The impact struck right where the first punch had landed, and again, Michael felt his vision go dark for a second. Then the jogger was off him and backing away.

Michael rolled onto his right side, clutching his

injured hand into his chest and trying to open his left eye. Every part of his body was throbbing in agony, and adrenaline still raced through his muscles like wildfire.

The man's voice came from above him. "Fucking psychopath! I should call the cops!"

Michael groaned and opened his eyes just wide enough to see through the teary film. He wasn't sure when or how he had started crying, but he was furious that it had happened once again. He choked back a wheezing sob and leered murderously up at the blurred image of the robin egg tank top.

"Why don't you?" It took all the strength Michael could muster to spit the words out. He wanted to sound venomous and spiteful, but instead, his voice just sounded quaky and pathetic.

The jogger just shook his head, rubbed the side of his face, picked up his dog's leash, and started to back away. Michael wanted to say something more, but he couldn't think of anything other than the unbelievable amount of pain he was in. With a sigh of disgust, he let his head fall back on his neck and to the ground.

For the first time, he noticed the smell of something foul that was extremely close to him and growing stronger with the breeze. He tentatively let the fingers of his left hand explore the back of his head. His hair was matted down and wet there, and he drew his fingers back at once in surprise. Michael didn't want to look, but he had to know for sure.

A quick glance at his hand revealed green-brown feces on his fingertips and under the nails. Michael moaned and frantically rubbed the stains against the dark denim of his pant leg. About halfway through trying to remove the excrement from his hand, he remembered that the back of his head was still covered in dog shit, and that his fingers were the least of his worries.

Slowly, painfully, Michael got to his feet. Cars whizzed by on the road in front of his apartment building. Apparently, no one had been that concerned about the full-on brawl transpiring on a city sidewalk next to a busy street. He had heard no car horns, and no one had stopped to come to his defense.

Indeed, it looked like business as usual. Michael saw an old woman checking her mail across the street, but she was focused on what she was doing and paid him no mind. Other than that, there were no pedestrians in sight.

He turned around and discovered Tucker at the foot of the stairs leading up to the front of the building. The Sheltie looked concerned, but whether or not it had actually participated in the fight was unclear. His leash was limp to one side, and when he noticed Michael staring at him, Tucker trotted right over and placed his front legs against Michael's shin.

Michael turned to look in the direction the jogger had gone. Off in the distance, several blocks away, he could just make out the bright blue of the tank top and the black gym shorts.

He couldn't believe it. The man was jogging again, as if nothing had happened. This lunatic who had started a fight over a little pile of poop in the grass, who had threatened Michael, beaten Michael, broken his thumb perhaps, and shoved his head into that same pile of manure, was now running free. He and his stupid French bulldog had escaped scot-free.

Michael wondered if the man was in pain, and if his punches had inflicted any real damage. But how could they have? If the jogger had been hurt, he wouldn't still be jogging. He would be reeling, injured, licking his wounds like Michael now was. That was what he deserved, after all.

Where was the justice? Michael's thoughts raced, and as they did, he began to feel the pain in his body less and less. His focus remained with the man jogging away, running away from the crime he had just committed. The jogger was getting away with it, Michael realized. Something had to be done.

Michael picked up the fallen leash and led Tucker up the steps and into the building. Wordlessly, he glided past the inquiring faces of two people he did not recognize who were waiting in the lobby for the elevator. He knew they must be wondering what had happened to him, and he wondered himself at just how bad he looked right now. Michael imagined his appearance in his mind's eye, his face battered and bloody, his hair matted with grass and excrement. Maybe he looked more badass now, at least.

But there was no time to examine his reflection or to talk, so he opened the door to the parking garage and moved quickly to his car. Michael opened the door just long enough for Tucker to jump in before getting in himself.

He noticed his dog was trembling slightly in the passenger seat. The only time the two of them went for car rides together was to the vet, so undoubtedly, the animal was panicking. Michael started up the car and put a hand on Tucker to try and calm him, wincing when the dog moved underneath his right thumb unexpectedly. He pulled the car up to the electric gate, waited for it to open in silence, and then turned out and onto the street.

It didn't take long for Michael to spot the big man in the blue tank top jogging along the side of the road with his French bulldog in tow. Michael slowed down considerably, and whenever he needed to, he pulled off to the shoulder entirely and waited for the space between them to grow again. His black Corolla followed the jogger along the route, always keeping an appropriate distance so as not to be seen. Michael knew the man wouldn't recognize his car, but he didn't want to take any chances of the man seeing him through the windshield.

The day was still overcast and grey, but the threat of rain seemed to be slowly diminishing. Those huge thunderclouds he had seen when he first brought Tucker out had for the most part moved on, and the sky was a bit brighter in their absence. Michael read the clock on his dashboard. It was almost 1:30 p.m. now. Somewhere, Jeanette was probably on her lunch break, assuming she had come in to work like normal today.

Michael shook his head. Jeanette could wait.

Up ahead, the jogger veered off onto a side street. Michael accelerated slightly, making sure to keep his eyes on the road and on the car in front of him.

When he came up to the intersection, he took his foot off the gas and stole a quick look. The man was now jogging from the right sidewalk over to the left diagonally across the street. Michael made a quick note of the street's name and read the yellow-orange sign below it that declared this was 'NOT A THROUGH STREET'. He smiled to himself victoriously, then returned his gaze to the traffic in front of him.

Michael drove a further two blocks before turning right onto a cross street. He sped down the tree-lined road until he came to another intersection, then turned right and floored the gas, cutting across the same two blocks before rolling to a stop at the street the jogger had gone up.

Michael looked left and then right, but the jogger was nowhere in sight.

"*Fuck.*"

He swore under his breath and turned left, easing the car to the side of the road and against the curb. Michael crept the Corolla up the street along the edge, weaving around the occasional parked car while still giving enough space to allow a driver every now and then to pass him coming the opposite direction on his left. Feverishly, he scanned the houses on both sides of the street for movement, for any sign of where the jogger might have disappeared to.

"Come on, come on..."

Michael muttered the words to himself, swiveling his head from side to side as he coasted up the street. Before long, the road ahead emptied into a cul-de-sac, and Michael followed the contours to turn around and begin heading back down the street, still searching. He passed the street he had come over on, and up ahead was the original road he had followed the jogger on.

When Michael reached the end of the street, he pulled off to the right and put the car in park. Tucker was still quaking in the seat next to him, so he reached over with his good hand and ran his fingers through the dog's fur.

Fearfully, he looked down at his right hand. Half

of his thumbnail was missing, and where it should have been, the skin was pink and inflamed. The bleeding had stopped, but in its place, a white pus was quickly forming. The finger itself didn't look crooked, but of course, that didn't mean it couldn't still be broken, sprained, or dislocated.

Michael examined his reflection in the rear-view mirror and began to assess the damage. On the left side of his face, a black eye was forming fast, and his lip was fat and swollen on that side as well. A small cut on his cheekbone gleamed bright red. Thankfully, all of his teeth were intact and accounted for.

The reek of the car's interior reminded Michael of what was still caked in his hair. He didn't dare turn his head to examine the source of the smell, for fear the sight of it would make him lose control and vomit. The odor itself was bad enough, and Michael was surprised it had taken him this long to really notice it. He rolled the windows down and turned the air conditioner on, then returned his gaze to the mirror, this time looking not at himself but back at the quiet street.

After ten minutes of inactivity, he turned the car around and began to drive up the street a second time, moving even slower this time around, peering through every window in every house he passed. Michael circled through the cul-de-sac and was coming back down the road when a flicker of movement caught his eye.

He thought he saw bright blue pass by a window near the front door of a small brick ranch-style home. Immediately, Michael hit the brakes and waited, idling the car in front of the house.

He could have sworn he saw the exact shade of blue he had been looking for. The color was unique, and even in the dim, pewter haze of the day, the shirt had seemed to glow like a neon blue daiquiri. Michael waited patiently, and his focus had all the intensity of a predator stalking its prey before the strike.

Sure enough, his eyes had not deceived him. Moments later, the color materialized again, and this time, Michael was ready for it. He followed it up to the man's face and recognized the bulging white eyes even through the glass panes of the window.

There was no doubting it was him. The jogger moved past the window and out of view again, but Michael had seen enough. He memorized the address of the house, and then drove off toward the main street and back to his apartment complex.

CHAPTER TWELVE

Tucker was relieved to get home, having staved off a perceived trip to the veterinarian's office. Michael was relieved, too. It meant he could tend to his wounds and his hair.

The first thing he did was head straight for the shower. The hot water stung his face, and he had to keep tilting his head so that the left side was out of the pressure of the stream. Without using his thumb, he scrubbed at the back of his hair with both hands, trying his best not to notice the small clumps that fell to the floor.

After three rounds of shampoo, the smell was gone, and his hair felt normal and clean to the touch. He took this time to examine the rest of his body. Apart from a few bruises on his torso, Michael looked relatively unscathed down there.

Unfortunately, his face was a different story. Michael got out of the shower and applied Neosporin to the cut on his cheek and his swollen lip. He looked in his medicine cabinet for anti-inflammatory drugs, found some ibuprofen, and decided it was the best he could do for the pain. Delicately, he rubbed a dab of ointment onto his thumb, then wrapped it with a

Band-Aid that wasn't designed for the end of a thumb.

Finished, he attempted several movements with the digit. With excruciating slowness, he was able to bend the joint down and back up again without assistance. Upon initial examination, at least, it seemed as if it wasn't broken.

When he was as satisfied as he could be, Michael put fresh clothes on, threw his dirty ones in the washing machine, and powered up his laptop computer. A search for "hit-and-run in Los Angeles" immediately brought up links to news reports that had been written hours earlier. Michael felt a lump form in his throat as he painstakingly went through every article he could find.

The deceased was Arthur Bennett, sixty-five, husband of Lea Bennett, father of two, grandfather of five. Michael immediately recognized the face from the pictures, and it made his heart sink. He didn't want to read anything more about the victim or his life, but he had to be sure in every article that nothing was known as to the identity of the man's killer.

Thankfully, it appeared nothing was. No witnesses were mentioned in any of the articles. One piece stated that the police did not have any leads, while another asked for anyone with information to call a certain number. There was an approximation of the time of death, and thus the time of the accident, which Michael knew to be roughly accurate.

In every article he read, there was no mention of clues or evidence regarding the vehicle that had struck and killed Bennett. This was the biggest relief for Michael. As far as he could tell, no one was searching for his car or for him.

Michael had to take a step back and remind himself that although his car was technically the murder weapon, he himself was not a murderer. It was absolutely crucial for him to remember that.

Drew had been behind the wheel, not him. Michael was asleep when the accident had happened. There was nothing he could have done. It was his car, but he wasn't the driver. So surely, the fault wasn't truly his.

Obviously, he still felt complicit for leaving the scene of the crime, but what else could he have done? At the end of the day, it was Drew Baskin who killed Arthur Bennett, not Michael Cavanaugh. Really, that was all that mattered.

He cleared his search history, exited the browser, and closed the laptop. Michael was still then, sitting on his couch with the computer on his lap, staring into the far wall of his apartment. Tucker sat at his feet and watched him with big, wet, brown eyes. Moments passed.

A buzzing sound broke Michael from his trance. He looked down to see his phone glowing on the cushion beside him. Again, he recognized the number as the credit union calling. He had to admire his boss's persistence, despite the fact that he truly hated the man.

The only thing Michael and Hamid had in common was their mutual love of smoking cigarettes. Perhaps Hamid thought of Michael as a friend, as he always seemed to time his cigarette breaks perfectly to coincide with Michael's. Either that, or maybe he was just lonely. Regardless, Michael often found himself making the most awkward kind of small talk with his boss, and he had soon gotten into the habit of sneaking out the back staircase to take his breaks just to avoid these conversations.

When Michael had first started working at the credit union several years ago, he had borne Hamid no ill will. Although the man wasn't overly friendly, he was cordial enough with his employees, and he seemed to manage the office competently. Hamid often encouraged his employees to use up all of their vacation days, and he would remind Michael whenever he had the chance that he should "go see the world" while he was still "young and fit." Michael even found himself beginning to like and respect his boss for a time.

That is, until Jeanette was hired.

It started with the wandering eyes. Michael couldn't help but notice Hamid's difficulty in keeping his gaze above Jeanette's neckline while speaking with her. The twice-divorced Armenian sexagenarian would waddle over during slower periods of the day and begin making chitchat with the both of them. Before long, however, he would square himself entirely toward his attractive female employee, and his eyes would dip repeatedly and unapologetically down her cleavage.

If it bothered Jeanette, she never let on. She was always better at playing the corporate game than Michael was. Sometimes, Michael even wondered if Jeanette seemed to like the attention.

Her reactions only served to spur Hamid on, though. After a while, the wandering eyes became occasional light touches, which in turn, became firmer and more frequent over time. Michael was forced to observe this process from a front-row seat, all the time growing more and more uncomfortable. He considered talking about it to Jeanette, but since she never seemed to mind or verbally object, he supposed it wasn't his place to fight her battles for her.

Michael realized over the years that a large part of his concern was probably also rooted in jealousy. He began to feel protective of Jeanette, and it got to the point during these moments where he would abruptly stand up and leave the row of tellers to go to the bathroom or go outside, hoping to show his disapproval of their inappropriate interactions through a dramatic exit.

It never seemed to work, though. When Michael had cooled off and returned to his seat, sometimes he would still find the two of them gossiping and laughing together.

Michael soon found his jealousy turning to disgust and then even to outright hatred. Hamid began making jokes at Michael's expense, hoping to solicit the occasional laugh from Jeanette. Michael started ignoring Hamid entirely, and as time went on, he became increasingly withdrawn and reclusive at work from all his associates. Michael limited his major conversations to Jeanette, but even those were few and far between. As soon as the credit union was slow or empty enough to permit such a dialogue, Hamid instinctively would detect the lull and move in on Jeanette anyway.

Any respect or appreciation Michael might once have had for his boss was now long gone. And as he presently looked down at the phone number on the screen, he realized with a sudden euphoric clarity that he simply didn't want to work there anymore.

What was the point? Michael didn't want to (or

need to) work, ever again. The last thing he wanted to do with his final days on Earth was spend them under fluorescent lights, cutting cashier checks and watching Hamid's grubby, wrinkly, little fingers molest his infatuation.

Plus, Michael realized he still had some time to kill before his major plans for the evening were set to begin.

He refilled Tucker's water and food bowls, grabbed his keys and cigarettes, and headed back down to the parking garage and his car. Michael felt much more relieved driving the black Corolla knowing now there weren't police helicopters searching all over the city for it. He pulled out onto the road and began the short commute to his workplace.

Deep down, Michael knew what he was doing now was unnecessary. He could just as easily accomplish this task by continuing to let the phone go to voicemail, ignoring the calls and allowing his silence to do the talking for him.

Michael had spent the vast majority of his life avoiding conflict and swallowing his emotions. Reason, logic, and his own mother had taught him long ago to 'choose his battles', and that sometimes, it was best just to 'turn the other cheek' or 'roll with the punches'.

For decades, Michael had lived and died by these abominable expressions, platitudes, and catchphrases, and now he found himself resenting them.

Where had they gotten him, after all? He was almost thirty, and he had absolutely nothing to show for it. Dead-end job, no savings, no girlfriend, no hobbies. He had only ever had two *real* friends, and one of them was dead now, while the other was a self-centered, borderline-psychotic asshole. His car was old and unreliable, his own dog had stood by and watched him get his ass kicked by a juiced-up French bulldog owner, and the one girl he had ever really liked probably thought he was a rapist now.

Michael didn't know whether to laugh, cry, or scream. Probably some combination of all three.

What he did know was that this time, he wasn't going to stand on the sidelines and just wait to see what happened.

He recognized Jeanette's car in the parking lot of the Glendale credit union. So, she *had* come to work after all. She was braver than he gave her credit for. Michael wasn't sure if he would have come to work the next day, had their roles last night been reversed.

Maybe he would have a chance to speak with her before he was done. It wasn't something he had planned for on this latest adventure, but he was open to the possibility, at least.

Out of habit, he began to circle back toward his usual parking spot under a loquat tree in the corner. At the last second though, Michael changed his mind, veered left, and parked sloppily in the first available spot he saw. He cut the ignition and exited his car, not bothering with the locks or the sunshade he usually administered to the car's windshield interior.

Once inside the lobby, he hit the elevator call button, grew impatient, and took the stairs instead, bounding up two steps at a time. Michael began to feel his heartbeat accelerate, and his palms, underarms, and forehead started to sweat. The danger of the situation was very real to him now, and so was the excitement and the adrenaline.

He threw open the stairwell door when he reached the third floor, raced quickly down the carpeted hallway, and rounded into the credit union office without stopping to acknowledge Gina, the receptionist greeter at the front desk. His time was precious, and he couldn't afford to waste it on people he knew only peripherally and didn't really care for.

It gave Michael quite a bit of pleasure seeing the abnormally long line of guests waiting to be serviced by a teller. Tuesday afternoons were not a particularly busy time for them typically, but it appeared that Michael's absence had slowed down normal operations.

Instead of the scheduled three employees, only two sat behind the counter. Michael spotted his nameplate behind a closed window and smiled to himself. Clearly, Hamid had not been able to find another employee to come in on such short notice.

One of his coworkers spoke Spanish, and he was busy speaking it right now with an agitated mother of two. The kids clawed at each other and at their mother's legs, and she would punctuate her disagreement with the teller by occasionally swatting at her offspring in annoyance.

At the other open window, a man tapped his fingers on the countertop impatiently, waiting on the pretty young woman working in front of him. Michael almost, *almost*, wanted her to look up and see him there, but Jeanette was glued to her computer screen, obviously stressed and overwhelmed by her work. Ultimately, Michael was glad she did not see him there and then, because his real business was with the man in the office across from the tellers' window.

Hamid Arakelyan had more hair on his body than

on his head. Fine silver strands sprouted with reckless abandon from behind his shirt collar, and Michael imagined a salt and pepper forest probably grew in places he didn't want to think of. Mercifully, the man dressed formally – almost too formally. Michael had never seen him without a button-up shirt, blazer, tie, and slacks, even on 'casual Fridays'.

Hamid was sitting behind his desk, phone in hand and at his ear, when Michael entered. The credit union manager had his back to Michael and appeared to be listening intently to whoever was on the other line. His free hand massaged his forehead, and he rocked the black office chair back and forth on its tilt rhythmically.

Michael cleared his throat, and his boss turned slowly around in his chair to face him. Hamid's eyes went wide for a moment, then narrowed quickly, and his lips curled into a frown. "Ani, I have to go… I'll call you back." He hung up the phone and took in Michael's appearance. "Michael… what happened to you?"

It took Michael a full moment to understand the question. He had not been prepared for that kind of reaction, but he had also forgotten entirely about his bruised and bloodied face. Worse, the mention of his appearance suddenly made Michael remember the pain he had forgotten in his excitement, and all at once, it came rushing back.

"I got in a fight. That's not important though. I'm here because I wanted to come in and quit in person. You can stop calling me, or having Gina call me, or whoever call me, because I won't be coming into work today, and I won't be coming back into work ever again." He paused to let the words sink in and have their full effect. "Okay?"

Hamid looked half-puzzled, half-surprised. He leaned forward in his chair to replace the phone on its base.

"No, that's not okay. What would make you think that any of this is okay?" He spoke in a thick voice, his words tinged by a slight Armenian accent. "You don't show up today, and you don't call out. And now you walk in with a black eye that you won't explain, and you want to quit without any advance notice?" Hamid laughed gruffly with incredulity. "No, Michael, that is not okay with me."

"Well, to be honest, I don't really care whether it's okay with you or not. I didn't even have to come in here today. I could have just never shown up again, but I'm tired of my phone ringing off the hook, and I don't want to think about this shitty place anymore. So once more, I'm telling you not to contact me further, ever again. I quit."

Michael soaked in the look of mounting frustration on his ex-boss's face, and then turned to leave. There was no point in elongating this conversation, or in making it overdramatic, or confrontational, despite his contempt for Hamid.

He had probably played out dozens of 'quitting fantasies' over the time of his tenure at the credit union, and this certainly was not one of them. Michael had always envisioned it to be a passionate, furious, or even violent episode between them. But that was fantasy and this was reality. He had no real desire to do anything outrageous or unconventional. His decision to quit, and to do so in person, had been spontaneous enough.

Apparently, though, Hamid was not as satisfied with the way their dialogue had concluded.

"Excuse me, Michael, but we're not done here. If you do intend to quit, you need to sign a termination agreement, and we have to sort through your paperwork with HR. It's not as simple as just walking in and then walking right out of here–"

"Actually, it is."

Michael cut him off and continued walking from the office. He looked across the line of guests, and this time, Jeanette met his gaze with her own. He wasn't sure how long she had been aware of his presence in the credit union, but now she seemed to be taking him in fully. He couldn't quite read the expression on her face... was there surprise there? Alarm? Maybe even a touch of curiosity?

Impulsively, Michael changed plans and crossed over toward her countertop. A young man was counting bills in front of her, but Michael sidestepped him as he approached her window. She sat back in her chair, her eyes still locked on Michael's features, and her right hand reached up to touch her throat absentmindedly, and perhaps even a bit defensively.

"Michael, your face..."

"Can I talk to you for a second?"

She turned her focus to the man in front of her, who also seemed surprised by Michael's sudden proximity.

"I... don't think now's the best time..."

"It's actually really important that I talk to you now. I'm not sure if I'll have another chance."

Jeanette was at a loss. "I'm sure you can see how busy we are right now."

Her tone was definitely accusatory. She flashed an apologetic smile to the young man and began to count the bills he had laid out before her.

"I'm sorry, sir."

"That's okay, it's not your fault." The man made sure to direct this response at Michael.

Behind him, guests seemed to be taking notice now, some murmuring discontentedly at this intruder who had barged his way up to the front of the line.

"Michael." This time, it was Hamid's voice, not Jeanette's, that spoke his name, and Michael saw the manager walking toward him from his office.

Hamid's cheeks flushed red with embarrassment, and he was clearly trying to control the volume and tenor of his voice, but mostly unsuccessfully. Evidently, the last thing he wanted was a scene, especially with the credit union as busy as it was.

Michael turned back to Jeanette. "Please, just give me a minute of your time. We can go talk outside, or in the break room, or wherever you want…"

Jeanette was resolute. She shook her head before continuing on counting the money, now aloud.

Michael leaned forward against the counter, imploring her.

"This has nothing to do with last night, I swear—"

"*Michael!*" It *was* Jeanette that time, and her cheeks flushed redder than Hamid's.

The young man standing next to Michael apparently had had enough, and, seeing her reaction, took it upon himself to intervene.

"Hey, man, why don't you leave her alone?"

Michael turned on the stranger. "Hey, *man*, why don't you mind your own business?" Hamid was there, then, stepping between the two of them with upraised palms.

"I'm so sorry, sir." He apologized softly to the guest before turning to face Michael, and his eyes were dangerous. "Please leave now." His voice was slow and deliberate, the voice of a man who had spent decades in charge.

Michael, however, was unfazed. "A minute ago, you wouldn't let me leave your office, and now you're throwing me out?!"

"I'm going to have to ask you to leave."

"Oh, I heard you the first time. I'm not coming back, so you got what you wish for. Just let me have a second to talk to Jeanette."

"I'm going to have to ask you to leave *now*, Mr. Cavanaugh."

Hamid was having trouble controlling himself. It was clear that even with all his years of experience managing employees, he was now decidedly out of his element, and was improvising as best he could in uncharted waters. The red of his face had morphed to a deep purple, and he reached forward to try and guide Michael away by the shoulder.

Quick as a cat, Michael batted the hand away and turned once more to Jeanette.

"Jeanette, *please*! We don't have much time left, and I care about you! I need to talk to you *now!*"

Her face betrayed both shock and fear. The situation was quickly getting out of hand, and Michael had the absurd realization that, to the others, it must have looked like he and Jeanette were lovers having a fight or dealing with a break-up.

Here he was, the heartbroken boyfriend, fighting

for one last chance at forgiveness and redemption. Maybe some of the credit union members even figured that Jeanette was responsible for giving him the black eye and the cuts on his face. But that wasn't the case, obviously, and Michael had no time to discredit assumptions.

A hand on his back made him spin around. One of the bolder guests had taken it upon himself to assist in defusing the situation.

"Take it easy, buddy." The guest pulled his hand back and raised both palms.

Michael stepped back and saw all the eyes on him. Self-consciousness began to gnaw at him, and he realized he was shaking. His teeth and fists were clenched, and he was breathing like a cornered animal with its back against the wall.

They would all be dead soon, these people. Soon, how much money they had in their savings and checking accounts wouldn't matter at all. Nothing would matter. He wanted to tell them that, then… to scream it at them until the horrible truth sunk in. Michael wanted to watch their faces crumble at the news, and to see what Hamid's reaction would be like then, knowing his life was over.

For a second, Michael even debated telling them all, right here and now. But he knew that no one would believe him. He would be dismissed as a lunatic; as a ranting, raving, former employee who had gone off the deep end. They would disregard him the same way he and Drew had disregarded Aaron that night, the night before Drew's wedding, before the flash in the sky that Aaron had predicted and warned them about actually happened, and then everything changed forever.

He didn't care about Hamid Arakelyan, about the young man with the bills of cash, about the imposing man standing in front of him now with his palms upraised, or about any of these people.

Michael did care about Jeanette, though, and he knew then that he couldn't live with himself if he didn't tell her the truth. She, and only she, deserved that knowledge, to do with as she would.

Hamid and the man who had put a hand on Michael's back were both slowly advancing on him now, and Michael knew he would have it rough trying to overpower the barrel-chested 'hero' guest if he had to, so he began to retreat. One last time, he called to the woman at the window.

"Jeanette, please! Please come talk to me! I'm sorry about what happened last night, I am, but this has nothing to do with that! I just need–"

His words were cut short by a grunt of pain and surprise. Michael turned and saw he had backed right into the door. The silver handle rammed him in the kidney, and the pain caught him off-guard and interrupted his thoughts.

Gina, the receptionist at the front desk, was standing to his left with her hands clasped together, panic etched across her powdered face. Michael saw the expression on his former coworker's face, and he resented her naked fear and animosity. He wasn't some monster that had invaded their workplace; he had been nothing but polite, civil, and pleasant to all of his coworkers over the years.

Michael turned his attention one last time toward the bank of tellers. The young man still stood at her window, but Jeanette's focus was trained on Michael, just like everyone else in the room.

She made no move to follow him, though, and her eyes just stared back at him sadly. Michael noticed she was wearing a yellow blouse. It was his favorite color on her. He was sure that he had told her that sometime in the past at work. The soft color complemented her tan, olive skin perfectly, and it brought out her eyes and smile vividly.

Had she worn yellow intentionally? Had she worn it for him? Was it a sign that she had not given up on him, despite all that had gone wrong the night before?

Michael's thoughts raced faster than his heart, but she remained still and motionless on the other side of the glass. Hamid stepped into focus, moving a foot closer and then pointing out the open door.

"*Out!*" He said it as if he were speaking to a disobedient dog or a child.

Michael felt cold fury bubble up inside, and for a second, he thought about attacking the fat man. He could still make one of his quitting fantasies come to life, right here in front of everyone.

But doing so would almost certainly bring the police, and Michael would have to make a break for it. For all he knew, Gina, or one of the guests in line, had already called the police, and Michael knew the last place he wanted to spend his final days on Earth was in a holding cell or in a prison. Besides, he needed no extra attention after the accident last night.

Swallowing his rage and his pride, Michael took one last pleading look at Jeanette, and then moved quickly out the doorway and down the hall. He opened the door to the stairwell and descended the steps as quickly as he had come up them, feeling far less than satisfied with how the events in the credit union had transpired.

Any sensations of excitement or elation that had accompanied his initial conversation with Hamid were long gone, replaced by a growing sense of desperation at his failure to adequately communicate with Jeanette. Perhaps he never should have tried to talk to her in the first place, but he also hadn't been lying when he told her that they might never have another chance.

As he exited the stairwell into the building's main lobby, Michael pulled his cell phone from his pocket and began to search his contacts. He walked out into the sunny October afternoon toward his car, looking up at the third-floor windows as he moved across the parking lot, hoping to see her face staring down at him from above.

Instead, he was disappointed to find only the shadowed face of his former boss, peering suspiciously out at him through parted blinds. Michael took the opportunity to flip him the bird. He realized Hamid must have been watching for him, making sure he wasn't going to come back. Michael fished out his keys from his pants pocket, got in his car, and returned his attention to the phone in his hand. After he found the number, he dialed it and held the device up to his ear.

As expected, the call went straight to voicemail. Michael listened to the recorded greeting message, waited for the beep, and then started talking as rapidly as he could.

"Hey Jeanette, it's me, Michael. I know you're working still, and I can't even begin to tell you how sorry I am for embarrassing you like that just now. I hope you don't delete this message and that you hear me out, because I don't know how else I'm going to be able to talk to you. Really, I need to be able to see you and talk to you in person, face-to-face, because there's no way I can tell you everything over the phone, or in this message. So, if you'll see me later, I don't know… at your place, or my place, or… even a public place, I guess, as weird as that sounds, I'd really appreciate it. Whatever you're comfortable with. I know that last night was just awful and it's really not what I want to talk to you about. What I have to talk to you about is so much more important than that, and I don't know how else to convey that to you over the phone right now. But I am sorry for my actions last night, and for what happened, if that makes you more comfortable and more willing to meet with me. Again, this has nothing to do with—"

An automated woman's voice cut in, informing Michael that he had reached his time limit for this message. Michael swore, ended the call, then hit 'redial' and waited for the phone to go to voicemail again.

"Hey, it's me again. Please call me back and let me know when I can talk to you. It's extremely important. Thanks. Goodbye."

He hung up and set the phone down on the seat beside him. Michael glanced into his rear-view mirror to see if Hamid was still watching him. Sure enough, the fat man still stood in the window, now with the blinds drawn entirely. Michael could see his face and body clearly now and noted the hands on his hips. Obviously, he wanted to be seen. Hamid stood still as a statue, waiting for his former employee to leave the premises.

Something about the man's frame in the window

created déjà vu for Michael, but he couldn't place the sensation at first. Where had he seen this before? It seemed all too familiar...

And then, his brain made the connection. In Hamid, Michael could see his next-door neighbor; the stocky, white-haired, steel-eyed old man who routinely stared him down from his balcony window at unreasonably early times of the night. His mind connected the dots between them, and for a minute, it was not the suit-clad Armenian manager staring down at him, but the silent bully from next door.

Michael scowled at the reflection in his mirror and found himself reliving old revenge fantasies against both his boss and his next-door neighbor, often combining the two people into one person for his purposes at the moment. He smiled devilishly, relishing the opportunity to inflict imaginary harm on his foes. Somehow, it made everything feel better.

His memory lighted on a particular episode of violence he had dreamed up not that long ago for this very same office window he was now gazing up into... but this one had not involved his boss or his neighbor.

Michael racked his brain for the target of this loathing. Who had he seen himself throwing through that window? It had been a recent fantasy of his, something he had concocted the day he chased that kid on the bicycle. He had imagined fucking Jeanette in front of the credit union guests and Hamid. In his mind, Aaron and Drew had been there, he recalled, cheering him on, and...

Lillian. Michael smiled to himself in triumph. That's who he had seen in his mind's eye, yelling at him, sneering at him with her ugly, bony features, and her acerbic personality. He had grabbed her then, socked her in the face, and thrown her through that very window, only to watch her fall screaming to her death in an explosion of brilliant, beautiful red. Even now, the fantasy gave him sadistic joy and pleasure.

The only sad thing was that such fantasies were just that: fantasies. In reality, the person in the window was not Michael, leering down victoriously at the ruin he had made of Lillian, his enemy.

In reality, Michael was the ruined wreck on the ground, sent scurrying to his car by a hairy old Armenian who now loomed above him from behind the plate glass window in his daydream.

It just wasn't fair.

Michael cycled through his contacts again until he came to the letter 'L'. Why he had not deleted her number long ago was a mystery to him. Perhaps he had only kept it for this very moment. Something in his subconscious had made him retain the number all this time, knowing that one day, he would be able to use it against her.

The only reason he even had her number to begin with was because of Drew and Michelle. It was their boneheaded idea to set the two of them up a couple years ago now, and the plan had famously backfired. That first blind date had been the longest two hours of Michael's life, and maybe Lillian's as well.

Thinking of it now made him cringe. There were few things or people that Michael hated more on this planet than Lillian Ross.

He debated whether to call her or just send a text. Making the call meant there was a decent chance of her picking up, which would mean hearing her voice and having to carry on some kind of conversation. Michael could avoid all of that by sending a simple text.

Of course, there was always the possibility that she had deleted his number from her phone entirely. Maybe she had even blocked him.

After mulling it over for a few seconds, Michael made up his mind to send her a text. If she got it, great. If not, then nothing was gained or lost either way. All he knew was that the thought of hearing her voice on the other end of the line repulsed him. But if he couldn't throw her through a glass window, maybe this was the next best thing...

It took Michael the better part of five minutes to word the message exactly the way he wanted it. When he was finally satisfied, he hit 'Send'. The text was delivered instantly, and Michael repeatedly read over what he had written with a vicious glee.

Lillian – this is Michael Cavanaugh. You wouldn't know this, but Aaron Hillison killed himself because he correctly predicted a cosmic event the morning of Drew and Michelle's wedding. That was the light we all saw in the sky. It's called a gamma ray burst, and it hit the Earth, and now it's just a matter of time until the world ends, as crazy as that sounds. If you don't believe me, ask Drew. He has all of Aaron's research as proof, and he can confirm all of this. I'm telling you this because I think you should know, and you should start preparing yourself. If there's a hell, I really hope you're going to it.

Michael still wasn't sure if the last sentence was a good idea or not. It was his favorite part of the message, but it could also make the rest of the text seem less reliable and believable. He didn't want Lillian thinking this was all some sick joke; he wanted her to really accept the fact that she was going to die, and he wanted to personally be the bearer of that news.

Truthfully, the chances of Lillian reading the text message and believing any word of it were slim. Again, for all he knew, she had blocked him from her phone altogether.

But sending the message gave Michael at least a fraction of the pleasure he received from his fantasies. Plus, this was reality, too. Everything Michael had told her was true, and if she chose not to take it seriously, then so be it. Either way, Michael hoped she would be one of the first to go on this side of the planet, and preferably from skin-melting radiation rays rather than drawn-out starvation, although either means would do.

Hamid had finally left his post at the window, and Michael realized he was long overdue to have left the building's parking lot by now, too. Again, he could not risk getting arrested, not when there was so much more he had left to do tonight.

Michael backed out of the parking space and sped across the asphalt, casting one last optimistic glance through his windshield toward the third floor. But she was not there.

No matter. He was still too busy riding the high from his text message to feel any true dejection. Maybe Jeanette would call him back, and maybe not. Maybe he would see her again before the end of all this, and maybe not. He had given it his best shot, and there was nothing more he could do now. Michael tightened his grip on the steering wheel and turned out onto the open road.

He had bigger fish to fry tonight.

CHAPTER THIRTEEN

Night came slowly for Michael. Smoking a cigarette, he sat on his balcony and watched the sunset sluggishly fade over the hills in the distance. Every so often, he had to stop himself from touching or playing with his various wounds, as his fingers had minds of their own.

Michael's left eye was swollen up to the point where it was hard for him to keep it open, and the skin there was a dark mixture of blue, black, purple, and green. The gash on his cheekbone glistened in the dying rays of sunlight, wet from a fresh layer of anti-scarring ointment.

He chuckled to himself. As if scars mattered anymore... But old habits were hard to break. Michael had a whole medicine cabinet full of pills, lotions, tonics, and other drugs for an assortment of health-related possibilities, the vast majority of which he never used. To say that he was a hypochondriac might have been a bit of an overstatement, but it wasn't too far from the truth. Michael had tended to his wounds again almost immediately upon returning to his apartment from the credit union.

His fat lip remained plump and pussy, and it was

the primary target of his exploratory fingertips right now. Initially, he had a difficult time keeping a cigarette in his mouth, as he usually smoked from the left side of his face. But after some careful maneuvering, Michael had managed to find an acceptable level of overall comfort, and he now settled into the deck chair to bide his time and wait for the cover of darkness.

Every now and then, Michael would glance over toward his neighbor's balcony, thinking perhaps he had heard a sound from inside the apartment. He wanted the man to come out, or even the small Asian lady.

Let her try and accuse him of something now. Michael itched at the thought of confrontation. One look at his bruised and battered face might be enough to scare her back inside.

The man might be braver. Maybe he had seen worse things in a war he had once fought in as a younger man, perhaps in Vietnam or Korea. Michael had no way of knowing whether the man was a veteran or not, but he had always sort of assumed as much in his imagination.

If the old man wasn't afraid, then maybe he would stand in the doorway again and stare Michael down. Michael wanted him to. He found himself willing the man to appear, to step out from his hiding place behind the sliding glass door into the last light of day. If he did, Michael was ready for him. As ready as he ever had been.

Feeling bold and reckless, he went inside to his kitchen, dug around in a seldom-used cabinet, and returned to the balcony with a small bottle of Scotch. Michael had never been much of a drinker, and he certainly didn't make a habit of drinking alone.

Primarily, he had started drinking in high school just to fit in and had continued doing so in college as a member of his fraternity.

Sure, there were nights with Drew and with Aaron post-college where he would find himself drinking more than he could really handle… and Michael always paid the price dearly for it the next morning. Drew, on the other hand, still seemed miraculously immune to hangovers, especially considering the copious amounts of hard liquor he regularly consumed.

But the strong stuff was exactly what Michael needed tonight, so he had rummaged through that dusty liquor shelf to find the bottle with the highest alcohol percentage by volume. Scotch wasn't his drink of choice, but it served better than the old bottles of Kahlúa, peppermint schnapps, and triple sec he also came across in there. Michael briefly contemplated grabbing a rocks glass but ultimately decided against it, and now he sat, bottle in hand, steeling his nerves for what was still to come.

His first swig went down easier than expected. The Scotch had been a gift from his mother, sent for his birthday through the mail a long time ago. He imagined it must have been expensive, but its true value was lost on him.

Why his mother thought it an appropriate gift for her son, he could not say. As far as he could remember, he had never, ever, indicated to her a taste for Scotch, whisky in general, or, for that matter, any type of alcohol whatsoever. Maybe it was just the best she could do for a man that had long since outgrown her and who now lived many miles away.

He took another pull from the bottle, clearing

away thoughts of his mother. Again, Michael turned to face the neighboring balcony, but there was still no one there, unfortunately.

Michael checked the time on his phone. It was almost 7 p.m. Surely, the man was home from work by now. He usually seemed to get home around 4 or 5 p.m. An early evening for a man that presumably started his workday at an ungodly hour of the morning.

Someone was in that apartment; the sliding glass door was wide open, only the screen door was shut, and he could hear the soft murmur of a television drifting across the air. Other than that, though, he still heard no voices and no barking from the terrier they kept inside all day. Michael lit up another cigarette and even tried to blow some of the smoke in the direction of the screen door, hoping perhaps that might garner the reaction he thirsted for.

Still nothing. Disappointed, Michael lifted the bottle to the good side of his mouth and gulped down more of the liquor. It made him gag slightly, and he sputtered a short cough. Michael had swallowed too much too fast, and some of it felt like it went down his windpipe accidentally. He coughed again until his eyes watered, and then checked back on the next-door balcony.

Where was the man?

Michael felt the slow, steady burn of the whisky roasting the coals between his stomach and his heart. He set the bottle next to him and put a hand on his chest, intrigued by the strange sensation. It had been a very long time since he last drank whisky, and he had forgotten this aspect of it. He liked the feeling... and decided to have some more.

By 7:30 p.m., the sun was gone, and the moon was out. Twilight had given way to dusk, and then dusk to full-blown darkness. Michael hadn't bothered to turn on the exterior light over his balcony patio. The cool night air felt soothing to his cuts and bruises, and the alcohol only further helped assuage the dull aches and pains of his body.

He finished off the last cigarette in his pack and stubbed it out in the ashtray next to his chair. Michael reached for the bottle of Scotch but found it empty. Surprisingly enough, he didn't feel nearly as drunk as he figured he would. His brain still seemed relatively sharp, and his movements were mostly fluid and controlled.

Michael took the empty bottle and ashtray inside. He threw out the bottle, dumped the ashtray, replaced it on the balcony, and went to examine Tucker's food and water bowls. The supply in both was good, so Michael went into his bedroom to change.

He felt a little foolish assembling this outfit, but he also knew that it was the best choice for what he had to do. Black pants, black shoes, and a black sweatshirt. Michael examined his reflection in the mirror and couldn't help but smirk to himself. He looked like a bank robber. All he was missing was the trademark ski mask or pantyhose pulled down over his face.

Michael had to dig behind an old oaken dresser in his closet to find the last item he was looking for. When at last he came across it, he decided he was ready to go.

The final thing he did inside was to pour himself a glass of water from the kitchen sink, down it, and then exit swiftly through the front door. He chose to bypass the elevator, instead taking the stairs all the way down to the street level of his apartment building.

By the time Michael was outside again, he could feel the Scotch working on his brain. He was not drunk yet, but perhaps he would be very soon. This was a different kind of intoxication; a slow burn that worked on his nerves steadily but slothfully. He continued to enjoy the buzz as he made his way down the main street he had driven on only hours earlier.

Most of the evening traffic commute had died down, but there was still a steady stream of cars going both ways along the road. Michael wondered if any of the drivers inside them could see him walking along the sidewalk, or if his dark clothing really did help him blend in with the trees and bushes that lined the walkway.

Occasionally, he would pass a jogger or someone out walking their dog. He didn't shy away from making eye contact with any of them, possibly seeking to gauge their reactions to his attire. If anyone was suspicious, they sure didn't seem to look it. Most people didn't even meet his eyes, and those that did would only give him a polite nod or smile as they passed. This was good. Maybe it was only Michael himself who thought he looked like a textbook criminal.

A couple of teenagers on the sidewalk stared longer at him, and he turned to notice them whispering to one another after he passed by. One seemed to be gesturing to his own eye and laughing, which at first Michael didn't understand, but then he remembered his black eye and his fat lip, and he could assume that these injuries were the source of their discussion. Michael had done his best to treat and then conceal his wounds, but apparently, even the dark of night could not cover up everything.

No matter. As long as no one stopped him, they could think whatever they wanted about him.

The object he kept low and at his side was much more questionable than his clothing, but he was doing the best he could to hide it behind his right leg as he walked. No one seemed to notice it, and even if someone did, what could they possibly do or say? This was a free country, after all, and there were no rules against what he was wearing and carrying. Besides, he would only be on this busy street for so long.

The night air felt charged with electricity. Michael's buzz was in full-blown swing now, and he walked with a renewed sense of determination. He couldn't stop now. The Scotch had been just enough to tip him over the edge, and he liked his newfound sense of courage and fervor.

After all, he was in a new world now. A world without a future, and with no guarantees or consequences. If there was to be any justice, he would have to be the one to execute it himself.

Michael turned right off the main road at the proper intersection. The neighborhood looked different in the dark, as could be expected. Earlier, his rage had blinded him to most of his surroundings, but he had driven up and down this dead-end street several times, scanning the buildings furiously with every pass, and now he began to recognize certain features: a mailbox here, a flower bed there.

Most of the houses were bright on the inside, alive with the activity of their tenants. Michael could make out some of their faces; kids running around playing with one another, families sitting down to dinner or to watch television, people in their kitchens and in their living rooms… All going about their nightly routines, all oblivious to the secret that spelled their coming end.

He wondered how they would react if he told them the awful secret destiny of the world. Disbelief, of course. That was only natural. Nothing he could say would probably help to convince them. People only heard what they wanted to hear, and a harbinger of doom would receive no welcome in any of these houses. Michael sighed and wondered if ignorance truly *was* bliss.

It was a question that he didn't have an answer for, and the more he thought about it, the more distracted and angrier he became, so he decided to let it go. As much as he resented being thrust into the horrible truth and then having to forcibly, painfully swallow it, nothing he said, thought, or did could change what had happened.

There was no going back now. He hadn't been afforded a choice, and so he had to press on with the burden of knowledge on his back and with revenge on his mind.

The small brick house was exactly where he remembered it; to his left, about halfway up the street. He checked the address plate on the front just to make sure, but there was no mistaking it. Michael had memorized the very shape of this building, and even in the dark of the night, he knew he had come to the right place.

A pale flickering light came from within the glass pattern of the panes on the front door. Michael could just make out the soft sounds of a television drifting toward him from behind the thick wood. He tried to identify what was playing in the other room, but the sound was too muffled.

With annoyance, Michael looked up at the exterior light glowing above him on the stoop. It felt like he was in the spotlight, and he was extremely aware of his visibility from the street. But what could he do about it? If he unscrewed the light bulb from its socket, he would certainly be harder to see, but there was also a strong chance that the door would not be answered at all. And if it wasn't, then he had done all this for nothing.

Michael's palms were sweating now, and he felt his grip on the instrument at his side begin to loosen. He set it down against his leg and wiped both hands on the front of his pants. Michael knew that he needed to be absolutely prepared, and that a slick grip was not possible for this to work.

He debated one final time whether he should have brought a covering for his face, but in the end, he was glad he hadn't. Better to be seen and recognized. That would make this all the more rewarding, seeing the reaction and knowing deep down in his bones that he had won. Michael picked up the object and hid it once more behind his right leg, took a deep breath, and pressed a finger to the small, glowing doorbell button.

Immediately, he turned his head to the side, and even took a small cautionary step back out of the direct halo of the stoop light. Michael needed to be seen, but he didn't need to be seen well. There were so many factors at play here, and he couldn't afford to do anything that might jeopardize the door not being opened in the first place.

Michael thought he heard a sound behind him and turned so fast he gave himself whiplash. The neighborhood scene was still and quiet. His eyes raced to locate the source of the sound, until they came upon two glowing green orbs underneath the belly of a car parked across the street. Light bounced back at him in their reflection, and the cat's eyes shone with watchfulness.

With the discovery came relief. As long as it wasn't a person, he was okay... at least for now.

The sound of footsteps brought his attention back to the space where he was standing, and Michael had to fight his instincts to turn and face full front as a figure materialized just at the edge of his vision behind the windows of the front door.

A light came on from inside. The shape behind the windowpanes seemed to hesitate, and Michael shook off the thought that this whole thing had already gone wrong. It was late, but it wasn't *that* late. And anyone burly and aggressive enough to confront a total stranger wouldn't be afraid to answer the door at this time of night.

His ears registered the sound of the deadbolt being drawn, and then the door was swinging inward. A figure was there in his peripheral vision, but Michael still hadn't turned his head around completely so as to see the face. He had to be precise, and he had to be quick.

"Can I help you?"

The voice was the same, and that was all he really needed. Michael turned his head to look at the figure, and there were the bulging white eyeballs set in the familiar, stocky, leathery face. They grew wide with recognition and instant alarm, but before the jogger could react further, Michael threw his left arm forward and shoved the man in the chest. Taken by surprise, he staggered backward away from the door and into the foyer of his house.

In one fluid movement, Michael stepped over the threshold and into the hallway, sweeping his left hand down to meet his right as he lifted the object into view from behind his leg.

His first swing was too wild, too sloppy, as the wooden bat collided with the man's outstretched hand, even though Michael had been aiming for his side. With a sharp *crack*, it made contact with the bones in his forearm and palm, and the man screamed in agony.

Michael had to have more control; he couldn't let this situation get away from him.

Pulling his injured limb in toward his body, the man retreated back in pain and lowered his gaze out of instinct to see what had happened. Michael swung again, and this time the bat connected with the meat of the man's left shoulder. The jogger screamed again and fell to the ground, trying to shield his face and head from his assailant.

The man was making way too much noise, and from somewhere in the back of his mind, Michael remembered the front door was still wide open. He struck downward again with two quick blows, both at the man's feet, and the crumpled heap on the floor pulled them up toward his body defensively with another series of cries and moans. Michael took advantage of the moment and turned to grab the open door, flinging it shut with one hand before turning back to the figure on the tile below him.

The man was trying to crawl away, but Michael was upon him once again. What started as a wail for help became more of a gurgled howl of anguish, as Michael brought the bat down on him again and again. The jogger curled up in the fetal position, struggling helplessly to shield himself from the blows, but there was nothing he could do. Michael began to see bright red spots forming on the man's skin, and above the cacophony, he suddenly became aware of barking.

At the last possible second, Michael looked up to see the French bulldog as it came charging down the hallway. It caught him by surprise, and before he could react, the animal had clamped its small jaws down on his shin and was tearing at his pant leg.

Michael shook his leg, more startled than actually hurt, but the dog would not let go. It growled deeply as it attacked. For a moment, Michael couldn't help but feel some jealousy at this animal's protective nature over its master, as Tucker had done absolutely nothing of the sort earlier that day.

Then again, neither had this animal. Maybe the bulldog had sensed its owner was never in any kind of real trouble against Michael before. Or maybe it was just used to the man getting in fights with complete strangers while out on jogs. There was no way of knowing.

But there was no mistaking the danger in this situation, and the canine was aware of it. Michael kept shaking it from his leg like a rag doll, but the dog's jaws held firm. Out of pure desperation, Michael brought the bat down on it, consciously attempting not to use the same amount of force he had used on its master.

It was enough, though. With a high-pitched yelp,

the dog let go and scurried back a few steps. But then it came at him again, and Michael began to realize that the night was quickly spiraling out of his control. Between the dog's frenzied barking and the man's anguished cries for help, there was a good chance that a neighbor or someone outside had already heard something, and maybe the police had been called.

Seeing the blunt wooden bat make contact with the tiny furry dog had also snapped Michael out from his vengeful, righteous state, and he suddenly began to feel very foolish and very cruel. The jogger had got what he deserved, no question, but the dog was just a dog, dumb and innocent. Michael would never abuse an animal, and yet he had done just that... albeit out of self-defense.

The man was still moaning on the ground, wrapped up in his own body, making himself as small and protected as he could. Blood streamed from several gashes across his arms and head.

Michael stepped back toward the door, desperately fending off the snarling bulldog with the end of his weapon, trying with all his might not to cause it any substantial harm. He used his free hand to find the doorknob, and with grasping fingers, managed to wrench it open. Michael then kicked his foot frantically at the dog's face, trying his very best to keep the snapping teeth at bay.

When he was outside again, he took one last look at the man before swinging the door back toward the frame. But the dog would not let up, so Michael knocked it once across the face with the end of the bat, and when it yapped and finally drew back, he slammed the door shut.

The barking continued from the other side of the door as Michael turned to face the street, his vision sweeping both ways to process his surroundings. As far as he could tell, he was alone, and the racket of noise had brought no one down upon him yet. The houses across the street were still illuminated from within, but he saw no movement there. Even the cat had seemingly disappeared.

Wasting no time, he took off at a brisk pace toward the main road, conscious not to draw any more unnecessary attention to himself. He wanted to run, but he knew what that might look like, and he didn't need to arouse any suspicion.

Michael noticed his muscles trembling, and he made a new, concerted effort to calm himself and steady his breathing. Adrenaline still raged through every fiber of his being, and his knuckles were white with tension.

He looked down at the baseball bat and noticed dark red-brown stains on the wood, glistening wet under the pale pink glow of overhead streetlights. Michael crouched down on the sidewalk and jerked the bat through tall blades of grass in the front lawn next to him. Back and forth he worked it, turning the instrument with his hands to try and wipe it clean.

All his efforts seemed to do was smear the blood around, and it filled in the dried cracks along the wood, much to Michael's intense dismay. He swore under his breath and began walking again, closing in on the road before him.

Just as he came to the end of the sidewalk, an SUV came whirling around the corner. The headlights lanced through the air and cut across Michael's frame, and he almost froze. As the car turned onto the street behind him, he was just able to make out the face of a woman behind the wheel, and he watched her eyes take him in with an indecipherable look before the vehicle was moving off. The sudden appearance of the car had taken Michael off-guard, and he was again acutely aware of his all-black clothing and the bloodied baseball bat in his hand.

Sensing an opportunity, Michael veered off toward a row of bushes on his right. The thick, flowering hedge surrounded part of a small stucco house with no lights on inside. He made sure the SUV had trundled off up the street and into a driveway further up, then quickly rounded the front corner of the house and followed the bushes along the side of it until he came to a fence. Michael then stabbed the bat into the scraggy green and brown branches of the shrubbery, every now and then pulling it back to examine the surface.

It didn't seem to be working. If anything, the stains had been worked deeper into the grain of the wood. Michael realized how ludicrous he must have looked right now, furiously scrubbing a baseball bat into some poor homeowner's manzanitas, and images of true crime reenactment shows began to pop up in his head.

He was acting absurd; he hadn't killed anyone, as much as he would have liked to kill that jogger. There would be no manhunt for him, no search for a murder weapon. He probably could walk back along the road, baseball bat in hand, and no one would notice anything out of the ordinary. This was Los Angeles, after all.

Still, the prospect of walking along a busy road with a bloody baseball bat at this time of night made him uneasy. He had come across runners, dog walkers, and more than a few other pedestrians on the walk over here, and there were sure to be more on the walk back.

Plus, traffic still flowed in both directions up ahead. All it took was one bored LAPD officer passing by in a cop car, seeing him, and getting curious, and that would be it. How could he possibly remain calm and reasonably explain the stained baseball bat in his possession? He was also publicly intoxicated, and that would not help his case in the slightest.

Michael made a decision, stooped down, and carefully nestled the bat as far under the bushes as he could. He slid it back into the underbrush, and then stood up and took a few steps back to examine his handiwork.

Apart from some fallen petals and leaves, the plants looked much the same as they had before. The baseball bat was not visible to the naked eye. If the yard was watered by sprinklers, it might never be found. The only way it could possibly be discovered would be by hand, should the homeowner or a gardener crawl under the bushes to water them individually. That was good enough for Michael.

Again, he turned back toward the main road, looking back just to make sure that no one was following him. The SUV must have pulled into a garage, because it was no longer on the driveway he had seen it turn into.

All was quiet; all was still. Michael wondered if the man had called the police by now. If so, it was high time for him to be on his way.

Sans weapon, Michael felt much more confident

walking alongside the trafficked street. He pushed up the sleeves of his sweatshirt to his elbows and wiped sweat from his forehead and upper lip. Michael walked at a measured clip, faster than he normally would. His heart still fluttered in his chest, and his clothes were sticking to his skin. He couldn't wait to get home and take a cold shower.

For the first time since his walk over, he allowed himself to smile… and even laugh a little. It felt good to breathe the cool night air and feel the wind on his face as he strode along the pavement. Every step he took was a step further away from the scene of the crime and a step closer to safety.

More than that, it was a step closer to 'getting away with it'. The jogger had 'gotten away with it' earlier, but now it was Michael's turn, and he was determined to have the last laugh.

He replayed the look of shock on the man's face when he had recognized Michael. It was just too good. And then that first sensation of the bat connecting with his bones… Michael had never experienced anything like that. All the pent-up rage, frustration, and humiliation he had felt earlier had come roaring out of him with every strike of the baseball bat.

Every blow was justified; every drop of blood spilt was payment for what Michael had lost at this man's hands. An eye for an eye, after all. Decades of feeling helpless and worthless had been corrected, at least for those precious few moments of sweet revenge. The jogger had gotten exactly what he deserved, and Michael felt exonerated. He was in control now.

Before he even knew it, he was outside his apartment complex, and he moved past the grass outside the front door with a concentrated look at where everything had transpired just hours earlier. Tucker's droppings were still visible, smeared into the lawn where Michael's skull had been.

That memory just made Michael even happier, knowing now he had left the perpetrator in a shattered mess on the floor of his own home. The man would think twice about ever asking anyone to clean up after their dog again. Maybe he would even think twice about ever coming back this way.

The thought of someone out there living in fear of him was a new discovery for Michael, something he had never dreamt possible. He liked the idea of it; he liked the idea of being considered wild and dangerous.

Michael took the stairs up to his apartment level, peeling the black sweatshirt off as he went. If someone saw him half-naked, he didn't care. His chest, stomach, and back were all sticky with sweat, and he dug moist black lint out from his navel as he padded down the hallway. The energy and excitement of the walk back had begun to recede just a tad, and Michael remembered how drunk he really felt, both on life and on the Scotch whisky itself. He came at last to his apartment door and inserted the key.

Surprisingly, it was already unlocked, and the door swung right open. Michael was alarmed at first and stood in his doorway warily looking about.

The lights were on, but he had left them on. After racking his brain for a minute, which was admittedly a little foggy, he came to the conclusion that he must not have locked the door on his way out. It made sense; he had been a man on a mission, and his mission was now accomplished.

Satisfied with himself, Michael tossed his sweatshirt onto the kitchen counter and grabbed the empty glass he had left in the sink basin, filled it with water from the faucet, and gulped it all down greedily without taking a breath. When it was empty, he refilled it, took another hearty sip, and then moved into the living room toward the thermostat.

"Phew… it's hot in here." He said it to himself and to Tucker, who was staring up at him from the couch with big, wet, brown eyes.

Beside the dog sat a man.

CHAPTER FOURTEEN

Michael dropped his glass, which fell with a soft thud and rolled onto the carpet, spilling out the remainder of water over the floor. He couldn't get out a scream because his tongue caught in his throat, and the resulting sound was more of a grunted whimper.

"Hey, Mike."

Drew had one hand on the dog, the other along the side of the sofa arm. His face was shadowed but visible in the light spilling in from the kitchen. Michael lit a lamp and picked up the fallen glassware.

"Jesus, Drew, you scared me. How'd you get in here?"

"The front door was unlocked. I knocked, but there was no answer. I tried calling you, too, but you must not have had your phone on you."

Michael's eyes went to the kitchen counter. He had indeed left his cell phone behind. Drew's eyes followed him as he walked over to retrieve the device and check the screen. Michael had missed two calls from his friend, but that was it. He couldn't have been gone for that long, anyway.

"What the hell happened to you?"

Michael turned back to him. Drew must have read

the blank expression on his face, because he gestured up at it.

"You look like a battered housewife."

Dumbly, Michael lifted a hand to his features before understanding finally kicked in.

"Oh, yeah, my face. It's a long story, actually."

He walked back into the kitchen to refill the glass. From the faucet, Michael turned to look at Drew, and his eyes glinted maliciously.

"You should see the other guy."

Tucker licked at Drew's hand, hoping perhaps for a treatment like the one he had received from Jeanette. But Drew kept his focus on Michael, and his hand was motionless on the dog's fur coat. He drummed the fingers of his left hand along the edge of the sofa arm, waiting for Michael to re-enter the living room.

"Can I get you something to drink?"

Drew shook his head. "No, I'm fine." He swept his gaze up and down Michael's body, then returned it to his face. His look was penetrating, incisive… and it made Michael a bit uneasy. Somehow, it seemed unfamiliar.

"Have you been drinking?"

Michael sat down across from Drew on a chair and laughed.

"Is it that obvious?" He took another big swallow of the water and relaxed into the cushioned armchair. "You'd be proud of me, actually. I killed a small bottle of Scotch all by myself tonight."

Drew looked unimpressed. "That's two nights in a row, now. People will think you're an alcoholic."

Michael shrugged. "What can I say? I learned from the best." He raised his water glass to salute Drew, took a sip, and set it down on the coffee table in front of him.

Drew didn't blink. "Why so chipper?"

Michael laughed and scratched at his bare stomach.

"I've known you for ten years, and I've never, *ever* heard you use the word 'chipper' before." He paused. "I don't know, why are you so serious? And more importantly, what are you doing in my apartment right now? I'm the one who should be asking the questions, not you."

"I'm here for a number of reasons. Not the least of which is because Lillian called me from work today about a text message she received from you."

Drew let those words sink in, watching Michael's reactions to them carefully before continuing.

"Originally, I was going to give you a call anyway and see how you were doing, in light of what happened last night. But after my conversation with Lillian, I decided I needed to come over here in person."

Michael's eyes moved to the water glass in front of him. Honestly, he had completely forgotten the text message to Lillian in all of the night's excitement. Michael was even ashamed to admit he had forgotten how this whole day had started: waking up to the horrific, unimaginable reality that they had hit and killed a man the night before.

It had all been lost in the last few hours. His mind had been so singularly focused, and even now, it was hard for him to accept these other truths.

Drew went on. "Normally, I wouldn't give three shits about what Lillian has to say, but she's Michelle's best friend, and Michelle is my wife now, in case you've forgotten. So, *naturally*, she only called me after she'd

227

already talked to Michelle. Which meant that I had to defuse the situation, not once, but twice today."

Michael looked up. "Did you tell them the truth?"

"Are you fucking kidding me?" Drew's voice rose for the first time. "No, I did not tell them the truth. I don't even know what 'the truth' is. Some star *supposedly* exploded on our wedding day and it's *supposedly* destroying the planet, even though we haven't heard anything or seen anything since. I told you that I wasn't going to tell Michelle any of this; it was never my plan. And yet today, she's asking me question after question about Aaron and NASA and the sky that day, and I'm trying to play dumb and pretend like I don't know anything about what you're talking about." He shook his head. "I hate feeling like an idiot, Mike. And I really don't like lying to Michelle."

"You didn't have to lie to her–"

"You didn't have to get involved! You didn't have to text Lillian! She read to me what you wrote her. What good did that do? I know you hate her, she knows you hate her, she hates you back. Fine, good. Everyone knows you hate each other. But why did you have to send her that text? What was I supposed to say to that?!"

Michael felt the need to defend himself as his temper began to rise. He knew he had to control it, to measure his emotions, otherwise he would never be able to articulate himself in this state.

"Listen… ever since *this thing* happened, you've been telling me over and over again that this is our chance to do whatever we want, do whatever we please. That nobody has to do anything they don't want to do, ever again, because none of it matters.

228

Over and over and *over* again, you've forced me to do things against my will, and put me in the most uncomfortable situations. I've gone along with it, every time, because I couldn't argue with your logic. And now you're telling me that I was wrong for acting impulsively and doing this one little thing that I wanted to do?"

Drew put his hands on his thighs. "This 'one little thing' has blown up into a 'big fucking thing'. But not for you, for *me*. And that's not fair, because I'm not going into your life and fucking things up—"

Michael laughed sharply, sarcastically. "You've got to be kidding me! What do you call last night? 'Not fucking my life up?' You drove my car through another human being! Remember that?"

Drew raised his index finger in warning, and his jaw set rock-hard. His dark brown eyes looked even darker then, hidden as they were in the dim light of the room and beneath thick eyebrows.

"Don't, Michael. Don't go there."

Michael started to protest, but the look in Drew's face was murderous. His friend lowered his voice to just above a whisper.

"If you want to talk about what happened last night, we will talk about it now... and then never again. But we will *talk* about it, at a reasonable volume, because it's a delicate matter that shouldn't be screamed about like a hysterical confession." His eyes flicked meaningfully toward the sliding glass door of the balcony, which Michael must have left open.

Annoyed at being scolded like a child, Michael quickly stood and walked over to slam the door shut. He didn't want to hear reason right now, least of all from this man. Everything Drew had said was so beyond hypocritical it almost came across as hilarious, and Michael didn't know whether to laugh at the absurdity of it all or scream at the injustice.

He returned to his armchair and sat down heavily across from Drew, sighed, and rubbed at his temples with his fingers. Michael growled and closed his eyes. His head was starting to throb.

Drew started in again. "So, what do you want to talk about?"

"I don't want to talk about anything. I just want you to go." Michael said it through gritted teeth and closed eyes.

Everything had gone so right for him up to this point. He couldn't have hoped for a better night, and now it was all crashing down around him. The drunken enthusiasm of his victory had splintered and cracked under the tension in the living room now, and it seemed that his hangover had arrived earlier and with greater ferocity than he would have thought physically possible. Michael moaned into his hands and looked up again.

"Please, just go. I don't want to talk about it. I don't even want to think about it anymore." He smiled bitterly. "Maybe you're right. Maybe we should just never talk about it again."

Drew studied Michael warily. He licked his lips and leaned back slightly against the couch.

"I won't force you to talk about it if you don't want to." He paused for a long moment. "But I need to know you're not cracking up."

Michael tilted his head quizzically. "What? 'Cracking up?' What does that even mean?"

Drew leveled his gaze. "When I left you late last night, you were a mess. Which is understandable... considering what happened. Michelle ran to the grocery store this morning, and on the way there, she told me she thought she saw your car parked on our street, a couple houses down, but she didn't see you in it. When she came back, the car was gone. This was *hours* after I left you last night, Michael.

"Then I get this call from Lillian, and she tells me about that awful text you sent her, and I have to spend half an hour convincing her it must just be some weird, cruel prank your twisted mind came up with. Fast-forward an hour later, Michelle gets back from pilates class and I have to go through the whole thing *again* with her, but in greater detail, because she can't understand why you would think any of this is funny. I tell her I'll talk to you, I come over here, and your front door is unlocked, you're not answering your cell phone, your lights are all on, but you're not home. And now you walk through the door with no shirt on and your face looks like it got in a train wreck."

Michael shifted his weight in the armchair. "What's your point?"

"My point? My point is that I'm concerned, Mike. I'm your best friend and I'm worried about you."

"Are you worried about me or are you worried about yourself? You didn't seem that worried about me when you left last night. After everything that had happened, you just got out of the car and walked away, like it was just another night. You said yourself that I was a 'mess', and you say you understand why, but I bet you slept just fine last night." Michael's voice wavered, and his eyes began to water. "I mean, seriously, Drew... *what are you?* Did that affect you at all last night? What we did?"

"Of course it did."

"Really? Because, somehow, I don't believe you. I look at your face and your eyes, and I don't think it did. So, I think I'm in the right here for 'cracking up', as you call it. I think most normal people would have a pretty hard time *not* 'cracking up', given the circumstances. After everything that's happened, after everything we've learned, I think I'm doing pretty damn well for myself. Better than most people would have done in my shoes."

Michael stood up abruptly then and carried the empty glass to the sink, set it down, and turned back to face his friend on the couch. His voice was dismissive at first, but grew louder as he continued, until it was a full crescendo of emotion.

"You didn't come over here for me, you came over here for you. So, let me tell you what you want to hear. No, I will not text Lillian again, nor will I say anything more to her, Michelle, or anybody in your life about what's happening out there... even though every single one of them has a right to know. I guess they'll all find out soon enough, anyway. No, I will not talk about what happened last night ever again, so rest assured your little secret is safe with me. I'd say your conscience is clear, but I don't know if you even have a conscience anymore. And finally, no, I don't owe you any explanation for what happened to me, or what I've been up to. But don't worry, it in no way compromises or inconveniences you and the fucked up, make-believe universe you think revolves around you!"

Drew sprung up, but before he could move or

speak, there came a pounding sound from the wall to Michael's right. They both turned to face it.

It was a quick series of percussive thumps, followed by a few seconds of silence. The noise was coming from the other side of the kitchen wall, where Michael knew his apartment connected to his neighbor's space.

It stunned Michael at first, and then it started again: low, steady bangs echoing against the wall. Now, Michael knew it was no accident; the sound was deliberate. Enraged, he smacked his fist against the wall, answering back with a furious hammering of his own against the hollow surface.

"Mike!" Drew sounded hoarse, and Michael whipped his head around.

"What?! This is my apartment, not yours! I've said everything I'm going to say to you. Get out!"

Drew took a cautious step toward him and raised his palms. Michael went to the front door and swung it open, took a step back into the kitchen, and pointed out toward the hallway.

From the wall behind him, the thumping sound came again, and Michael wheeled around to answer it, smacking his palm this time against the wall, as loud as he could. The sounds from either side of the wall overlapped, till it seemed they were striking at the same time almost, like a violent form of Morse code between homes.

From out of his periphery, Michael saw movement, and he turned to see Drew approaching rapidly. His friend still had his palms upraised defensively, but he had moved all the way across the living room to the edge of the kitchen table, and he couldn't be further than six feet away now. Michael stepped back so that his spine was against the wall, and he could feel the reverberations of the impact coming on the other side.

Drew's hands went higher, but he didn't blink. "Easy, Mike, just calm down–"

"Get out!" Michael took in Drew's hulking frame, and he suddenly felt very threatened, pinned against the wall in the cramped corner of his small kitchen.

He was not about to let this happen… not again. Not in his own house this time, not after everything he had suffered earlier, and not after everything he had done to make it right. Michael was different now; he was in control.

Quickly, he dropped his fingers to the handle of the drawer and pulled it out and open. Michael reached from memory to the right, and without looking, found a kitchen knife and raised it up protectively. It wasn't quite a serrated steak knife, but the edge was sharp enough, and with enough force…

Drew's eyes widened at the sight of the blade, and he stopped moving instinctively. His jaw dropped, and he looked incredulously at Michael. Drew's lips moved silently, and he seemed to mouth the question, *'Really?'*

But Michael was resolute, and he took half a step forward.

It was enough. Drew retreated back toward the doorway, his eyes trained on Michael's, and without another word, he slipped out into the hallway and out of sight.

Michael held his position for several seconds, poised for anything. There was the sound of a door shutting, and then silence. He had forgotten the wall thumping entirely, but now he realized that it, too, had stopped.

Carefully, Michael moved toward the doorway, knife still in hand. He peeked around the corner of the frame toward where Drew had disappeared but saw only the closed metallic door leading to the complex stairs.

A noise to his left made him spin back around, weapon at the ready.

The small Asian woman had materialized, half-hidden behind her front door. Bizarre orange light spilled out from behind her, and Michael realized he had never seen inside their apartment before. He barely could now; all he could make out was a tall floor lamp with a burnt orange lampshade, fringed at the bottom, that silhouetted his mysterious neighbor and bathed the wall behind her in an unusual shade of colored light.

She scowled at him from behind the door, and it occurred to him that this was the first time he had ever seen her without her large black sunglasses on. Her eyes were beady, dark, and bloodshot, and now they glared accusingly at him. It looked like she was prepared to say something. But then she saw the knife, and she gasped audibly.

Michael lowered it quickly to his side and took a step back into his own doorway. The woman's initial fright turned to alarm, and then she seemed to find enough courage from behind the protective shield that was her front door to shriek something out.

"What are you doing?!"

It was only the second time he had heard her speak. Her voice was shrill and thick with accent. Michael felt frozen to the spot, as if her words had put a spell on him. Then she jutted her chin forward in what could only be described as a movement she intended to be intimidating or aggressive, and the bizarreness of it finally broke Michael from his stupor.

Swiftly, he stepped back inside his apartment and closed the door in front of him, then brought his eye to the clouded, milky peephole in the center of the wood.

Her appearance was even stranger through the distorted view of the barely functional glass. Michael watched her open the door just a bit wider, still staring at his apartment suspiciously. She was rigidly motionless for what felt like minutes, then she turned and barked something unintelligible behind her. The little woman opened the door a bit wider and faced his apartment once again.

A shadow swept along the wall behind her, and then the old man was there, standing beside the woman in blue jeans and a white undershirt.

Michael held his breath from behind the door, keeping one eye up to the peephole, struggling to see all that was happening. He watched the man's mouth move as he muttered something to the woman at his side, and she leaned up toward his ear to reply, all the time keeping her face on Michael's front door. She pointed a thin bony hand at his apartment and said something with her eyes wide, shaking her outstretched arm forcibly with every word.

The old man nodded, adjusted his thin wire glasses on his nose, and moved slowly across the way. Michael heard the woman cry out the word *"careful!"* as the man approached his front door.

At the knocking, Michael drew back from his peephole. He held his breath, as if it might give him away, and tensed his muscles in stillness, careful not to make a sound.

After several short raps at the doorway, the man waited, then knocked again, this time a bit more vigorously. Michael's palms were sweating, and he felt the knife slipping in his grasp, so he tightened his grip on it.

Slowly, Michael brought his eye back to the peephole, and there he was: hair white and oiled as always, his old balcony nemesis, closer than he had ever been before. The man's nose was pink and purple with broken blood vessels, enlarged comically in the fishbowl effect created by the peephole. His steely eyes were lifeless behind the thin silver wire frames, and his lips curled downward. They parted then, and he spoke.

"Hello in there. I know you're in there." He waited for a reply, and when none came, he knocked again. "*Hellooooo.*" The old man sighed with impatience and shifted his weight. "I know you're in there. Can you come out and tell me what's going on over here?"

The little Asian lady hissed something at him from her perch behind the door. When he didn't immediately respond, she repeated herself, louder this time, though whatever she was saying was still unintelligible to Michael.

This time, the old man lifted a hand to silence her, nodding his understanding. He knocked again, three sharp taps of his knuckles against the wood.

"Is everything all right in there?" He waited again for a response, and when none came, he continued. "We heard shouting. Is everything okay in there?"

As slowly and as quietly as he could, Michael drew the lock on the door shut. It made a soft click as it set into place, and the man must have heard it too, because he immediately dropped his face toward the sound.

"I know you're there... I can hear you on the other side."

Michael kept his eye pressed against the small peephole in diligent observation, though the contact was uncomfortable and tickled his lashes. He kept having to switch eyes, as both would begin to water after too long, and blinking made it nearly impossible to see out.

The woman hissed again at the old man, and now he seemed to listen right away, changing his tactic on the spot.

"We're going to report a disturbance. Do you want me to call the police? Because that's what I'll have to do."

Michael backed away from the door and closed his eyes in frustration. He deliberated with himself quickly before placing a hand against the door lock. Michael considered opening it, but changed his mind, and instead returned his eye to the peephole and spoke through the wooden door.

"There's no disturbance in here."

The man looked a bit surprised to finally get a response. He took a moment to look back at the woman in his own apartment, then faced front again.

"My wife and I heard shouting."

Michael swallowed and shook his head. "I had a disagreement with my friend, but he's gone now. So, nothing to worry about." He paused, then added one last thing. "Thanks for checking."

The old man seemed skeptical. "We heard banging on the wall."

Michael grimaced. He was having a hard time holding his tongue. Here was the man who had long tormented him from across the way, challenging his right to enjoy a cigarette on his own property, staring him down night after night without saying a word. He had to know how much Michael resented him for this. Surely, he wasn't stupid.

Yet at the same time, there was no way of knowing this for sure, and here now was the perfect chance to finally let him know, to unload on the old man and speak his truth. Michael fingered the blade of the knife with his thumb, replaying in his mind countless past episodes of their silent confrontations.

In every single one of them, Michael had lost, always wilting back into his apartment. He felt himself quivering with rage at the memories.

"Yeah, I heard banging on the wall too!" Michael snarled the words through the door, careful to lace them with as much impact and anger as he could.

His neighbor processed them as well, and then leaned his face forward slowly. Inch by inch it grew larger, until the man had brought his own cold grey eye up to the peephole. Michael heard the tiny clink of the man's glasses lens as it butted up against the small round dome of the peephole.

There was no way he could see through it, Michael knew, because that wasn't the way these things worked. He knew this, but still the man seemed to be staring right into him, his pupil and iris just centimeters away from Michael's own.

The man didn't blink... he just stared. His pupil seemed to dilate before Michael and grow larger until it filled up the whole space, and all Michael could see now was blackness. His own eye watered, and his lashes tickled against the glass. He tried not to blink, he tried to stare back, but he could feel himself faltering and failing.

His knife hand floated up at his side, and his free hand went to the lock. He brought the point of the knife to the door. As if it had a mind of its own, the blade moved up the grain of the wood, scraping across the surface ever so softly, like a rasping whisper. Michael seemed to be moving involuntarily now, as the fingers of his other hand drew the lock open gently, and again, there was a soft click.

Nothing moved then, and Michael waited, one hand tensed around the lock, the other pressing the silver knife against the door.

Finally, Michael blinked. Relief washed over him at once, and the black sphere before him began to shrink and pull back with the man's dwindling face.

The neighbor had heard the sounds, too; Michael was sure of it. He had the strangest feeling that the old man had also seen everything on the other side of the door. From the tiny peephole, Michael watched him take a step back from the door and crack his index finger knuckles with his thumbs. His expression was unreadable, but Michael thought he saw the muscles in the man's jaw spasm several times.

Then, the old man turned slowly and walked back toward his own doorway, where the woman was waiting for him expectantly with an upturned chin. She mumbled something to him as he walked past her, but he didn't answer.

Michael followed him out of sight behind the door and watched his shadow play along the orange wall until it disappeared completely, and then only the woman remained. She looked vengefully across at Michael's apartment, made one last strange derisive smacking sound with her mouth in his direction, and then ducked her head back inside and flung the door shut.

Michael waited for at least a minute at the door, straining to see or hear what would happen next. At one point, he thought he heard the woman screaming something, and he debated whether to crack open his door to try and listen better. But just as he was watching their door, he knew that they could be watching his. He had repelled them successfully, at least for now, and he did not need them coming back.

It was the first time Michael had ever won. He had never seen the back of the old man's head before; he had never watched him walk away or retreat. Michael smiled to himself and pulled away from the door. His victory was complete. In one night, he had conquered many. He set the lock again on the door and replaced the knife in his kitchen drawer.

Feeling bold, he slid the glass balcony door open wide and stepped outside into the night air. Calmly, regally, he pivoted his head to examine the neighboring balcony.

It was empty, but Michael could still make out the faint orange glow of the lamp inside. Their glass door was open, as it usually was, with only the screen in place. Michael strained his ears to try and pick up conversation, but he could hear nothing over the sound of the cars below. He reached for his cigarette pack and was disappointed to find it empty.

Oh well, Michael thought. You can't win them all.

When he was satisfied with his time out in the open on the balcony, he went back inside, leaving his own sliding door open this time. The sounds of the city were calming to him tonight, and they helped take his mind off his headache.

Michael realized he hadn't eaten in a very long time, so he helped himself to some leftover spaghetti sitting on a ledge in his refrigerator. Tucker sat at his feet as he ate, alert and primed to move on any food that might fall to the floor. Michael noticed his companion, cut a meatball in half, and shared the tasty treat with the dog, who gobbled it up gratefully.

His stomach full, Michael took some aspirin with a glass of water and got ready for bed. He took one last look from his balcony across the way at his neighbors' apartment. The light was gone now, and all seemed dark and quiet inside. If they had indeed decided to call the police to report a noise complaint or a disturbance, surely at least one of them – and probably both – would have stayed up to deal with law enforcement. Evidently, the confrontation through his front door had been enough to placate the two of them.

Michael turned out the rest of the lights in his home and then collapsed into bed. His muscles ached from the activity of the long day, and he was beginning to sweat out the alcohol in his body.

Tucker had beat him into bed and seemed to already be peacefully asleep on the pillow next to him. The dog gurgled contentedly as Michael gave him a light scratch behind the ear. Michael couldn't help but smile. He was thankful for the companionship, and realized bitterly that he was pretty much alone now in the world.

Aaron was dead. Michael had driven Drew from his home at knifepoint just an hour earlier. And, not surprisingly, Jeanette hadn't returned any of his phone calls.

The small Sheltie was all he had left.

Sleep came quickly, and with it, vivid dreams. Michael wandered aimlessly through a strange village. He was somewhere in South America, he thought.

Everyone around him was dying. Old women wailed in the streets and asked him for help in a language he could not comprehend. Some fell to their knees to beg to him, while others begged to their god or gods. Large flies buzzed around the shrunken bodies of children, some wrapped in bloodied, tattered rags, and the sun beat down harsher and hotter than he had ever felt before.

He tried to find shelter, to hide beneath shanty roofs or in the shade underneath rainforest canopies above, but there was no escaping the persistent heat. His skin changed copper and then black before his eyes, and everywhere around him, there came high-pitched screams from distant corners of the jungle. He touched his fingers to his forearms and felt the charred flesh slide off his bones, and he, too, was screaming for help now, but no sound came out. Dead skin fell like paper ashes from a fire, and he looked up to see dark shapes falling from the branches high above him.

Howling apes, birds, and other mysterious creatures came crashing down to the forest floor, all exploding in thick clouds of dust upon impact with the ground. He was breathing them all in now, and the smoke was choking his lungs. Michael tried to run away, but his legs were heavy with the weight of his body breaking down.

At last, he twisted and gave up, surrendering to gravity. The earth rose up to meet him, and his fall was broken by a carpet of dry, black leaves. Vaguely, he became aware of his body rotting and decomposing, and small centipedes, spiders, and other insects began to scuttle over what was left of him.

He looked up into the sky, through the swarm of dying animals and scattered branches, and the sun grew brighter and brighter until all he could see was white light. Then it swallowed him whole, and he felt himself die.

CHAPTER FIFTEEN

From somewhere in that great bright silence came knocking, softly at first, like the echo of rain falling into a deep well far below. Michael had closed his eyes in a last desperate attempt to avoid his death, but it had come for him all the same, and with it, came the excruciating pain of being burned alive.

There was no relief or release in that moment, just indescribable pain and merciless silence. But the knocking was an intrusion, something that didn't belong here in the illusory playground of his subconscious. It continued until Michael could no longer dismiss it, and he felt his mind tear away from the world of his dreams and nightmares like a power cord being ripped from a wall socket.

The cruel, white light was gone, replaced by total darkness. His body was sweating beneath sheets and a blanket. He kicked the covers off and let the cool night breeze trickle over his legs, arms, and torso. The knocking came again, and he realized it had not been a dream, but rather had been what had woken him up from one.

It was much louder now, and he sat upright in bed. Michael checked the alarm clock on his nightstand:

12:43 a.m. He wasn't sure what time he had crawled into bed or how long he had been sleeping now. His jaws opened wide to release a yawn, and Michael reached for the lamp on his bedside table, flicking it on. Slowly, unsteadily, he swung his legs out from under the covers until his feet made contact with the floor.

Tucker was nowhere to be seen. Again, there came a firm knock from the other room, rhythmic and persistent. Michael couldn't possibly imagine who would be at his door at this time of night. He rose to standing and stretched his spine out before pulling on the discarded black pants on the floor. Next, he reached under his bed for two old slippers he seldom used and wiggled them on over his feet as his eyes adjusted to the growing light.

His body had left dark sweat stains on the bed sheets, and he took a second to try and reflect on the intensity of his dreams, but they were quickly fading from memory and retention. Faintly, Michael reminisced on dark canopy leaves and the brightness of the sun, and still he could feel a blistering, relentless pain across his skin... but the vivid details and specifics of the visions were all but gone by now.

The events of the night came trickling back as his mind reverted back to its conscious state. With a pang of dread, he remembered the encounter with his neighbors, and he wondered now if the old man or his wife had returned to further harass him. Michael stumbled into the main room of his apartment to try and find his black sweatshirt, equal parts asleep, drunk, and hungover at this point, and fumbled the light switch on. He couldn't remember where he had last left the shirt.

Michael did see Tucker, though, waiting for him with tail wagging and face pressed against the front door. The Sheltie had never been much of a barker, for which Michael was thankful. The small terrier next door more than made up for the both of them, yapping every single time Michael passed by in the hallway.

Again, there came knocking at the door, and Michael decided to momentarily forgo the shirt and instead check the peephole to spy who was on the other side. Warily, he pressed a bleary eye up to the glass, steeling himself for the expected sight of the wire-thin glasses and oiled white hair of the terrier's master from next door.

Instead, two unfamiliar green eyes stared back at him from the other side of the glass. The man was dressed in a crisp navy-blue uniform and was flanked on either side by men in similar attire. Gleaming silver police badges adorned their shirtfronts, and each man's belt carried the full arsenal of expected equipment: nightstick, radio, handcuffs, gun.

Michael felt a lump form in his throat, and the beating of his heart began to quicken. Why were there police at his door? It made no sense. He had neutralized the threat from his next-door neighbors at least an hour or two earlier; he was sure of it. Michael had done just enough from behind the wooden shield of his front door to send both the old man and his hissing little wife back to where they came from.

He had then enjoyed the thrill of his first real victory from the hotly contested site of the battlefield itself: his balcony. The apartment next door had gone dark, the orange lamplight was extinguished, and all had been quiet ever since.

Michael had listened specifically for further sound of their voices, or for any kind of indication that they might be making good on their threats and calling the cops on him. But time had passed, nothing had changed, and he had fallen asleep confident in his total conquest and evasion of all possible consequences.

Nevertheless, there was no mistaking the very real presence and problem of the men on the other side of his front door. Michael watched the officer in front raise his hand to patiently knock once more on his door. He wondered how many times the man had knocked now, and how long they had been standing outside his door.

Perhaps they were almost ready to give up, and if Michael could just hold out a bit longer, they might determine that no one was home, and move on. That being said, he had turned on all the lights in his apartment and had made no efforts to muffle his approach to the door. Were the officers aware of this? Could they see the sudden light spilling out from beneath his door?

Michael's thoughts raced as he struggled with what to do. Even if they did move on eventually, he was certain that they would be back.

And what was he really afraid of anyway? The officers were checking up on a noise complaint. Surely, this was a routine operation for them, and as soon as they saw Michael – half-dressed and clearly just woken up – they would be able to rationally determine that whatever kind of commotion had transpired earlier was no longer occurring. They could search his apartment, for he had nothing to hide; no battered girlfriend, wife, or child tucked away in another room.

Really, it would be his word against his neighbors', and if it came to that, he was confident in his ability to talk his way out of whatever minor ticket or citation the police would try and give him. His record was clear; he had never had so much as a speeding ticket. These LAPD officers were simply doing their job, and they were probably just as eager as he was to wrap this up and get on with more important duties.

Carefully, Michael wiped the last bits of perspiration from his brow and the back of his neck, dried his hand on the front of his pants, and drew the lock open. He wrapped his fingers around the cold door handle and turned to open it, letting out one last quick breath to try and calm the butterflies in his stomach and chest.

The officer who had knocked seemed mildly surprised when the door opened. He had his hand raised to knock again, and now he lowered it back to his side.

Two of the three men were taller than they had initially appeared through the warped view of the peephole: the officer in front of Michael stood at least three inches above him, and the man to his right was even taller. This officer sported a thick black mustache to match bushy caterpillar eyebrows and dark obsidian eyes. Something about his stature and appearance reminded Michael of Drew.

The third policeman stood the furthest from the door and was shorter than his comrades. He must have been just looking at the neighboring apartment, because his head now swiveled to face front at the sound of Michael opening his door. This man had bright red hair, kept short and bristly by a military-style crew cut. His skin was pale, and his high forehead shone with the reflective gleam of the hallway light above him.

Michael couldn't be sure, but it seemed like this man was sweating, and perhaps more nervous than the others. Even more unsettlingly, this officer kept one freckled hand flat on his upper thigh, but the other rested faux-casually on the handle of his weapon. His fingers weren't necessarily clutching the butt of the handgun, but there was no way that they were there by accident either, and Michael noticed it.

The man in front with the green eyes smiled thinly at Michael and rested his hands on his hips. There was almost a look of recognition in his eyes, like he was seeing an old friend for the first time, and the queerness of it unnerved Michael. He had never seen this man before, so there was no reasonable explanation for that expression of familiarity, however subtle.

Michael wondered what to say. Everything that came to mind seemed like some cliché out of a movie or a TV crime procedural: 'Evening, officers,' or 'What can I do you for?,' or 'Is there a problem, officers?' Each phrase seemed more suspicious than the last.

Mercifully, the man in front of him spoke first.

"Good morning." The words were a bit unexpected, and his voice was softer and kinder than Michael would have imagined. "Sorry to bother you so late, or so early." There was a lengthy pause then, until it finally dawned on Michael that the officer appeared to be waiting for a response.

Michael cleared his throat, blinked, and croaked

out a hoarse reply.

"Th– that's okay." Another throat clear. "Excuse me. I was sleeping."

Michael half-heartedly thumbed a gesture back toward his bedroom, as if it was somehow proof or confirmation that he was telling the truth. It was impossible not to second-guess his every word, his every movement, his every facial expression. He had to try and relax and get out of his own head. Again, he reminded himself that he had done nothing wrong. Innocent people have nothing to fear and nothing to hide.

The officer in front of him nodded politely. "I'm sure you were."

He seemed to mean it when he said it, but Michael couldn't quite be sure. There was no overt sarcasm or suspicion in the officer's tone, yet something about it just didn't feel as relaxed and conversational as the man's easy smile wished to convey.

"Do you live here alone?"

Michael responded quickly. "Yes, sir."

Again, the officer nodded good-naturedly, and he let his gaze move down to the animal at Michael's feet. Michael had forgotten his dog, who was well-trained enough to sit patiently at his feet, rather than to bullrush strangers at the door. But now, Tucker saw that this stranger's attention was on him, rather than on his owner, and he began to wag his tail hopefully.

The policeman looked back up at Michael. "Is this your dog? May I pet him?"

The two questions came successively without a break between them. They caught Michael a bit off guard, but he nodded his acquiescence all the same.

Before he finished gurgling out an additional "of course," the officer had squatted down on his hamstrings and extended upturned fingers to the dog. Tucker barely sniffed at the proffered hand before licking at it and then moving forward, tail wagging furiously now, as the officer began a vigorous scratch around his ears and chin.

Michael's eyes were still on this interaction when a voice brought his attention back up. It came from the man with the darker features and the thick black mustache.

"What kind of dog is that?" The question startled him momentarily, as up until now, only the first officer had spoken.

Michael cleared his throat again before speaking, hoping this time he had finally dispatched all of the phlegm and grogginess.

"He's a Sheltie." And then he added further clarification. "That's short for Shetland Sheepdog."

The mustached officer nodded his understanding. "Kind of looks like Lassie."

It wasn't quite a question or a statement, so Michael wasn't sure if or how to answer him. He just nodded his own head in agreement.

The first officer stood back up, and Michael brought his eyes back to the man in front of him. From below, he could just make out a faint whimper from Tucker, who was unsurprisingly disappointed by the sudden stop in attention.

The officer returned his hands to his hips and spoke again. "What's your name?"

"Michael. Michael Cavanaugh."

"How long have you been asleep for, Mr.

Cavanaugh?"

Quickly, the focus had shifted from his dog back to himself, and Michael began to feel his temperature rise under the officer's gaze. Gone was the bizarre but kindly familiarity with which he had first looked at Michael. Since rising from his squat, the knocking officer's eyes were colder now, and the warm laugh lines and wrinkles etched in his face had all but vanished, replaced by a firm mask of resolute dutifulness.

It took Michael a second to answer. "I– I'm not exactly sure. At least a couple hours, if not more."

"Do you work late?"

"No, I don't usually."

"But you did today?"

"No."

"Did you work today?"

"What?"

"Did you go to work today?"

The questions had come furiously, relentlessly, and without warning. Michael's uneasiness intensified, and he debated whether or not to lie.

Up until this point, he had no reason to be untruthful. Michael had no reason that he knew of to be untruthful now, but for whatever reason, it just didn't sound like a good idea to admit to the police that he had not gone into work as scheduled, but rather had gone in extremely late and made a huge scene out of quitting his job.

"I did."

"Where do you work?"

"I work at First Glendale Federal Credit Union."

Michael turned to look at the third officer, perhaps

subconsciously, because this man at least appeared to be almost as nervous as he was.

"Is there a problem, officers?" Michael regretted the words the moment they came out of his mouth. Of all the contrived expressions, he just *had* to use that one. "I mean, is there a reason you're here? Or something I can help you with?"

No matter what he said, it sounded bad. Somehow, every conceivable expression sounded guilty, or defensive, or both. Michael reminded himself that he had rights, and that one of those certainly was a right to know what these men were doing on his doorstep at this time of night.

The first officer with the green eyes took in all three questions, analyzing Michael carefully before deciding how to respond.

"We're following up on two separate but related reports of aggravated assault, one occurring earlier tonight around 9 p.m., and the other sometime between 12 p.m. and 1 p.m." The man paused to let the information sink in and observe Michael's reaction to it. "We have reason to believe that the first incident occurred outside this apartment building, and that the assailant in both incidents is a resident here."

Michael felt like someone had just sledgehammered him in the gut. The blood rose to his cheeks, and he could feel his ears turn bright red and his face go white-hot.

In short, he was floored. Michael had opened the door cautiously but optimistically, prepared to defuse anything but this. What once was a mere noise complaint or a report of a domestic disturbance was in fact much more serious. A lot more serious.

Everything was starting to make sense, and Michael felt very, very exposed. He had forgotten all about his injuries, but each and every one of them now jostled for his attention. His black eye felt blacker and broader than ever. The gash on his cheekbone must have been a mile long and deep as a ravine. His fat lip felt comically large, and he marveled at how it hadn't affected his speech more up to this point. His face was battered and bruised, and now it seemed to light up like a flashing neon sign that read 'GUILTY'.

Even the officers' interactions with Tucker made more sense. Surely, they knew what they were looking for: a man that fit Michael's description, with injuries to his face and body, living in this apartment building, and with a dog that fit Tucker's description.

Michael swallowed hard and hated himself for being so stupid. What had been the point of the dark clothes and the stealth of waiting until the cover of night to attack the man at his home? He had purposefully left his face uncovered so the jogger could recognize him and understand why he was being punished.

But of course, the man would call the police... and of course, he would know *exactly* where to find his attacker. The jogger had seen Michael lead a Sheltie back up toward the front door of the apartment complex, clearly heading back inside. He knew what Michael looked like, what his dog looked like, and what the apartment looked like. The man could tell the police exactly where to find the perpetrator, only there was no way he knew which apartment Michael lived in.

But now, they had found him. And it was too late for Michael to run. And there was nowhere to hide.

Feebly, he tried to control the muscle spasms in his face. For half a second, he considered throwing the door shut and barricading himself behind it.

But the first officer who had knocked was too close to him, and the other two weren't far behind him, either. The redheaded cop still had his hand on his gun, and now Michael realized that the other police officer with the black mustache also had both hands on his belt. He didn't remember when this physical positioning change had happened, but clearly, it had happened at some point during the line of questioning.

Michael knew why they were here now. Worse, he knew that they knew he knew. He could see it in their faces; in their locked jaws, in the new placement of the dark-haired cop's hands, in the trembling fingers of the redheaded cop, itching atop his weapon. And he could see it in the green eyes of the first officer, watching his every move, waiting anxiously to see how Michael would react next.

His mouth dry as starched cotton, Michael stammered. "What do you want with me?"

It was all he could think to say. Michael felt as if any moment now he might pass out. His vision swam between dark and light, and fleeting stars crackled before his eyes. His knees were weak, and he could feel all his muscles quaking violently below him. Any second now, he would collapse into a heap on the floor, and they would have to drag him away.

There was a sudden noise to his left that caught Michael's attention. A door had swung open just a bit, and the little Asian woman peeked her face out from behind the crevice.

"That's him! He had the knife!" She squealed the

words across the narrow corridor, and her eyes were wild and white with vengeance.

The redheaded officer had nearly drawn his gun at the unexpected disruption, but the lead officer reacted quickly, lifting his left hand to stop the younger man while simultaneously saying the name "Tom" in the direction of the mustached cop. The dark-haired officer – presumably Tom – moved quickly toward the other apartment door.

"Ma'am, I'm going to ask you to stay inside."

The lead officer kept his attention on Michael all the time, leaving his companion to take care of this new intrusion.

"That's him, though! He's the one!" The woman screeched at Tom, who was advancing rapidly on her doorstep.

But just before he could reach it, she closed the heavy door shut again. Tom waited a second to see if she had truly retreated, and then turned his attention back to Michael. Still, he kept himself positioned between their apartments, perhaps wanting to be close enough to deal with the woman should she reappear once more.

The temporary commotion had jilted all of the officers in different ways… perhaps none more so than the redhead. He looked ready to draw his pistol at a moment's notice, and he didn't dare take his eyes away from Michael. The lead policeman brought both of his hands back to his hips and took the slightest of steps toward Michael.

"We just want to take you to the station and ask a few questions… if you'll cooperate." The officer put an extra bit of emphasis on those last three words, and his meaning was clear. Michael felt hot tears welling up, and somewhere in the back of his mind, he wanted to scream at himself, '*Not now! Please God, not now!*' But a salty bead broke free and traveled down his cheek all the same, and for the last time, Michael wondered if he could run away, or perhaps wake himself from this moment, as if it were just a bad dream. But his fear, his absolute and utter terror at what was happening, would not let him forget reality.

From somewhere in the fog, he found his voice, miniscule and childlike.

"Okay."

He wanted to beg for mercy… or else to beg for death. This wasn't happening. Somewhere, some way, he still had a hope of escape, of rescue or release. He thought to call on his mother, his father, or on God. He needed someone, *anyone*, now more than ever. Where was Drew? Where was Aaron?

Strong hands helped him move forward, and in a slow-motion daze, he felt himself being led down the soft carpet of the hallway. Vaguely, he was aware of the first officer on his left and of the younger redhead on his right. Each had hands on his arms, but somehow, it felt that there were hundreds of hands on him, and thousands upon thousands of clenching fingers steering him forward, pressing him inward and together, controlling his body and forcing him forward, always forward.

The mustached officer, Tom, must have been behind him, he thought, keeping an eye on him from the rear. He wondered if the little Asian woman and her husband were watching him now, satisfied with his capture and apparent arrest. Had they called the police after all, as well? Or had they only spoken with the officers when they appeared at their own door, looking for a man that fit the jogger's description?

Michael would never know. The thought occurred to him that he might never see these walls again, these wooden doors, these fluorescent lights. Only a few hours earlier, he had glided down this very same hallway, returning like a conquering hero, riding a high of ecstasy, justice, and strength. His heart and soul had felt ready to burst with joy, and now he felt sunken in and nauseous. Michael gagged and fought back bile in his throat, and the thousand fingers tightened on him reflexively, moving him faster now, down the stairwell and out into the cold, dark night. It was all a blur.

Some part of him wondered about his apartment and about Tucker.

"But – my dog…" The words came from someone else's throat, and he no longer recognized the speaker.

"He'll be fine."

Michael wasn't sure who had spoken to him. He wasn't even sure if someone had.

The biting wind outside gnawed at his flesh, and he became aware that he was shirtless. Two police cars emerged up ahead, black and white and formidable. Then, a door was being opened and he was being shoved inside. Once his legs were clear within the cabin, the door slammed shut behind him and locked.

Michael eased his spine upright. The black leather of the seat was cold as it touched his bare skin, and he felt goose bumps break out across his body. He tried to take in his surroundings; the thick Plexiglas partition separating the car's front seats from the back, the shiny black material of the car's side panels and doors, the driver-controlled locks, the dimly-lit computer screen, and the strange controls configured in the dashboard. Michael wondered absently if he was expected to put on a seatbelt.

The three officers had a brief conversation outside the vehicle. Whether their voices were intentionally hushed or not, Michael wasn't sure, but he couldn't make out anything from inside.

Eventually, the officer named Tom moved away toward the other police car. The redheaded cop circled round the front of the car Michael sat in and approached the passenger door to get in.

Once he was inside, Michael caught the officer looking back at him in the rear-view mirror. The man looked less nervous now, and the sweaty gleam on his high forehead had given way to a sea of freckles that extended down across his nose and cheeks. The ruddy brown flecks and dots were soon bathed in alternating red and blue as the car behind them turned on the roof lights. Taking his cue, the young officer reached forward to turn on the lights of this vehicle, as well.

From outside to Michael's left, the third policeman opened the driver door and entered the cabin space. He reached for his radio and softly muttered a stream of words and numbers that meant nothing to Michael, and then he reached for his seatbelt. His partner followed suit, and the green-eyed officer started the engine and slowly eased the vehicle out onto the main street in front of Michael's apartment.

Neither car used a siren and neither sped. As soon as both vehicles were out and moving along the road together, the flashing lights turned off. At no point did either officer in the front think to speak to Michael, or really to each other. Instead, they drove in deliberate silence, punctuated only occasionally by strange voices speaking codes across the radio.

They drove past dark houses and empty sidewalks. Michael's hands were clasped together in his lap, his feet heavy and flat on the floor. At times, he found himself staring mistily into space, peripherally noting a change in color on an overhead traffic light and the slowing of the car as it rolled to a temporary stop, only to gradually lurch forward again when the light turned green.

At one point, he looked out the window to his right and witnessed a familiar stretch of street leading off the main road. Somewhere up that particular lane was a little brick house on the left, home to a ferociously protective French bulldog that maybe was missing its owner right now.

They passed the side street quickly, and Michael couldn't quite see far enough up the darkened road to recognize the house. But he knew it was there all the same, halfway up and on the left.

He wondered if anyone would ever find the baseball bat he had tucked away under those scraggly bushes further down. Michael wondered just how seriously the jogger was hurt, or if his injuries were life-threatening. Was he in a hospital by now, and if so, was he in critical or stable condition? The man was still squirming and grunting when Michael had left, but who knew what kind of internal damage or bleeding may have been inflicted. He supposed it was not entirely out of the question that the man had died...

Michael shook that idea from his brain hastily. The first officer had said nothing of homicide, only of 'aggravated assault', whatever that meant exactly. He had an idea of what both words meant literally at face value, but their precise legal and criminal definition was more of a mystery to him.

For the first time, a stream of questions began to run through his mind, one right after the other. Did he need a lawyer? Had he been read his rights already and just not heard them? Would they put him in jail? Could he post bail? Who could he call? Would he go to court? If he lost, what would his sentence be?

Michael had never so much as been sent to the principal's office growing up. The idea of getting in trouble had always been a terrifying concept to him, and so he had lived most of his life consciously avoiding risky situations and amoral individuals. And up until the past week or so, he had mostly succeeded.

But then Drew's wedding happened. More importantly, then the light in the sky happened.

Michael marveled at how often he was able to forget about it. It had been less than two weeks, and still, it could slip from his mind so easily, like an important to-do list item that he could never remember to take care of.

Of course, there was nothing to 'take care of' in this situation. The sequence would take care of itself, as Aaron had accurately predicted. Nothing anyone could do would stop the chain of events, and it was only a matter of time until people started dying – if they hadn't already in other parts of the world.

Michael closed his eyes, found his breath, and collected his thoughts. If this was to be the end of days, he could not, *would not*, spend it behind bars.

Whatever happened, he had to get out.

CHAPTER SIXTEEN

Soon, the cars were pulling into designated parking spaces at the police station. Michael looked out his window, studied the façade of this unfamiliar building, and wondered where exactly in the city he was right now. For most of the drive over, he had been lost in his own thoughts and feelings, rarely taking in the world passing by outside the glass. Figures dressed in deep blue uniforms materialized before him, and then the door opened slowly outward into the night.

He was more prepared for their hands this time, and also more helpful himself. Whereas earlier he had been led sluggishly in a daze down from his apartment, this time he walked more freely under his own power. He recognized the officer Tom up ahead holding the door open for them. Michael was immediately grateful to be inside; without a shirt on, the breezy October night had felt at least ten degrees colder than it probably was. The air inside the station was warmer by comparison, though still a bit chilly for a half-naked man.

Michael was led past a smattering of people; some dressed in uniform, others more casually. He made eye contact with at least one officer: a young woman not much older than himself, who even seemed to smile back at him from her computer. Her gaze was more inquisitive than anything, yet her smile seemed genuinely pleasant and polite to Michael. For the most part, the police station seemed quiet for this time of night, and Michael found himself relieved at not being paraded past rows of onlookers.

Through several doors and hallways they went, until at last, his escort brought him to an unmarked metal door. Michael wondered if they had brought him to a jail cell, but when the door was opened, he saw instead a small room with a table and two chairs on either side of it. He was struck by just how much the room resembled interrogation rooms on some of the late-night shows he used to watch; plain grey walls, plain white floor tiles, plain dull pewter table, and two plain steel chairs.

Unlike in the movies or on TV, though, this room did not have one bright overhead light burning down on one of the chairs, the classic hot lamp used to sweat out confessions from handcuffed killers and rapists who wore menacing faces and grisly tattoos. This room had several overhead lights, all boring white fluorescent rectangles that just as easily could have served a high school classroom as a police interrogation room.

"Have a seat; someone will be in shortly."

It was the first policeman, the driver of his car, who spoke to him now. He gestured toward the table and chairs. Michael slowly moved over to the indicated destination and reached for the nearest chair back.

"The other chair, please."

Michael drew his hand back from the metal sharply, like he would from an open flame. He turned back toward the doorway, and the green-eyed officer gestured at the chair furthest from the room's entrance.

"Sorry." Michael muttered the word quickly and walked around the table to take the far seat. He couldn't help but flinch when his uncovered skin touched the cool steel of the chair's back, and the policeman must have noticed the reaction, too.

"Officer Langley is bringing you a shirt to wear."

The news took Michael a bit by surprise. It was an unexpected kindness, and he was sincerely grateful for it.

"Thank you."

He realized he was shivering a bit now, and Michael tried to make a concerted effort to stop. But it was harder than he thought; the chair he had been assigned was positioned directly underneath an air conditioner vent. Michael wondered if this was intentional... a subtle, seemingly harmless strategy for making the people brought into this room more uncomfortable.

Officer Langley turned out to be the redheaded cop who had rode shotgun in their cruiser on the way over. He came in a few minutes later with a generic oversized t-shirt that could have come from Goodwill or Salvation Army.

Langley walked a few steps into the room and then tossed the shirt over to Michael, who wasn't at all expecting it to be thrown. Nevertheless, he fumbled it out of midair and put it on. The shirt smelled clean at least, but was not very thick, and Michael still felt cold even with it on. He sat as far forward in his chair as he comfortably could, careful to avoid making more contact with the chilled metal seat back.

And then both officers turned and left him, with the green-eyed man giving him one last mysterious look before swinging the heavy door shut behind him. Michael heard the sound of a lock from the outside, and then it was quiet once again, save for the steady whir of the air conditioner and the faint buzz of the fluorescent tubes above him.

He looked around the small room and noted that all the walls were the same except for the one that contained the door he had come through. Two large panels of dark glass bordered the lone entrance/exit, each about five feet off the ground, three feet high, and five feet wide. Michael saw his own dull reflection in both panels, and figured they had to be made of one-way glass. He wondered if anyone was watching him right now from the other side of those windows, studying his face or his movements.

The thought made him look up toward the ceiling, and sure enough, he now spied two small black domes he hadn't noticed before, one in each corner of the room where the walls met the ceiling. Michael turned around, and there were two more cameras in the other corners of the room.

He faced front and clasped his hands together in his lap. Michael noticed his right leg bouncing up and down on the toe of his slipper nervously, so he stopped himself and made his body as still and calm as he possibly could.

How long he sat there for, he could not tell. It could have been ten minutes; it could have been two hours. Michael tried to keep his mind off the grim reality of his present situation, but the task was daunting. There were no distractions in the room to steal his focus, and nothing of note to look at or study.

Occasionally, he would find his gaze drifting up and into one of the small hidden camera domes in the high corners before him, but then he would catch himself and bring his attention back to the surface of the table or to a tile on the floor. Never in his life had Michael felt so totally scrutinized and unclear of what to do with his hands, his face, or his thoughts.

Finally, there came the soft click of a lock being switched, and the grueling monotony was dispatched by the opening of the door in front of him.

A middle-aged woman dressed sharply in a grey wool pantsuit and white blouse shut the door behind her and crossed into the room. In one hand, she carried a thin manila file folder. Everything about her appearance came across stoic and austere: the dreary hue of her clothing, the crisply-pressed collar of her shirt, the total absence of jewelry or makeup, the tight bun of brown hair with the occasional streaks of grey.

Everything, that is, but her nails. Her fingernails were painted a garish volt yellow, with the fourth fingernail on each hand tinted robin egg blue in contrast. They were dazzlingly bright amidst the otherwise drab backdrop of this woman in this room, and Michael couldn't help but stare at them as she lowered herself into the chair across the table from him. The woman laid the file folder down on her side of the table, placed her hands atop it, and let out a deep sigh.

"Hello, Mr. Cavanaugh. I'm Sergeant Torres."

She made no offer to shake his hand, nor did she wait for a response. Her tone was direct and efficient without being antagonistic, and Michael thought she sounded a little tired, too. Torres let her eyes move freely up and down his face and torso, taking him in without ever really leveling her gaze or staring. Clearly, she had been doing this for some time, and Michael wondered how long she had been in the force.

"Thank you for cooperating with our officers so far. First off, do you have any questions for me?"

It wasn't quite what Michael had expected to hear, and he shifted in his seat. It had been a long time since last he spoke, so he took a quick second to clear his throat.

"Well, I guess… I mean – do I need a lawyer?"

Sergeant Torres seemed unsurprised by the query.

"You don't need a lawyer unless *you* think you need a lawyer. We just want to ask you some questions and see what you have to say for yourself first."

That answer was significantly less than reassuring to Michael. Again, he shifted uneasily on the edge of the chair.

"*Should* I have a lawyer here, though? Am I a suspect?"

Sergeant Torres responded promptly once again, as if she had anticipated this question too.

"In my cases, I like to say that everyone is a suspect and no one is a suspect. It's all part of the investigation."

She drummed her vivid nails along the steel tabletop a couple times, then crossed one leg and relaxed back into her seat. Somehow, she looked a lot more comfortable in her chair than Michael felt in his, though he knew both pieces of furniture were identical.

"Let me put it to you this way: We both know why you're here. It's no great secret. There's really nothing to gain by waiting. This isn't a taped confession; I didn't bring a recorder in here, or even a notepad and pen. Trust me, there will be plenty of opportunities for all of that, for lawyers and official statements and interrogations, for 'he said/she said' mumbo-jumbo, if – *if* – you want to go down that path." She paused. "Right now, though, it's just like they told you earlier: We have some questions for you. But at the same time, yes, we already have enough to have brought you in, obviously. So, keep that in mind. Okay?"

The information had been rattled off so quickly that it took Michael a second to process all of what he heard. In the end, he still wasn't convinced he didn't need an attorney here. But this was completely new territory for him; he had no idea what he was doing, or what he was supposed to be doing. The best he could muster was a small but uncertain response.

"Okay."

Sergeant Torres gave him a perfunctory nod, opened the file folder, and then charged right back in, only occasionally glancing down at chicken-scratch notes on the white pieces of paper in front of her for specific details.

"Good. Well, let me tell you everything we know. Yesterday, around approximately one o'clock in the afternoon, a man named Louis Sanzo claims to have engaged in a verbal argument with another man outside of the apartment address you reside at. According to his report, this man – let's call him 'M' – was on his way back inside the building when Sanzo decided to confront 'M' about not picking up his dog's waste."

Torres allowed herself a beat, then half-smiled to herself and to the paper.

"Only in L.A."

She continued. "When 'M' refused to pick up after his dog, Sanzo continued to argue with him, until 'M' became violent and struck Sanzo across the face. 'M' then continued to violently attack Sanzo, who, out of self-defense, finally retaliated until such time as he was able to neutralize his assailant and make an escape down the street."

Torres focused on Michael for a moment, studying his reaction, then pressed on again.

"Despite this incident, Sanzo did not call the police at this time. However, later that night around approximately 9 p.m., Sanzo claims to have answered knocking at his door, where he discovered a man that fit the same description as 'M', dressed differently but with his face fully exposed and recognizable. 'M' then proceeded to attack Sanzo once again, but this time, with a weapon, believed by the victim to be some kind of baseball bat or other blunt object. After suffering a number of bodily injuries including several broken bones, contusions, loss of blood, and the blinding of his left eye, Sanzo claims that 'M' then left his house abruptly."

Another pause, this one longer and more pregnant than the first.

"Alarmed by the commotion, Sanzo's neighbor, Ms. Loretta Rich, came to the house to check on him, and saw Sanzo on the ground through the glass windows of the front door. She entered his home, and upon seeing his condition, immediately called 911, at which time police and paramedics were able to respond to the scene."

The lengthy account had crushed Michael beneath

its considerable weight.

At first, he had listened attentively for possible lies or exaggerations on the part of this man, Louis Sanzo. Michael had poised himself for a rebuttal, and he could barely contain himself when reliving certain points of their initial encounter, eager to spill details of all the jogger's brutalities to this woman.

Torres had no idea how much the jogger had pushed Michael, relentlessly goading him about something as trivial as dog poop, until finally, Michael had had no choice but to respond physically. Even then, this bully, this Louis Sanzo, had embraced the fight, pounding Michael into submission, embarrassing and annihilating him for all the world to see.

And then, just like that, the jogger had walked away scot-free, leaving Michael a shriveled wreck in front of his own home, a beaten and bloody pulp covered in dogshit and humiliation. And all of this simply because Michael accidentally forgot to pick up after his dog.

He had been so ready to retort. Michael was no idiot. Torres selecting the letter 'M' for this mysterious assailant was no accident. Surely, she must have noticed him chomping at the bit during her report, turning red with rage, eager to defend himself when given the slightest chance to do so.

But midway through her speech, Michael's fury had cooled considerably. No matter how justified he had felt at the time, he found it hard to deny any of the points in the timeline of events she presented.

Even if Sanzo had *brutally* defended himself against Michael, he was, after all, only defending himself. Michael had indeed thrown the first punch.

And the entire second episode of assault had sickened Michael to hear it retold. Words like "victim," "weapon," and "attack" were hard to argue with, and they stung Michael like vicious wasps.

The worst part of all, however, was the last bit. Torres had said something about the man's bones, his blood, and… his eye. Just hearing the sentence and thinking about what it meant made Michael's stomach twist and heave, and his cheeks began to burn with hot shame and a newfound sense of dread. If that was true… if the jogger really had been blinded…

Michael couldn't think about it anymore. He stared at the papers in the folder on the table, wondering where in the black and white that grotesque string of words was hiding. When it became clear that no response was coming, Sergeant Torres continued.

"You don't have to comment on anything I just told you. However, let me make it clear how things stand on our side. From Sanzo's report, we can reasonably assume that 'M' lives in your apartment building. We know that he is a young man in his mid-twenties to mid-thirties. We know what his physical description looks like. We know what kind of dog he owns, and that he was home today at the time of the first assault. We know that the same man who attacked Sanzo the first time almost certainly attacked him the second time as well, and we can confirm this when Sanzo is healthy enough to do a positive I.D. for us. He still has one good eye left, after all."

She stuck those words into him, one by one, and chronicled their impact.

"And, most importantly, I know what I'm looking at across from me right now: a young man with a matching dog from the apartment building in question, who has a number of cuts and bruises across his face and hands. A man who, according to his next-door neighbors, got into a loud and lengthy argument with another man late last night, before driving this second man at knifepoint from his apartment, and then threatening his neighbors, as well. Which is, all in all, an entirely separate offense, but pretty poorly timed in its concurrence with the aforementioned incidents of violence."

Again, Torres leaned back in her chair, folding her arms across her chest and gripping each sleeve with the gaudy fingernails.

"So, I guess it's your choice. You can answer a few simple questions now, without all the fanfare and theatrics. Or you can wait in a holding cell until we show Louis Sanzo a photo of you and see what he has to say. Your choice."

There was no choice. Laid out bare before him was only the grim and inevitable reality that he could not escape. There was no denying the case against him and lying about it now would only do more damage down the road when the evidence was indisputable. Michael swallowed hard and steeled what courage he had left.

"What do you want to ask me?"

Sergeant Torres wasted no time. "Did you assault Louis Sanzo yesterday afternoon in front of your apartment building?"

"I hit him, yes, but he wouldn't let up about the whole dog poop thing. He was threatening me–"

She cut him off. "Did you also assault Mr. Sanzo with a deadly weapon later that night at his house?"

"It was a baseball bat, not a deadly weapon–"

"Do you know Mr. Sanzo personally?"

"No, I've never met him before. He was jogging–"

"How did you know where he lived?"

"I followed him back to his house. I mean, after he beat me up, I got in my car to try and see where he went–"

"So, you stalked him back to his house?"

Michael's eyes watered. "I didn't stalk him!"

"You followed him, though?"

"At a distance, yes, but–"

"And then when you found him and found out where he lived, you decided to come back later that night, then. Why? For the cover of darkness?"

"Well, I – I mean, no... it wasn't – planned out, like that..."

"But you did wait several hours after the initial assault, and then came back to his house that night, dressed all in black, and you severely beat him with a baseball bat, did you not?"

"I, I did, but–"

"Is the baseball bat in your apartment now?"

Michael hesitated. Sergeant Torres did not.

"Is the baseball bat in your apartment now?"

"I don't know."

"You don't know?"

"I don't know."

She scowled. "Later last night, did you attack another man in your apartment?"

"No!"

"Then why were you holding a knife outside your doorway?"

Michael didn't know what to say. She pressed on, relentless.

"Who was the man in your apartment last night?"

"Just a friend."

"Why were you arguing with him?"

Michael couldn't believe the way things were going. The room was spinning around him now, faster and faster.

"It wasn't a big thing... it was stupid."

"Then why did you have a knife in your hand?"

"It wasn't even a real knife! It was a kitchen knife, a butter knife—"

"Did you try to use it on your friend?"

"Of course not! Ask him – you can ask him! Drew Baskin. That's his name. Ask him." His eyes rolled to the ceiling. "I can't believe we're even talking about this right now!"

Deftly, Sergeant Torres produced a pen from somewhere in her jacket and jotted something down on the paper in front of her. She spoke as she wrote.

"Your neighbors say you threatened them."

Michael's blood boiled, and for a second, the policewoman came back into sharp focus, and he screamed at her.

"That's not true! That's a lie! I didn't do anything to them... they banged on the walls, I banged back, and the little bitch saw me holding a knife – a kitchen knife! That's it, that's the whole story. I went back inside and went to sleep. I didn't threaten them or anybody. They've always had a problem with me. They've always been like that!"

Torres raised an eyebrow at his outburst. Michael was panting, his chest heaving up and down. Some small part of him realized how ridiculous he must have looked and sounded, but he didn't care. It was one thing to sit through the whole gruesome account with the jogger, but this business with Drew and his neighbors was completely ludicrous and absurd.

"I'm sorry, but I'm not going to sit here and try to defend myself for things that didn't happen. I've told you everything you wanted to know about the jogger, Mr. Sanzo, and you haven't even let me tell my side of the story about that yet, and now you're changing the subject to this stuff that isn't true, and you're not giving me the chance to defend myself – to speak even!"

He was running out of breath, and raw, thick, pulsating emotion was making his voice break.

"I know I should be allowed that. At least that! I'm allowed a right to *speak*, for fuck's sake, and to defend myself, am I not?"

Sergeant Torres took in the sight of the quaking man across the table, sighed heavily, and closed the file folder. Her voice was calm as she stood up, and it had that note of weariness to it again.

"You are allowed those rights, Mr. Cavanaugh… but not right now, and not with me. You'll have your chance to tell your story, when you have your lawyer, and Louis Sanzo has his… and we bring in the voice recorder, the pen, and the notepad."

She smiled wryly down at him. "I'm going to book you now on two counts of assault and one count of aggravated assault with a deadly weapon. If you wish, we can contact Mr. Baskin directly and see if he intends to press charges, or if he is willing to corroborate your stance that last night's encounter was a non-issue. We will also be in further contact with the eyewitnesses from next door. An officer will be in shortly to get your full information, take your fingerprints and mugshot, and inventory any personal property you may have on you. Any inventoried property will be returned to you upon such time as you are released. A bail hearing will be scheduled for you within the next 48 hours. You will be allotted one phone call before you are taken to a holding space."

And with that, Torres turned and strode to the door, opened it, and left, without so much as a look back.

Michael was alone in the room once again, only this time, he could not sit still. His hands were still shaking with all the pent-up rage and injustice swirling within his chest, and there was nothing he could do about it. He needed a release, but none was there. As much as he felt like flipping the table or hurling a chair across the room, he knew he couldn't. So far, he had avoided any handcuffs or physical restraints, and he wasn't about to give them any cause to administer them now.

Instead, Michael stood up and began to pace the room, rubbing at his forehead and face with his fingers, but careful to avoid his black eye and other wounds. At one point, he even found himself examining his ravaged lip in the mirror of the one-way glass. What did it matter who saw him on the other side… he was already under arrest anyway.

When at last an officer did come to begin the booking process, most of Michael's angst had subsided. He led from the room down a hallway and into other rooms, each more indistinguishable than the last, as this strange new man asked him questions, filled out forms, and took his fingerprints and photos.

Michael moved through the process in a

disengaged daze, drained of his fight as well as his despair. For the most part, he just felt tired now. He wondered how long it had been since he last experienced a full night's sleep. Everything normal seemed so distant now, blurred and distorted by the bizarre new reality he had been forced into.

There was really only one person he could call… and even then, Michael wasn't sure if that person would answer. Thankfully, it was one of the very few phone numbers he still knew by heart, and he tried it all the same, holding onto a wisp of hope that someone would answer. Michael looked around for a clock on the wall to see what time it was, but none could be found. It had to be very, very early in the morning by now… but even of that, he was unsure. Time had ceased to exist in that interrogation room.

After four long rings, someone picked up.

"Hello?"

Michael sighed with relief. "Drew, it's Michael." He remembered their last encounter at his apartment, and realized he had no time to waste. "Please don't hang up or anything; I really have to talk to you."

There was only the sound of silence on the other end. Michael waited, half expecting to hear the beep of a disconnection. But none came immediately, so he forged on.

"I know this is going to sound crazy, but… I– I'm in jail, man." Michael looked around. "Well, not jail. Not yet, anyway. I'm actually at the police station if you can believe that. I'm not sure which one, but I think I can find out from someone at some point." Still, no response. "Drew?"

Michael thought he could hear Drew's familiar

heavy breathing coming through faintly over the line, but he wasn't positive. He strained to hear better through the old plastic receiver.

"Are you fucking with me?" The voice was gruff and groggy, but unmistakably Drew's.

"No, I'm dead serious."

Another pause. "Why are you at the police station?"

"It's a long story, actually, and I don't know how much time I have. They told me I get cut off at a certain point, so I have to make this quick." He tried to formulate his thoughts the best he could. "They're going to schedule me a bail hearing over the next couple days. If you can, I'd like you to be there. I also need you to help me... They're thinking of charging me for what I did last night, or what my fucking neighbors thought they saw. Assault or something ridiculous. They're saying I threatened you and them with a weapon." Michael paused. This had to be delicate. "I need you to tell them that it's not true."

"But it is true."

Michael had been afraid Drew would say that. Thankfully, he was also prepared for that response.

"*Come on*, Drew, I didn't assault you or anybody. I know things got a little heated between us, and the knife thing was dumb, it was a mistake... but I guess I just felt threatened or something, and I grabbed it." He forced out an artificial laugh. "I just as easily could have grabbed a fork or a spoon. I mean, it was a kitchen knife I found in a drawer. It's not like I came at you with a butcher's knife or a gun or something."

More silence on the other end. Michael decided to change his tactic.

"My neighbors are saying I threatened them, too. And you know they're just trying to get rid of me. They've never liked me, for whatever reason... just because I like to smoke on the balcony sometimes, or stay up past seven o'clock, God forbid. I mean, it's ridiculous. I didn't threaten them."

"I don't know that."

The words came as a surprise, and they hit Michael hard. He recovered as gracefully as he could.

"What?"

"I said, I don't know that. I don't know what you did after I left, after you came at me with a knife."

Michael's heart sank. "What are you talking about?"

"I don't know that. I don't know what you did to your neighbors. I still don't know why you did what you did to me."

"Drew—"

"You pulled a knife on me, Michael. I don't care what kind of knife it was. You pulled a knife on me with a look in your eyes I've never seen before. I didn't recognize you then. I don't recognize you now."

"What do you mean you don't recognize me now?"

"You tell me you've got everything together. Then you attack me. And now you're in jail?"

"I'm not in jail yet—"

"You're at the police station, you're under arrest... for what? For what you did to me or the neighbors? Or did you do something else?"

Michael sighed. "It's a long story—"

"No, I don't want to hear that. Why are you calling me right now? What do you want?"

"I told you, I need you to come down and tell the police what really happened last night…"

"No, I don't think you want me to tell the police what really happened last night, Michael. Because I will tell them what really happened."

"I told them to ask you about it anyway. They're going to talk to you one way or another, so you might as well–"

"FUCK!"

The exclamation was so loud it hurt Michael's ear. He recoiled from the phone, his face wincing with pain and shock.

"FUCK, MICHAEL!" Drew was definitely breathing heavily now. "How else can I make it clear to you that I don't want to be involved?! I'm tired of this shit! I don't want to go to the fucking police station, I don't want to talk to some fat fucking cocksucker and lie for you! I don't want to be *involved!* I don't know what you've gotten into, what fucked up shit you're doing with your life, but for the last fucking time, leave me and Michelle out of it!"

"*I'll tell them about the man we killed!*" It erupted from Michael in a hoarse whisper, and even then, it came out far too loud.

Immediately, Michael looked around, convinced someone had heard him. But the only person within earshot was the officer who had led him into this room of phone banks, and he was still positioned just outside the closed door, speaking with another policeman. Nevertheless, Michael made a more concerted effort to control his volume.

"I will. I'll tell them everything."

He knew now he had crossed the point of no

return, and there was no going back or second-guessing. It was the only card Michael had left... and he was just desperate enough to play it.

"I'm sorry, but I will. You don't understand. I hurt somebody pretty badly. This jogger, his name is Louis, Louis Sanzo, and he, well... it's a long story, but we got into a fight, and then I followed him back to his house, and I hurt him." The words sounded awkward coming out of his mouth, but there was no good way to say them. "I beat him up with a baseball bat, and I guess... I guess I..."

Michael found his voice cracking and his lip trembling. He had yet to feel genuine remorse for his actions up until now, but suddenly, he found himself pitying the man.

Uninvited, gruesome memories and graphic images of the body cowering on the ground, of the man trying to protect his face and shield himself from the flurry of blows... they all came flooding back to Michael.

And this time, the man bleeding on the floor wasn't the tormenter who had beaten the tar out of a weaker opponent. This time, he was a brutalized victim, a man who would never see again from one eye, who was probably physically and emotionally scarred for life. Michael began to cry into the phone, and now he was pleading with his best friend – his only friend left.

"Please, Drew. Please... I'm sorry I said that about the car thing. I didn't mean it. I didn't mean for it to come to this... any of this. I don't know how this happened... You're right, I don't know who I am anymore. Please... please..."

He begged and he sobbed, and he begged and he

sobbed some more, until he wasn't sure which was which.

At some point finally, his brain began to register another sound… and that was silence. Soft, painful silence. Whether Drew had hung up or his call had been cut off, he wasn't sure.

But the policeman came in all the same to fetch him, pulling him away from the phone and leading him firmly out of the room. The officer seemed unfazed by the display of emotion. Perhaps it was something he was accustomed to witnessing during these all-important single phone calls.

Michael had done his best to stem the tears and compose himself before being led back into a small holding cell with a toilet and two little cots, both built into the walls and facing one another. The officer closed the metal door behind him and locked it from the outside, then moved off and out of sight.

A long, thick window allowed people in the hallway to keep an eye on people inside the room, but for right now at least, the hall seemed empty and quiet. Michael was just glad he didn't have to share the room with anyone else. He hoped it would stay that way.

Seemingly alone now, Michael moved across the small space to empty his bladder in the shiny metal toilet. It took a few seconds for the urine to come, as Michael felt acutely aware of the window behind him, and he could not shake the awkward feeling of being on display. After several quick looks over his shoulder, finally he was able to go, and he closed his eyes and tried to expel all of his worries with the passing of his wastes… but to no avail.

When he was done, Michael sank down on the

edge of one of the cots. It could not possibly have been more uncomfortable. The thing felt like sheetrock and had absolutely no give whatsoever.

For a long time, Michael stared at the white wall across from him, wondering how much Drew had heard of his final plea, if any of it at all. Would he come tomorrow? Or today, rather? Would the cops come get him if Drew arrived?

Would he be allowed to speak to him again, perhaps this time through the connected phones on either side of the glass, like they did in the movies? Or would Sergeant Torres just come and let him know that Drew had explained everything, and that at least one of the arrest charges was being dropped?

Michael wasn't sure if he had gotten through to his friend. He had told him everything – or at least as much as he could in the short time of the phone call. Michael had left things a mess with Drew when last he saw him, and he wasn't sure he had done enough over the phone to win his friend back over. After all, Michael had somehow been dumb enough to threaten Drew again, this time verbally, just when Michael needed him the most.

Maybe he didn't deserve to be saved by Drew. And even if, against all odds, Drew took pity on his old friend and set the record straight with the police about the knife incident, there was still no escaping the noose when it came to Louis Sanzo. He was guilty; he had admitted it himself.

It didn't matter what kind of story he spun to the cops, to lawyers, or to a judge and jury. No matter how much he tried to convince them all how utterly wronged he had felt at the hands of this psychotic jogger, how Sanzo's claim of self-defense only went so far when Michael was being pulverized and pounded into a pile of dogshit, and how justified Michael had felt in exacting his revenge, all it would take was one look at the mess Michael had made of this man, and that would be it. Michael himself would want to be found guilty and punished.

What would that punishment be, exactly? He had no idea what kind of fine or jail time accompanied a conviction for aggravated assault. It didn't sound so bad, saying those words together.

Of course, it sounded worse if you tacked on 'with a deadly weapon'. But that was just a baseball bat, after all. It was a sporting good, something a kid might have at home. And Michael hadn't been trying to cause anyone's death with it.

Maybe, just maybe, if he could convince Drew to help him find a good lawyer, and if he really did a top-notch job of explaining just how crazy and overly aggressive this man had been during their first encounter, he could find a way to minimize his overall punishment.

For the first time in forever, Michael felt a morsel of hope. He reclined back on the cot and tried his best to shut out the bright lights in the room with his eyelids.

His right thumb was bothering him where he had lost half the nail, and the dull pain made it difficult for his mind to truly relax. Every time he felt the pain there, or on his lip, his cheek, or in other places along his body, he imagined what Louis Sanzo must have been feeling at that very same moment. Michael wondered how close or far away Sanzo was, and he wondered if Sanzo was having trouble sleeping, too.

The last thing Michael did before finally drifting off was to cover his swollen eye with a hand. He did it with a kind of dumb, morbid curiosity, and tried to imagine what life would be like with only one eye that worked. Eventually, both of his eyes went black, and Michael fell asleep.

CHAPTER SEVENTEEN

Seconds later, Michael was awake again. Rough hands shook him from a dreamless sleep, and he stared uncomprehendingly at the strange face above him. His heartbeat quickened as his eyes darted around the unfamiliar location, and his brain felt feverish and fatigued.

Some unknown assailant was telling him to "get up," and strong, calloused fingers were prying at his limbs and shoulders. Begrudgingly, he allowed them to haul his body up, and finally, Michael remembered where he was. Recognition began to set in with the officer who had first led him to this room post-phone call.

In a groggy, husky voice, he asked the officer what time it was and how long he had slept for, but the man just shook his head and replied a blunt, simple, "I don't know."

That was the extent of their verbal interaction. This policeman seemed intent on moving Michael as quickly as he could to some new destination and was either not allowed to or was simply uninterested in answering any of his questions. The officer's long legs and brisk pace made it difficult for Michael's stiff muscles to keep up, and at times, it felt like he was being dragged along the cold, sterile corridors of the station.

At last, he found himself in somewhat familiar territory as the officer opened a metal door and led him inside the interrogation room from earlier.

"Have a seat."

Michael didn't make the same mistake twice; he lumbered over to the far chair on the other side of the grey table and lowered his body into it, careful to avoid extra contact between his spine and the chair's back. Sure enough, the chair was still chilly to the touch, even through the fabric of his pants. The cruelly-efficient air conditioner vent above him was on full blast, and Michael felt small goose bumps break out along his arms and neck again.

His charge properly situated, the officer gripped his hands together behind his tailbone and this time decided to stand vigil inside the doorway, careful to maintain a stern and steady watch over his prisoner.

Neither man said anything. Michael began to wonder if maybe he had in fact slept longer than he thought. Maybe Drew had already come and set the record straight about the knife incident. For once, Michael hoped he would receive some good news.

He didn't have to wait nearly as long this time to find out. The door opened again, and in came Sergeant Torres, manila folder in hand. Only this time, she had backup with her.

A tall, gaunt man with sunken splotchy cheeks and thinning black hair accompanied her. He, too, was dressed more like a businessman than a police officer, though Michael did glimpse a silver shield on the belt of his trousers. His drab necktie was worn loose, and the top button of his shirt was open, exposing a few silver wisps of upper chest hair beneath a white undershirt. This man carried with him no papers or folders, just a small black folding chair that he had brought in from somewhere outside the room.

Presently, he opened it up and set it down next to the other silver chair, which he offered to Torres.

If Sergeant Torres had seemed tired during their first meeting, she seemed much more so now. Her eyes were heavier, and there was a certain slump in her shoulders as she sat down across from Michael. Immediately, she opened her folder and began rifling through her notes, which had doubled in bulk since last time.

Michael looked from her to this new man, and back again, wondering who was going to speak first. Torres did, though she seemed to be talking to either her stack of papers or her electric rainbow fingernails, not to her suspect. Michael had forgotten those nails, and once again, he found it hard to look away from them, like a moth being drawn to ten different technicolor flames.

"Mr. Cavanaugh, this is Detective Moorehouse, Homicide."

Michael blinked; he must have misheard her. He looked at Detective Moorehouse, who sat calmly with one leg crossed over a knee and with his hands folded together in his lap. Moorehouse had a permanent frown on his face, and his advancing age was showcased in the abundant creases and crinkles around the corners of his eyes and lips. He sat and stared at Michael, who made no attempt to conceal his open confusion.

"What?"

Always a step ahead, Torres seemed to have expected this reaction, and she nonchalantly repeated herself.

"Mr. Cavanaugh, this is Detective Moorehouse, Homicide."

Hearing the words a second time did not make them any more sensical. Michael's gaze roved both of their faces questioningly as his brain struggled to process what his ears had told it.

"What do you mean, 'homicide'?"

Torres looked up from her papers.

"Well, what does that word mean to you?" It sounded innocent enough, but there was no mistaking the subtle challenge in her tone.

Michael's thoughts went to a hospital bed somewhere, where a maimed Louis Sanzo was hooked up to an IV drip and a pulse monitor that suddenly flat-lined.

But that couldn't be. Michael's mouth went dry as sand. It couldn't be. A knot formed in his belly, and his eyes grew wide with horror. It couldn't be, but he had to know. As much as he couldn't believe it possible, he had to ask.

Neither cop looked ready to tell him anything more of his or her own volition. Both were waiting for him to put it together, like a schoolteacher patiently waits for a child to work out a problem.

"Is... did he... is he okay?"

It was Moorehouse who replied. "Is who okay?"

Why were they making him say it out loud? Michael swallowed hard and bit his bad lip accidentally.

He felt a sting of pain and the faint taste of blood, but it didn't matter.

"Louis Sanzo?" He croaked the words out the best he could.

Moorehouse studied him and took his time before answering.

"Mr. Sanzo is far from okay, from what I've heard." He tilted his head slightly. "But his condition is stable, if that's what you're asking."

Relief came and went quickly for Michael. It washed over him like the tide coming in, rinsing the cold terror of his greatest fear away. But then it was out again, and with it went clarity and comprehension. Once again, Michael was left puzzling why a homicide detective now sat across from him.

Torres decided it was time to chime in again.

"Your friend Mr. Baskin came in a few hours ago."

Michael's emotions were a rollercoaster. He felt more discombobulated than ever. Confusion had led to shock, dread, relief, more confusion... and now, even an unexpected dose of hopefulness and anticipation.

Drew must have heard the last of Michael's desperate pleas for help after all, and somehow had found it in himself to forgive his wayward friend. He had come to the station like Michael had asked him to. Had he set the record straight about last night's events? Michael wondered about who Drew had spoken to... perhaps this Detective Moorehouse had been the first officer Drew approached, and that would explain his presence now.

Torres continued. "We hadn't had the chance yet to track down his contact information, so I'll admit it was a bit of a surprise when he walked right into the station of his own accord and asked if he could speak with someone regarding you and your situation. I'm assuming you contacted him with your phone call?"

Michael nodded vigorously. "I did. I told him how important it was for him to come in and tell you guys what really happened last night with our argument, and how the whole thing was blown out of proportion. But I wasn't sure he heard me. The line cut out or something, and I wasn't sure how much time I had to talk."

Both officers listened carefully, and now Torres began to drum her fingernails on the tabletop, much like she had done during their previous conversation in this room. The blur of color kept trying to wrangle Michael's attention away from the matter at hand: his salvation.

Or, at the very least, his partial salvation. He had to embrace anything and everything that could be done to reduce the long litany of offenses he was being accused of.

The police sergeant sighed deeply. "Well, Mr. Cavanaugh, I'm not going to beat around the bush here. Your friend Mr. Baskin came in a few hours ago and had an extensive conversation with me. He told me all about what happened last night: that he had tried reaching out to you several times unsuccessfully before becoming concerned and deciding to visit you at home. He claims that your door was unlocked and the lights were on when he arrived at your apartment, so he decided to wait and see if you would turn up, which of course, you did. He then says the two of you engaged in a heated discussion which quickly escalated into a full-blown argument.

"Now, I asked you this last time we were in here together, and you wouldn't give me a straight answer. I'll ask you again: What were you arguing about?"

Michael felt unease creeping back in. She hadn't gotten to the all-important part about the knife yet and the encounter with his neighbors. Why did it matter what they were arguing about? What had Drew told her? He hesitated a bit before answering.

"I mean, it was stupid. It really doesn't matter..." The cops waited for more, unsatisfied with his dismissal of the question. "I sent a text to his wife's friend, that's all. Me and this woman don't get along, and we have a history, I guess. It was stupid. Not worth getting into a fight over, but that's what happened."

Torres pressed him further. "What did you say in the text?"

Again, Michael hesitated. He had to be careful what he said now.

"Does it really matter? We're talking about a text message here."

"Of course it matters. Everything matters. The two of you are best friends, yet last night you pulled a knife on your best friend over a text message. I have to imagine it matters quite a bit what you said in that message."

Michael began to feel heat. "Again, the knife thing, it didn't really happen that way... I felt cornered and he's... well, he's a big guy. I know it sounds stupid, but I really wasn't thinking straight, and I just grabbed the first thing I saw. I wasn't going to attack him with it or anything, I just wanted him out of my apartment."

"But why? You say you felt threatened, but he was

the one who found himself driven at knifepoint from your home. Had he come at you before that or made any indication he might try and hurt you?"

"Well, no… he was coming toward me, and like I said, I was emotional, and he was emotional, and he's a big guy, so I guess it was just sort of a snap judgment type of thing–"

"But why were you both so emotional? What were you arguing about? What did you say in this text message to Lillian Ross?"

Michael tried to catch his breath and stay in front of the sergeant's line of rapid-fire questioning. If she knew Lillian's name, then obviously Drew must have told Torres more than he had originally anticipated.

But just what, *exactly*, had Drew told them? Again, Michael tried to measure his thoughts and choose his words carefully.

"I sent her a text basically telling her how I feel about her and to go to hell. It was very harsh and very inappropriate, and I regret it. But it really has nothing to do with any of this… Drew and I had an argument that got a little out of control, I did something rash and unintentional, and then he left, and my neighbors saw me standing with a kitchen knife in my hand in the hallway. That's it. That's all that happened. Did he tell you that?" Michael looked from one police officer to the other. "What did he tell you?"

Both Torres and Moorehouse seemed to be processing his response. Torres ran a hand across her folder, and Moorehouse licked his chapped lips, always frowning, always observing. Michael still didn't understand why the detective was there, and so far, neither officer had made any attempt to explain the reason for Moorehouse's presence. It frustrated Michael beyond belief to be left in the dark like this and only further added to his edginess.

So far, the man had only spoken twice to Michael. Otherwise, Moorehouse had been silent as a ghost, and his pallid appearance reminded Michael of a corpse, lifeless and creepy.

Again, it was Torres who addressed Michael.

"Mr. Cavanaugh, who is Aaron Hillison?"

That question came far out of left field, and Michael's mouth hung open vacantly.

"What?"

"Who is Aaron Hillison?"

Michael's brows furrowed. "He's my friend. What... why are you asking me that?"

The police sergeant flipped through pages and pages of notes until she found what she was looking for.

"If our records are correct, you are the one who initially called 911 to report Mr. Hillison's death, were you not?"

"Yes, I did. What does this have to do with anything?"

"And the last time you saw him was at Drew Baskin's wedding, was it not?"

Michael didn't understand where this was going. "That's correct."

He turned his attention to Moorehouse for help or further explanation. The soft-spoken detective had once again tilted his head at an odd angle, like he was scrutinizing something he couldn't quite understand.

"Can someone please tell me what is going on here? Why are we talking about Aaron?"

This time, Moorehouse did speak. "How about we talk about Arthur Bennett instead."

Again, Michael shook his head, absolutely at a loss. He felt like he had stumbled into someone else's life, or was having someone else's dream, and nothing made any sense anymore.

"Who?"

Moorehouse wet his lips before repeating himself. "Arthur… Bennett."

The name sounded somewhat familiar, but Michael didn't know why that would be.

"I don't know who that is. Am I supposed to?"

Torres had been consulting her folder again, and now she extracted a piece of black-and-white parchment that she slid halfway across the table to Michael. He reached for it and brought it in closer so that he could make out the words.

It was a clipping from a newspaper, dated only a couple days earlier. The small article detailed a fatal hit-and-run in which sixty-five-year-old Arthur Bennett had been struck and killed while jogging late at night. He had been found dead just a few blocks from his home.

Michael remembered the article well. He had seen the online version of it and scoured it for any mention of information that might incriminate him, Drew, or his Corolla. It was one of many news links he had stumbled across that afternoon following the accident.

Two pairs of eyes were waiting when Michael looked up from the newspaper clipping. He felt his hands trembling and his heart beating much faster now. Somehow, the small red muscle in his chest had found its way into his throat, and it now worked overtime to strangle him from inside. He had to calm down. Tragic revelation was written plain as day all over his face, and there was little he could do to hide it.

Detective Moorehouse took the newspaper as his cue, and all of a sudden, the room was his. Michael now knew with a painful realization why this ghoulish figure from the homicide division was here.

"Michael." He leaned forward as he spoke his captive's name, ensuring rapt attention. "I don't know if you knew this man's name before, but I know you know who he is. Arthur Bennett is the name of the man you hit and killed with your car in the early hours of Tuesday morning."

Michael was blindsided. For the moment, he was speechless, his world rocked by a tiny piece of paper. It took everything he had to stammer something, anything, out.

"I... I didn't kill anyone—"

Moorehouse tilted his head and leveled his gaze like a rifle.

"Arthur Bennett is dead because you killed him while drunk driving. You hit him, you killed him, you panicked, and you fled the scene."

No, that wasn't true. Michael needed to speak, to cry out and defend himself, but his thumping heart was choking him. His voice was a sputtering whimper; his chest felt ready to burst.

"I wasn't driving! Drew was driving my car!"

The detective's jaw tightened. "Was it your car that killed Arthur Bennett?"

"Yes, but I wasn't driving it!"

"Were you drunk?"

"What?"

"Were you drunk that night?"

"Yes, but we both were—"

"Did you black out?"

Michael couldn't breathe. His lungs were being smothered by a shrinking ribcage, and he was suffocating.

These people were letting him die right in front of them. They didn't care that his taut skin was turning purple and that he was gasping raggedly for breath, as hot tears filled his eyes and their stony faces began to blur and distort in his view. Dark spots fluttered at the corners of his vision, and Michael struggled to stay conscious, to fight through crippling wave after wave of paralyzing electricity.

"Did you black out?"

"I – I – I can't breathe—"

Torres turned and put a hand on Moorehouse's leg, stood up, and exited the room altogether. The door shut behind her, and Michael was left alone with the pale detective. Through clouds of darkness, he could just make out the man's pearly, pointed cheekbones and chin, his cracked wormy lips, his unfeeling eyes. Who was this grisly figure, this phantom specter from the other side? Had he been sent to collect Michael, to reap his soul and suck the life from his body?

Moorehouse said nothing. He just sat, bony legs crossed casually at the knees, breathing shallowly from the small slits of his nostrils and watching Michael, waiting for him to do something, to say something. The man's patience was ironclad and eternal, and his steady, wordless presence did nothing to quiet Michael's violently splintering psyche.

The door swung open, and Torres came back into

the room. She returned to her seat and passed a small plastic bottle across the table to Michael. The sight of a familiar brand, the colors and wording on the paper ribbon, it all tugged at Michael's mind, and it was a comfort in this cold cage he did not recognize.

Water. He needed water. His shaking fingers fumbled at the plastic cap until finally he wrenched it free, and as steadily as he could, he brought the cool liquid to his dry lips and drank. It went down fast, and before he knew it, the wellspring was gone and the bottle was empty. He set it down on the table and panted like a dog, desperately trying to steady his body and brain.

Sergeant Torres reached for him with her voice, probing gently but firmly at the walls he had put up.

"Mr. Cavanaugh, you have to understand how all this looks to us in the big picture. First, we have a man at Cedars-Sinai hospital missing an eye and several pints of blood that's lucky to be alive. And we have accounts from both him and from you yourself that you put him there, bludgeoning him with a baseball bat in his own home.

"Second, we have not one, not two, but *three* individuals that say you threatened them last night, both verbally and physically with a weapon, even if it was 'just a kitchen knife'.

"Third, we have another victim who was run down by a drunk driver and left to die alone in the city street, and now we have not one but *two* people saying that not only do you own the car that killed this man, but you were in the car and you were drunk when it struck and killed this man who was out for a jog while his wife waited at home for him in bed. You admit to this yourself, and you say you weren't driving, but you won't deny the fact that you may have been blacked out.

"And less than three hours ago, we had a man in the station who came in and testified to all of this, on the record, and who claims to have been with you the whole night in question. Drew Baskin says you called him late Monday night to go get drinks at a bar in Hollywood, and that when you picked him up, he could tell already that you had been drinking heavily. He says he smelled alcohol on your breath, and that you admitted as much to him on the ride over to the bar.

"Despite this, the two of you continued drinking at the bar for another hour or so, until you were thrown out of this bar for public lewdness while engaging in sexual intercourse – potentially with a minor – in the bar bathroom. Mr. Baskin says he can provide a number of witnesses who can attest to this indecent, disorderly, and wholly troubling conduct, including several employees of the bar itself.

"He then says, despite his numerous protestations, you insisted on driving the two of them home. Mr. Baskin claims to have been drifting off to sleep when your car hit Arthur Bennett, and that when Mr. Baskin stepped out to examine Mr. Bennett and attempted to perform aid and call for an ambulance, you became hostile. You demanded that he get back in the car, for fear of onlookers or getting caught, and that when he at first attempted to resist, you began to threaten him, both verbally and eventually physically, as well. Afraid for his life, Mr. Baskin finally acquiesced, but only under the condition that he drive your car the rest of the way back to his house. You agreed. When you both arrived outside his townhouse, Mr. Baskin claims you began to threaten him again, this time including his wife Michelle, and stated that you would harm both of them should he mention anything of this accident to anyone. He then was forced to promise his silence and cooperation and did not see you again until late last night, after finding out from his wife that you had sent essentially a death threat to his wife's best friend."

Torres had spread a number of documents out before her for reference during this long and factual dissertation, and she took a moment's respite to sigh out an exhalation. She looked both tired and troubled.

"And this, of course, brings us back to the text message, and in a roundabout way, to Aaron Hillison. Lillian Ross forwarded the message she received from you to Michelle and Drew Baskin, who was able to provide it for us this morning. In it, you reference a 'cosmic event' that occurred the morning of the Baskins' wedding, a supposedly fatal and apocalyptic 'gamma ray burst' that Aaron Hillison predicted before his death."

She couldn't help but raise an eyebrow.

"Mr. Baskin states that the night before his wedding, you, he, and Mr. Hillison were spending time in the den of his townhouse when the topic of this cosmic event first came up. Although you both dismissed it at the time, a strange phenomenon did, in fact, occur the next day at around the same time Mr. Hillison had 'prophesied'. Shortly thereafter, Mr. Hillison decided to take his own life. He left a suicide note addressed to you, which you then shared with Mr. Baskin, along with other emails and documents found on Mr. Hillison's laptop that seemingly corroborated his doomsday theory as fact.

"Mr. Baskin says that from this point forward, you became increasingly convinced that the world was ending, and as a result, began to exhibit more erratic and irresponsible behavior, including a genuine disregard for the well-being, and ultimately the lives, of others around you. This culminated in a number of recent incidents, including your decision to abandon Arthur Bennett's body after being responsible for his death.

"According to your former manager at First Glendale Federal Credit Union, Mr. Hamid Arakelyan, whom we contacted today, you also created quite a public disturbance while quitting your job and harassing your fellow employees, Mr. Arakelyan himself, and a number of credit union members. You then sent the threat to Ms. Ross, twice attacked Mr. Sanzo – once with a deadly weapon – and then finally threatened and attacked two of your neighbors as well as Mr. Baskin before officers were able to bring you into the station for questioning."

Michael sat limply, dumbfounded and speechless. Her monologue had meant different things to him at different times.

At certain moments, he had found himself hurt and enraged by Drew's betrayal. Other times, he couldn't help but marvel at the wicked cunning with which his so-called friend had spun these lies and, even occasionally, the truth.

A lot of the time, Michael found himself reflecting on Arthur Bennett. Even if in reality he was not responsible for the old man's death, Michael had left the crumpled yellow heap alone in a pool of his own blood all the same, and he had done everything humanly possible to drive that gruesome reality from his brain and forget about his own role in the man's murder, accident or not.

More than anything, though, Michael had been absolutely struck by the policewoman's knowledge of Aaron and the light in the sky. Despite all Drew had told her, Michael still couldn't believe he had decided to include anything about this.

Time and time again, Drew had shot down the idea of telling anyone else about what was happening to the world. Even Michelle was left in the darkness of ignorance, much to Michael's uneasiness and discomfort. But Drew had come clean with this random stranger – a police officer, an authority figure, no less – and unloaded everything he knew about the situation to her.

And Drew had done it all just to save his own skin.

Torres was shaking her head sadly at the spread of papers before her.

"Where do we even begin with all this, Mr. Cavanaugh? Do you have anything you'd like to say to all of these allegations?"

Michael was more overwhelmed than she possibly could have been. Everything he thought he knew about his friend had changed in the past five minutes. His cautious optimism had been raped by the injustice of Drew's total, perfect betrayal.

What could Michael possibly say now? He was in too far... he was in too deep.

The worst part of all was that many of these claims against him were indisputably true; he had admitted to them already. The only meaningful thing Michael could try and dispute was who was driving his car when it killed Arthur Bennett… but even that, he was not sure he could prove anymore. His unruly and reckless behavior in the bar earlier that night had gone anything but unnoticed, and it was true he had already been driving drunk when he first picked up Drew from his house.

There was no definitive way Michael could see to prove he was in the passenger seat when Bennett was killed. It was his word against Drew's, and clearly, Drew had the upper hand there; his current record was spotless and pristine. Michael's, on the other hand, now boasted a laundry list of crimes, complaints, and accusations. It was a battle he could not possibly hope to win.

Instead, all Michael could do was try and sate his curiosity and wonderment. Tentatively, he looked from Torres to Moorehouse and then back again.

"What did he tell you about Aaron's research? About the sky that day?"

Torres sighed and raised an eyebrow. "He told us everything I just told you, Mr. Cavanaugh. What I want to know, and what I'm quite positive Detective Moorehouse wants to know, is whether you admit responsibility for the hit-and-run death of Arthur Bennett?"

Trancelike, Michael gave the slightest of nods. A new feeling had begun to descend over him: a bizarre calm, an almost Zen-like tranquility.

"I am responsible for what I did that night." But Michael still wasn't satisfied, so he decided to venture further into the abyss. "What I want to know is… what does it matter?"

Moorehouse snorted, and the noise caught Michael by surprise. The policeman's milky eyes flashed dangerously, and his frown darkened.

"'What does it matter?' Lea Bennett is a widow... because of you. His children are fatherless... because of you. Louis Sanzo will never lead a normal life again... because of you."

Michael shook his head. "You misunderstand me. I will never forgive myself for what I have done to those people, and how I've hurt them and their loved ones." He paused. *"But what does it matter?* What does it matter, really, that Arthur Bennett died two days ago, or if Louis Sanzo never sees out of one eye again? What does it matter if you put me away for six months, for six years, or for six lifetimes? We're all dead, anyway."

They still didn't get it. He could see the dumb ignorance on their faces.

And Michael had to change that. He owed it to the world to try and do some good before it all was over. A long time ago, Michael had tried to convince Drew to tell Michelle the truth, and he had tried to tell Jeanette the truth himself, as well.

He had failed both times, and now neither one of them would ever know what was coming: that ugly, awful fate that was moving faster than anyone expected.

It killed him to think of Jeanette right now... innocent, unaware, and unassuming. She deserved better than that, and Michael had failed her. That was his real crime, his real sin against his fellow man.

He felt no great sympathy toward Moorehouse, the detective who chilled his blood and made his skin crawl. But Sergeant Torres had not been unkind to him. She had brought him water and had at least tried to give him the occasional opportunity to speak and defend himself. Nevertheless, both officers were entitled to the truth.

"Don't you see? It's not bullshit. You said it yourself: 'a strange phenomenon did occur at the correct time'. 11:13 a.m. That was the time, to the second! I was there that day. I saw my watch, and I saw the sky. You said it best: 'Aaron prophesied it'. But he didn't prophesy it like they do in the Bible; he did it through scientific research. He and his colleagues, they knew this thing was going to happen, they discovered it themselves, and they were told not to tell anyone – *anyone!* Not their loved ones, not their family, *no one.* But he told me and he told Drew, and then it *did* happen. You can't deny what happened that day. Did you see the sky? Either of you? Or read the reports?"

Before they could answer, he caught himself.

"Well, you couldn't read the reports, because there were none! I looked online and in newspapers and on TV. I'm not an idiot. There was absolutely *no* explanation or coverage of what happened that day, other than some phony B.S. about a solar flare… and you know why? Because it was covered up! Just like Aaron and his colleagues were told to keep quiet, that's what's been happening in this country… Meanwhile, God only knows what's happening in parts of the southern hemisphere and in countries that we simply don't care about as Americans." His voice broke, and he struggled to contain the emotion in his conviction and his passion. "Don't you realize? People are dying! People are dying, the world is dying… and we're not being told anything, because nobody wants a panic on their hands!"

He fell silent and continued to look from one officer to the other. Neither said anything. Neither looked particularly moved by his speech, either.

Michael couldn't believe the blank expressions of indifference they both wore; not in the face of everything they now knew and had learned.

"Don't you care at all?" His voice was tremulous. "You're going to die." He said it as simply and as gently as he could.

Moorehouse snorted again, uncrossed his leg, and stood up slowly. He grabbed his little black chair by the seat and folded it up flat against his thigh, then looked down the barrel of his thin, crooked nose at Michael.

"I've seen the copied contents of Aaron Hillison's computer, and I've read the report on his suicide. It may interest you to know that your friend hasn't worked for NASA in almost ten months. He was let go, along with three of his other colleagues, for their unhealthy obsession with this 'discovery' of theirs, a doomsday conspiracy theory that was not shared by anyone with half an ounce of sense. When NASA wouldn't listen to them, they created a secret online society to continue their 'research' and swap ideas around about how it would all end: aliens, World War III, mass suicide, the Rapture."

He snorted again with contempt and made his way toward the door. Just before reaching it, Moorehouse turned around to face Michael again.

"I've been doing this for a very long time, and I've seen all kinds of people."

His grey, colorless eyes narrowed, and there was

genuine hate in them.

"People like you scare me the most. I'll never understand it." And then he was gone.

The news about NASA was surprising... but not altogether unexpected. Aaron had indicated to Drew and Michael that night his struggles with the morality of keeping their findings secret from the public. Maybe he and his small group of colleagues had quit, or even if they had been let go by their superiors, maybe it was just done to further discredit them should Aaron and his colleagues try and spread the truth of their discovery. News of the apocalypse coming from an ex-NASA employee 'let go' would sound a lot less believable than news coming from a current employee representing an organization as reputable and established as NASA itself.

Moorehouse's words didn't mean anything at the end of the day. Though Michael did wonder a bit why Aaron had never mentioned a split from NASA before.

Sergeant Torres gathered her notes together, straightening and arranging them into a more manageable bundle within the confines of the thin manila folder. She closed it, and with a weary sigh, pushed back her chair and stood up herself.

"Well, Mr. Cavanaugh, may I suggest that the next time you make a phone call, you dial the number of a good lawyer rather than a man you've threatened on numerous occasions, and one who also happens to know of your direct participation in an unsolved homicide."

She gave him a pitying, somewhat sardonic half-smile, and turned to walk to the doorway.

Much like Moorehouse though, something stayed

her exit, and with five colorful fingernails already on the handle, she still couldn't resist turning back to face Michael one more time. Torres hesitated before making up her mind, and for the first time in any of their interactions, her tone seemed more personable and pleasant. Her words came slower now, less robotic, more thoughtfully strung together.

"My son, he's ten, he's a bit of an amateur astronomer, you might say. My ex-husband got him a telescope last Christmas, and now he never puts it down." Torres studied Michael. "I saw the light in the sky that day. I'll admit, I've never seen anything like it before. It was... kind of frightening, but also kind of beautiful. At the time, I wasn't sure what to make of it, but I went on with my day after it happened all the same."

She paused. "Later that afternoon, when I picked up my son from his father's house, he knew exactly what had happened, and he couldn't stop talking about it. He called it a 'soft gamma repeater', or a 'magnetar'. I remember thinking that all sounded like something out of Star Trek or like one of his Pokémon cards, and I made that joke to him. But he took it all very seriously. He rattled off a bunch of words and statistics I couldn't possibly try to understand, and I remember watching his face in the rear-view mirror as he talked and as we drove out to get dinner. And I don't know if I've ever been prouder of him. It wasn't just his knowledge; it was his enthusiasm, and the passion of his conviction. So finally, I asked him if I had anything to worry about; if any of these fantastical things he was talking about up in space – magnetars, black holes, event horizons, apparent horizons – if any of this was something I should be concerned about here on Earth. And he just smiled this big, incredulous grin at me from the backseat, like I was the biggest fool on the planet, and he said, 'Of course not, Mom. You think I'd let you take me to Applebee's if they were?'"

Torres smiled her pitying smile again, pushed down on the handle, and swept out into the hallway.

He was not alone for very long at all. Moments later, the door opened again, and Michael recognized the officer who had booked him earlier and escorted him to and from this room. He went willingly with the policeman, eager to be rid of the relentless air conditioner and the bad memories associated with those four walls, the table, and chairs.

This walk back to his holding cell seemed longer than the previous time he made it, and there were more gawkers along the way now. It made sense. Michael did manage to glimpse a clock on the wall as he passed by a row of desks and noted that it was almost mid-day.

As such, the police station bustled with a greater number of employees, some dressed in suits, while others wore full navy-blue uniforms. All of them were going about their business, but many of them still found time to stare at Michael as he passed.

Maybe some of them had learned by now that this was the coward guilty of killing that poor old man who had been out jogging too late; the poor old man who simply but tragically had been at the wrong place at the wrong time, mown down by a drunk behind the wheel who was too afraid to stop and face the consequences of his actions.

Perhaps others knew him as the psychopath who had stalked and then beaten senseless yet another jogger in the wrong place at the wrong time, and all over a pile of dog turd.

His guardian brought Michael to a different cell this time, though this room looked exactly the same as his last, albeit a bit smaller. Instead of having the great luxury of two cots and one toilet, he now had just one cot and one toilet. Maybe it was a downgrade, but it didn't matter to Michael; again, he was just happy to not be sharing the space with a hardened criminal.

When he was alone, he felt out the cot to see if it was any more comfortable than his last bed. It was not. Despite Michael's exhaustion, he was in no mood to sleep, anyway.

Instead, he found himself pacing the confines of the small space, back and forth, back and forth. After a while, Michael was surprised to realize he had worked himself up into a small sweat, and so he went to try and sit on the edge of the cot.

The mattress, if you could even call it that, was so uncomfortable that he decided to sit on the floor instead. Michael moved to the center of the room and sat down cross-legged, facing the door he had come in through.

But the sight of the window in the wall, and the occasional men and women who passed by it, was distracting for him, so Michael instead decided to shift his body around until he was facing the far wall of the cell with his back to the door and the window.

Yes, this was right. He stretched his legs out in front of him. This was what he needed. A plain white wall to stare at; a blank canvas for his thoughts.

Everything had happened so quickly in the other room. Everything had happened so quickly over the past few days… the past week. He needed this now… some time for himself, and only himself.

It didn't matter what they said or what they did to him from here on out. Detective Moorehouse and Sergeant Torres could go on thinking whatever they wanted to think. Michael wasn't sure what Drew believed anymore, but really, he didn't care. His friend had betrayed him, and so his friend wasn't really his friend at all.

If the universe wanted him to be alone, he would be alone on his own terms, and not on anybody else's. They could move him from the station to a courtroom, or from a courtroom to a jail cell, and it wouldn't matter. Let them sentence him to whatever fate they decided. The whole thing was arbitrary anyway and out of his hands.

If nothing else, Michael had learned that now: what he could control and what he could not. Realistically, he would never see Drew, Michelle, his mom, his dad, his brother Everett, his dog Tucker, or even Jeanette, ever again.

And some of that was a sad thought, and some of it was not. But there was nothing he could do to change any of it. Facts were facts.

The world was ending. That was also a fact. Michael couldn't forget that, couldn't lose sight of it or let these people try and take it from him or convince him otherwise.

He had forgotten it somewhere along the way, lost it in a desperate rush to live out the little time he had left according to someone else's image of a thrilling life led without consequences and morality.

In some ways, many ways, Michael still agreed with

that ideal. A world without gods and governments required a certain change in philosophy. There was no longer any sense in fearing what might happen tomorrow with no guarantee of today.

And so, Michael sat alone on the floor, slowly sliding his slippers forward and backward, forward and backward along the smooth, white surface. He stared without feeling into the blank wall of his future, knowing that finally... he was in control.

COMING SOON

Realms

A love without dimension.

by

PATRICK MORGAN

SPRING 2021

©2020 Patrick Morgan
Photo credit: Robert Atchinson

ABOUT
THE AUTHOR

Patrick Morgan is a novelist, playwright, and poet. A graduate of the University of Southern California with a degree in theatre, Patrick has always enjoyed telling stories in one form or another.

After having spent a long and memorable stint in Los Angeles, Patrick currently resides in Austin with his dog Cider.

His two great loves are the ocean and the New England Patriots. He's also partial to Nacho Cheese Doritos dipped in cold Tostitos Salsa Con Queso (don't knock it till you've tried it).

You can contact him via his website at:

www.patrickmorganonline.com

CPSIA information can be obtained
at www.ICGtesting.com
Printed in the USA
LVHW041125051020
667944LV00001B/6